PASO DOBLE

Paso Doble

Pamela Rogers

SERENDIPITY

Copyright © Pamela Rogers, 2002

First published in 2002
by Serendipity
Suite 530
37 Store Street
Bloomsbury
London

British Library Cataloguing-in-Publication data
A catalogue record for this book is available from the British Library

ISBN 1-84394-027-2

Printed and bound by Bookcraft, Midsomer Norton

For Terry

Chapter One

SLIPPING QUIETLY OUT OF THE HOTEL, she crossed the road and walked quickly down the path towards the village, stopping for a moment to renew her acquaintance with the forlorn-looking donkeys plucking at the meagre grass in their scrubby field, then off to the left for the path to the cove. Nothing had changed. The smell of soapy water filled her nostrils as she passed the old washing trough, still steaming from the newly washed clothes hanging on the fence. Past the tiny orchard, over the first stile and round the winding path, she drank in the familiar scenery and relaxed into a leisurely pace. She clambered happily over the second stile, noting how rickety it had become, the bottom rail worn smooth and thin from countless boots. Crossing the dry river bed, she remembered the last time, when the river had been in spate, churning furiously, debris whirling along in its path, making it almost too dangerous to contemplate. Now the only sounds were the song of birds, the tinkle of a distant sheep's bell and the faint echo of a dog barking. The early morning sun was beginning to cast shadows on the high rocky sides of the valley, as she reached the tiny cove.

For a moment she hesitated, fearful that others might have got there before her, but, thankfully, the beach was empty and she picked her way carefully over the pebbles and boulders to her favourite spot, where she spread her towel on a broad, flat stone and settled herself down to watch the morning unfold. The cove was not fashionably picturesque, but had retained the dramatic appeal which had attracted so many artists over the centuries. The inlet was surrounded by high cliffs with huge over-hanging boulders, some of them teetering menacingly above the beach, itself a product of earlier falls. There was the famous rock from which Robert Graves used to dive, and where, later in the day, young bloods would vie to show off their skills. Seaweed lay piled up at the water's edge and on some days the smell was awesome, but today it merely added to the atmosphere which she drank in greedily.

The beach was in shade and she shivered in the cool moist air, but beyond the inlet the sky was already a deep, clear blue and in a couple of hours it would be too hot to remain where she sat. The little beach bar was deserted, though she could see people moving around in the café on top of the cliff and she knew that soon they would come down to put out the tables and chairs and prepare for the day's business. The sea was choppy and she watched a young cormorant dipping and diving and drying his wings on the rocks. The phut-phut of a motor boat disturbed the air, heralding the arrival of one of the men from the café. With unhurried ease he carried out his daily ritual of taking off the engine, standing it against a wall to dry in the sun, then dragging the boat off the beach and up on to the path leading to the café. In another hour there would be two or three more boats straggled untidily there.

The sound of voices floated down from the café, as cloths were spread and pots rattled. Soon there appeared a little procession, three women, a young boy and a man, wending their way down the path bearing crockery, a tea-urn and crates of bottled drinks, which they pulled along on a cart, negotiating the bumpy route over the beach to the bar. Laughing and chattering, they would have to make several more trips before the customers arrived, but seemed undaunted by this daily chore. The sun was creeping round and people were starting to arrive on the beach. Time to move on. The magic of this place had not dimmed, but she could not bear to share it.

The morning was still young and Laura decided to walk up to the village for coffee before settling down to write postcards and prepare to meet old acquaintances. It was just over a year since her father had died a week before they were due to come here as they had done for the past five years. She felt awkward on her own, though the two of them had always spent the holiday in separate pursuits, apart from mealtimes, and wished she could spare people the embarrassment of expressing their sympathy. Tonight would be especially difficult as it was the Queen's Silver Jubilee and there was to be a celebratory Gala Dinner by the pool in honour of the British residents. Dad would have loved it. He had lost a leg in World War Two and was staunchly patriotic, while remaining quite without bitterness towards the Germans. In fact, one of the things he always looked forward to in Deya was seeing his friend, Karl-Heinz, a veteran of the Eastern Front, swapping war stories and playing cards in the village with him and the local priest.

Bill Somers was not her real father, though she had known no other, her natural father having died before she was born. She was three years old when he married her mother and he had adopted her. The arrival of her half-brother, Michael, two years later had not lessened his affection for her.

He had worked hard to establish his own business as an accountant and the children had enjoyed a secure and happy childhood. Whenever she had a problem it was Dad she turned to and he always made time to listen and advise. Mum could be difficult, sometimes aloof and usually more concerned with what others might think than with what her children felt. Laura had worked hard at school and had qualified as a dentist. Her wedding to Tim, a fellow-student at Nottingham University, had been perfect, the marriage a disaster, and within two years she had had enough of the lies, the infidelities and the humiliation and had sued for divorce. Mum had been cold and distant. She should have stuck it out. Dad, sympathetic, not judging, told her that, whatever happened in the future, she could always come home.

Laura moved to Lincolnshire and eventually became a partner in a dental practice. She was sociable and attractive, tall, slim, with chestnut hair and dark brown eyes. There was no shortage of male attention, but, apart from a couple of low-key relationships, there had been no serious involvement. She went home to Tyneside several times a year and spent some happy times with Michael and his two little boys who adored her. When her mother's health began to fail, she sold her share in the practice and moved back, joining a local dental clinic to be near her parents. Her mother died and, since both she and Dad were exhausted, she had suggested a holiday. Dad had not had a real holiday for several years, apart from short trips to France on battlefield tours with the Royal British Legion. He and Mum had visited the USA on several occasions, but Mum would never go to Europe. Laura had been with friends to France, Spain and Italy and had particularly loved Majorca. According to the brochure, the hotel in Deya offered everything they both could wish for and so it turned out. The holiday became an annual event and they had both made lasting friendships over the years.

One such was Willy van Hoek, a South African who had fought with the Allies in the Western Desert in World War Two and, like Bill, had lost a leg. There had been some problem in South Africa in the early fifties about which he had never been explicit and he had made a hurried exit. The Government at that time was tightening up on the removal of diamonds from the country, but Willy had smuggled out over £80,000 worth in his artificial leg, which had enabled him to open a small hotel in Majorca. Over the years he had expanded his business interests on the island and now spent most of his time at his lovely house in Deya with his wife, Mathilde, known to everyone as Tilly, a delightfully eccentric Dutch lady of indeterminate age, who made pots and ran a sort of salon for artists and musicians, organising exhibitions and arranging musical entertainment in hotels and clubs around the island. It could not be said with certainty whether their union had received benefit of clergy, but the pair had been together for some twenty years and their home, a comfortable mixture of luxury and chaos, was a charming reflection of their warm personalities. Bill and Laura had been exploring the village on their first visit to Deya, when they had noticed an art exhibition in a courtyard and ventured in to look at the paintings. It was a very hot day and Bill sank down thankfully on a bench while Laura walked round the exhibition. She stopped to admire some pots and fell into conversation with the potter, Tilly, who had noticed Bill's gait and asked with disarming curiosity about the cause. The upshot was that they were invited to meet Willy and the four of them became friends. Laura had kept up a correspondence with Tilly and always spent a couple of afternoons with her when she came to Deya, finding her company at once exhilarating and restful. Today, however, she had other things on her mind.

Karl-Heinz was due to arrive in the late afternoon and Laura was hoping that he could help to throw some light on the mysterious items and documents, some apparently in Spanish, she had found at the back of a drawer when she was clearing the house after her father's funeral and which, inexplicably, he had never mentioned. She had written to tell him of Bill's death and Karl-Heinz had asked if he could do anything to help. Knowing that he was fluent in Spanish and that he had spent many hours over the years in Bill's company, she had sent the package to him and he had promised to try to unravel the contents for her. Since he had made his living as a private detective, she was confident that he would have the skills to solve the mystery, if mystery there was. Michael had been less than enthusiastic when she told him of her attempt to uncover the story behind the documents and why Dad had never said anything about them. It was like prying into someone's personal life, he told her indignantly. Everyone was entitled to a little secret if it did not hurt anyone. Dad had been abroad during the war and those things might have had some romantic memories which he would not necessarily want to share. He probably stowed them away after he married Mum and forgot he had them. Assuming, that is, that they belonged to him in the first place. He might have been keeping them for someone else who had never collected them. Now that he was dead there was no point in raking over things which did not concern them. Laura had laughed, called him an old stick-in-the-mud. He was the one jumping to conclusions about a possible romance and anyway, Dad had not been in Spain during the war, nor, as far as she knew, at any other time. It was more likely that they had been among their mother's things. She had been friendly with a Spanish girl at school and might have been keeping them for her. She had dug out some old photographs and Mum's school certificates to show Karl-Heinz. If the things belonged to someone else, she would like to think that she had done her best to find the rightful owner and return them instead of just throwing them away.

Back at the hotel, she avoided Reception and slipped quietly through a side gate into the garden, reaching her room without bumping into anyone. Drink in hand, she watched the poolside scene from her balcony and congratulated herself on having escaped Joanna. The vivacious little lady, a former ballet teacher, flitted gracefully between the sunbeds like a visiting butterfly, renewing old acquaintances and establishing new. Everyone knew the story. She had been widowed at the age of 40 and had used some of the insurance money on a cruise for herself and her two young daughters. Emil, a wealthy French bachelor travelling with his mother, had found her charming and irresistible and the ship-board romance had led to his entrapment, at fifty-one, in marriage. They made their home in Brighton, holidayed in France or on cruises and Emil made short visits across the Channel to attend to his businesses and see his Maman. All was relatively harmonious until Maman's health began to fail and Emil declared, to Joanna's horror, that she must come to live with them. Joanna delivered an ultimatum – Emil must choose between his mother and her. He chose Maman.

There followed an acrimonious divorce resulting in Joanna keeping the house, Emil buying an almost identical one less than a mile away. When Maman died, there was some thaw in the relationship, though they remained in their separate establishments, having dinner once a week, spending Sundays together and taking a holiday together once a year. Why they bothered, no one knew, since they spent little time together, squabbled when they did and indulged in spiteful remarks about each other. Emil, silver haired, silver tongued, always immaculate, still looked as if he had just stepped off a French film set and spent most of his time surrounded by ladies, while his ex-wife scornfully recounted how long it had taken him to perfect his toilet. Laura could not help wondering idly what went on behind the door of their shared bedroom.

There was old Frau Tauber, who had been coming to the hotel for over twenty years, talking with Hans and Dieter, a gay couple, gregarious and amusing. When Laura first met her she had a little mongrel dog, called Jack, which she took with her wherever she went. She liked to swim, but, since dogs were not allowed in the hotel pool, she took the bus every day to the private beach, where she swam in the sea with him sitting on her back. When Jack died, she mourned him for longer than she had mourned her husband and though she continued to come to the hotel, she could not bear to go to the beach and confined herself to the pool. She had no children of her own, but lamented the loss of other women's sons in World War Two and always made a fuss of Bill, whose injuries were a reminder of the evils of that conflict. Such a waste of youth and talent by all the nations involved, she would sigh. Would they never learn? Then there were the Nelsons, a frail, quaint old pair who seemed to have been caught in a time capsule of Old Colonial life. Though they could hardly walk, they took the hotel bus each day to the private beach and swam blissfully in deep water, oblivious to warnings about currents. Mrs Nelson ('The Memsahib') was thin as a stick, tanned to a deep mahogany colour and had a scar running from her breastbone, round her ribcage to her back, just below the shoulder blade. The sun was never too hot for her and she worshipped it without embarrassment in her bikini, looking up occasionally from her book to bark an instruction or a question at her portly, deaf and slightly confused husband.

Laura relaxed. She was going to enjoy this holiday.

Hours later, showered and dressed, she made her way to the pool-side bar where people were preparing for the festivities. Some of the British men were draping a large Union Jack between lampposts at the head of the pool, helped by one of the young Germans balanced precariously on a ladder. The hotel had risen to the occasion, providing a Gala Dinner on the terrace, followed by coffee and drinks round the pool. A small dance band gave a creditable rendition of 'God Save The Queen', followed by nostalgic tunes and wartime songs, some of which bore scant resemblance to the originals until someone guessed, producing an uproarious chorus and much applause. Frau Tauber sighed nostalgically as Laura approached, 'You are so lucky to have your Queen. Things have never been the same in Germany since we lost the Kaiser and I do miss the old ways.' Soon they were all drinking champagne, laughing and sharing jokes, experiences, hopes and fears, nationality aside, as they all toasted the Queen. Just as the meal was about to begin, Karl-Heinz appeared and was immediately collared by the Memsahib, who invited him and Laura to join their table. The old lady regaled them with hilarious tales of life in the declining years of the Empire in India, her husband smiling genially and nodding gently off to sleep as the champagne flowed. Everyone circulated and there was singing and dancing and laughter and tears. It was a magical evening and Laura felt that Dad was surely there in spirit.

Karl-Heinz loved Majorca. His father had been the German consul there when the Spanish Civil War started and he and his brother lived and went to school there for three years. He was fourteen when his father was recalled and posted to Turkey, but, despite the dangers he had faced from Republican air attacks, he never lost his nostalgia for the beauty of the island and the warmth of the climate and the people. As soon as he was old enough, he had enrolled at the military academy and had been proud to serve his country as an officer at the Eastern Front, but events there had sickened him beyond endurance and he remained bitter about the way he was treated by his homeland. Twice a year, for the past ten years, he had been coming to the hotel, at first with his wife, Ute, then, when she finally left him, four years ago, alone. He had made many friends over the years among the hotel's regular visitors and among the residents of Deya village, including the priest, Father Rafael, who had been on the island at the same time during the Spanish Civil War, though they had not met. When Bill Somers appeared on the scene, there had been an instant rapport, fuelled, no doubt, by their understanding of each other's wartime experiences, and he had been drawn into the little circle at Deya. Now Bill was dead and his daughter had asked his help in translating some puzzling documents written in Spanish which had been among his possessions. He knew Laura quite well, because she often accompanied him on the mountain walks organised by the hotel, in which Bill was unable to take part. He enjoyed her company and sometimes the three of them had dined together. He had never realised that Bill was not her natural father.

As the evening drew to a close, he could see that Laura was anxious for his opinion on the documents, but there were questions to be asked, some quite delicate, before he could piece together the full implications, which appeared to be very interesting and might prove alarming. This was not the time and place. They were both going on the mountain walk next day and there would be time to talk.

Chapter Two

Less than three weeks to the end of term and the end of the 1936 school year. Miss Gresham replaced the telephone and tried to collect her thoughts on how to deliver the tragic news she had just received. It did not seem possible that misfortune could strike for a second time in one young life and just at the time when all had seemed set fair for a successful future. Margot Chase had been orphaned at the age of six when her parents were killed in a car crash. There was only one living relative, her father's unmarried sister, who had immediately accepted responsibility for the child and had brought her up in a secure and loving home. Jane Chase was a fashion editor with a busy life, but she arranged her schedule to allow herself maximum time with her young niece. She could afford to pay for reliable help and the child grew up strong and happy. From the age of eleven, Margot had been a boarder at Sevenacres School, where she thrived academically and was popular with her fellow pupils. The school had an enviable reputation for academic achievement and social respectability. It was expensive, many of the girls coming from wealthy backgrounds, some from abroad, and had occasionally boasted the inclusion of a minor member of a foreign royal family. Many of its pupils went on to University, though in most cases a career was not essential or envisaged and a year at a continental finishing school would fill in the time and put the final polish on preparations for the young lady's introduction into society and the marriage market. Margot was not among the leisured set. She hoped to become an archivist and was due to take up a university place in October. Aunt Janey visited frequently at weekends to take Margot out to tea and school holidays included trips to France and Italy, sometimes 'working' holidays, when Margot, to the envy of her friends, would get to see a fashion show, sometimes just pottering around, but always interesting and exciting, because Aunt Janey's knowledge and enthusiasm made them so.

Now Aunt Janey was dead. Suddenly and unbelievably from a heart attack at the age of fifty-two. The call had come from the hospital where she had been taken when she collapsed in her office and there was no one to break the news to her niece, apart from the headmistress. Miss Gresham had dealt with bereavement before, but never in such a heart-rending situation. The VIth form girls would be on their mid-morning break now. She picked up the phone and asked the porter to send Margot to her immediately, then arranged for tea to be brought in, though God knew it would provide little comfort for the poor child.

When Margot arrived, her face anxious and questioning, Miss Gresham motioned her to a chair. 'My dear, I am afraid I have some very bad news.' The girl's face paled visibly and she looked as if she would faint. 'Aunt Janey?' she whispered. Slowly and gently, the headmistress formulated the words, the girl's eyes fixed imploringly on her face, her head shaking from side to side as she struggled to comprehend. Surely there must be a mistake? Aunt Janey was so full of life and energy, she was never ill, could not, must not, be dead. No, no, no! But she was. And this young woman, barely 18 years old, would have to deal, not only with the immediate intrusion of death, but its impact on her entire future, until now seemingly so secure.

Miss Gresham pulled herself together and began to deal with the practicalities. 'I will get someone to take you to the hospital and help with the arrangements.' There would be the funeral, of course and the sordid business of money. It was unlikely that the girl had any idea of her aunt's financial situation or whether any provision had been made for her in a Will. From her numb responses it was clear that there was no relative to take her in or help her through the ordeal. She knew her aunt's solicitor and the headmistress telephoned to explain the situation and made an appointment for her to see him later that day. Slowly, mechanically, Margot began to think. She asked if her roommate, Margarita, could go with her to the hospital and it was quickly arranged that the two girls would be collected by the school secretary, Mrs Porter, who would drive them there.

At the hospital the formalities were quickly dealt with. Looking at Aunt Janey lying still and cold, Margot suddenly felt shy and awkward rather than shocked. There was something obscene about staring at a dead person who could not defy one's gaze and she turned away quickly, giving a brief nod of identification. Outside, she began to shiver uncontrollably, though the day was warm, and Mrs Porter hurriedly ushered the girls into the car. Somehow the registrar and the undertaker were dealt with and they arrived at the solicitor's office on time for the appointment. There was a Will and, after a few small bequests, Aunt Janey had left everything to Margot. Apart from the house there was little money, for, although her salary had been sufficient to allow a good standard of living, school fees, and holidays, Aunt Janey's unfailing generosity had not left much for savings. Margot would have to consider whether she could maintain the upkeep of the house while at university.

Mrs Porter bought some sandwiches and dropped the girls at Aunt Janey's house, recognising that rest and privacy were needed, but that the presence of a young friend might help. She arranged to collect them in time for supper and that Margot would return to school for the remainder of term, though she would be excused from attending classes in order to allow her time to sort things out. Inside, Margarita found the kitchen and busied herself making tea and finding plates for the sandwiches. 'Eat,' she commanded when Margot shook her head and she bullied her gently until the food was gone and the tea drunk and the colour began to return to Margot's cheeks. 'What will you do?'

Margot shook her head. 'I don't know. I can't afford to keep the house if I go to university and if I sell the house I shall have nowhere to live out of term. I suppose I could take lodgings, but it would be expensive and I would need to keep the money from the house until I finished the course. Besides,' her eyes filled with tears, 'there are things I couldn't bear to part with, Aunt Janey's, my parents', and I have nowhere to keep them.'

Margarita put an arm round her shoulders and gave her a little shake. 'Hey, come on, you don't need to make any final decisions. Why don't you ask to delay starting at university for a year to give you time to think? Lots of people do that, even without the reason you have.'

Margot brightened. 'Of course! I could take a job – anything, waitress, shop assistant, while I'm deciding what to do.'

'Listen,' Margarita wriggled excitedly, 'why don't you come home with me for a holiday first? It would do you good and I would love to show you round.'

Margot stared, open-mouthed. 'To Spain?'

'Of course to Spain! Why not?'

Miss Gresham received the news with some relief, admittedly, but not without apprehension. Margarita Rosario Federica Martinez had been at Sevenacres for two years. With a Spanish father and an English mother, she was completely bilingual and her sophistication, easy grace and nonchalant attitude ensured her popularity. She was clever enough to get by without much application and Miss Gresham detected a touch of arrogance in the toss of her sleek dark head if she incurred a reprimand.

High-spirited and a natural leader, she was generally behind the pranks and practical jokes which disturbed the peaceful academic atmosphere from time to time. Miss Gresham permitted herself a wry smile as she recalled how poor Miss Cathcart, attempting to soldier on with religion and ancient history, despite advancing Multiple Sclerosis, had been a victim. Of course the girls were unaware of her illness, but her increasing vagueness and spells of trance-like silence were an unmissable opportunity. Margarita had ground up some green and white chalk and rubbed it into her face, pretending to be feeling sick, whereupon the bemused teacher, not realising it was a hoax, had left the classroom and assisted the girl to the sick bay. The slowness of Miss Cathcart's jerky gait and the girl's deliberate dallying gave the rest of the class time to tie up all the desks and chairs in a web of red knitting wool. In detention, given lines to copy from the Bible, they retained the papers which Miss Cathcart forgot to collect, so that next time they could sit and chat, the task already done. When Miss Cathcart finally succumbed to her illness, however, and her secret was revealed, it was Margarita who had organised a collection for her, contributing generously herself, and taken it with a beautiful bouquet of flowers to the sick teacher. She then organised a rota so that each Sunday two sixth form girls would visit and spend a couple of hours chatting with her or performing small tasks to make life more pleasant for the invalid. Wilful, yes, but with a kind, warm heart. She could certainly prove to be a friend in need.

The family was wealthy, her father an eminent surgeon in Barcelona, and the deepening troubles in Spain had prompted the decision to remove Margarita from possible danger. Her brother Rafael was in training for the priesthood in Valladolid and her sister Eulalia too young to be influenced by any of the growing political factions. For two years now, she and Margot Chase had been close friends and, though very different in personality, they seemed to complement each other. Margarita, restless, extrovert, funny, had bolstered Margot's self-confidence, while Margot's calm, sensible nature seemed to restrain Margarita's waywardness.

The headmistress could not suppress a niggling concern that Margot, vulnerable in her present situation, might be easily led by her stronger friend into situations she could not control, particularly in a foreign land whose customs and problems she did not understand, but, since there did not appear to be a better alternative, she would have to rely on Margot's innate common sense and trust that the Spanish family would protect her. The next three weeks passed quickly. Somehow they got through the business of the funeral, which was well attended by people from Aunt Janey's office and friends and neighbours, most of whom Margot did not know. There were no other relatives and Margarita fought back tears as she sensed her friend's utter desolation and the enormity of her loss. Together they began the task of sorting out Aunt Janey's belongings, Margot being unable to face it alone.

Among the many photographs chronicling Margot's childhood years were some taken with her parents, a happy, smiling couple, clearly devoted to their little daughter, but she confessed that she had only vague memories of them. There were some of Aunt Janey herself, others of relatives, long dead, and one or two people whom Margot could not recognise. Margarita had been out to tea with Margot and her aunt on several occasions and had been impressed by the chic, attractive lady whose amusing conversation brought a touch of glamour into the routine school life of her young companions. She wondered aloud if Aunt Janey had had any men friends and Margot looked up sharply. The thought had never occurred to her. Her aunt had many friends and her work had involved a great deal of social contact, so the opportunity for romance had been there, but there had been no evidence of a man in her life and she had never spoken of anyone in particular. Until that moment she had been indulging her own feelings of grief and loneliness, anger even, but suddenly she was assailed by a feeling of guilt. Had Aunt Janey given up her own life to look after Margot, choosing to remain unmarried in order to devote herself to caring for the child? Margarita hurried to reassure her. Aunt Janey had loved her work and had no doubt chosen her career in preference to marriage and a family. She loved Margot and felt no need of other children to make her life complete. Gratefully, with a watery smile, Margot hugged her friend. At last the distasteful task of sorting through documents and clearing clothes and personal belongings for which there was no further use was done.

Margot made arrangements with the Bank for payment of bills during her absence and for money to be available to her in Barcelona, packed her suitcase and closed up the house. Margarita had relayed their plans to her family, who were delighted to entertain her friend and had organised their journey by boat and train to Barcelona, where they would be met. Both girls were excited at the prospect of a holiday together and Margot's initial apprehension that she might be intruding on the family were laughingly dismissed by Margarita, who assured her that everyone would be glad that she had found such a nice, sensible companion. The language would not be a problem, since all members of the family spoke English, but Margot resolved to learn Spanish, keen to make the most of this unexpected opportunity. As Margarita described her home, Margot could see that she loved it.

'It sounds wonderful – how could you bear to leave it?'

Margarita sighed. 'My father gets uptight about politics and he was worried that some of my friends might get themselves into trouble, so I was just packed off out of the way. As if that would stop me thinking for myself!'

Pressed, she explained that Spain was in turmoil, people had lost confidence in the government and there were various factions battling for control. No, there was no danger where they were going, she assured an alarmed Margot. Her father would not have allowed them to return if there was any danger.

Chapter Three

THE CHANNEL CROSSING WAS SMOOTH, a light breeze ruffling their hair as the girls wandered about the deck. A young French family, arguing volubly, tumbled around splashing each other with drinks, the parents trying ineffectually to control them. Several couples, some with young children, were clearly bound for holidays in the South of France, relaxed and happy as they discussed their plans. Two elderly ladies, smartly dressed, sat drinking coffee and exchanging confidences, while their husbands disappeared into one of the bars. Most of the other passengers appeared to be businessmen, mainly English, preoccupied with their papers or talking confidentially with colleagues or contacts. No celebrities, spies or eccentrics and very few young people.

Margot shivered, though the air was not cold. It was as if a curtain had come down at the end of a play in which she no longer had a part. What lay ahead she did not know, but excitement overtook apprehension and she had no responsibilities other than to herself. Margarita was speaking to her and she collected herself quickly.

'Those boys over there...'

Margot turned to where two young men were hunched over the rail poring over a map.

'I wonder where they are going. Shall we go over and talk to them?'

Margot was not ready for such a bold step. 'No, please, let's wait. They might think ...'

Her voice tailed off and Margarita laughed. 'Hey, it's a ferry not a night club and they won't think anything! Doesn't matter, though, if you would rather not.' They went below for coffee and when they returned the two boys had been joined by an older man and were deep in conversation. Though they spoke in low voices, the words 'Barcelona' and 'fascists' were discernible and Margarita pricked up her ears. 'I thought so!' she exclaimed excitedly. 'There's going to be more trouble – Vicente said that they were forming International Brigades and I'll bet that's what those boys are about.'

Margot was aware of her friend's involvement with Vicente, to whom she claimed to be unofficially engaged and who wrote regularly to keep her informed of events at home. He was a political activist, a student leader in the anarchist CNT party, ready to fight to the death for the Republic, though quite what it was all about Margot had so far failed to grasp. The idea of young men from other countries, including Britain, going over to help some political cause put quite a different light on the situation and she eyed the two boys with a keener interest. One was tall with wispy fair hair framing his thin, angular face, large clear blue eyes, shyly downcast mostly, but sparkling with enthusiasm when speaking earnestly to his companions. His wrists protruded from the frayed cuffs of his jacket, which was clean and carefully pressed, but worn and either second hand or outgrown. An old duffel bag lay at his feet and his pockets bulged, presumably with last minute provisions pressed on him by a tearful mother. He looked as if he needed a good meal. The other was smaller, dark, with curly hair and neat, small features, restless and jerky in his movements. Bandy legs suggested rickets in childhood. Sharp eyes and the occasional flash of an impish grin gave the impression of a cheeky schoolboy out on a prank. He had a large, lumpy parcel, firmly tied with yards of string and a battered case which looked as if it contained a musical instrument, possibly a clarinet. The man talking to them was older, perhaps thirty, short, stocky, with a swarthy complexion and an air of importance, clearly, from his accent, as he instructed his charges, Spanish.

The ferry was approaching the harbour and Margot went to freshen up before landing. When she returned, Margarita was in conversation with the two boys and waved Margot over to join them. The Spaniard had disappeared. Frowning slightly, she approached the little group, the lads grinning and shuffling their feet with embarrassment as they were introduced. Tom, the tall one, blushed to the roots of his hair, while Jimmy stuck out his hand, saying, 'Ay, man, pleased to meet you!' They were from Tyneside, where there was no work, no money, no hope. Communist recruiters promised adventure, excitement and the glory of helping to bring about a more just government, not only for Spain, but for the working classes everywhere. They were bound for Paris, from where they would be directed to Marseilles to be smuggled on to ships bound for Barcelona or Valencia or to Perpignan, then over the Pyrenees under cover of darkness. As they said goodbye Margarita handed a slip of paper to Tom on which she had hastily scribbled down the name of a café in Barcelona where they could contact Vicente. Margot felt vaguely disturbed, but brushed away her misgivings as her friend shrugged smilingly, saying, 'That's the last we'll see of them!'

The train was not full and the girls spread themselves out, sleeping through much of the long journey through France. Occasionally, snatches of singing reached their ears and *en route* to the buffet car they passed a group of seven or eight rather scruffy youths huddled together, flushed with the effects of the cheap wine they were passing round and drinking straight from the bottle. Oddly, as the girls passed by, there was no ribaldry, the lads silently averting their eyes to look out of the window. It was the same on their return; talking ceased and silence hung heavily in the air until they were out of earshot, when the rumble of voices resumed. Margarita made no comment but was clearly uneasy. Bravado at a distance was fine, but this was getting a bit close to home. At Marseilles they boarded the boat for Barcelona. There was no sign of the youths and Margarita relaxed.

The heat was becoming oppressive and the girls were glad to retreat to their cabin, where they rummaged through their suitcases for light clothing, running cold water over their wrists and tying back their hair. There was a bustle of activity on deck as the ship came alongside and passengers struggled with their suitcases, jockeying for position for a quick disembarkation.

'Not long now,' Margarita assured her wilting friend. 'It will be cool in the house and we can have a dip in the pool later if you like.'

Margot nodded. The journey had been tiring and the thought of a swimming pool was bliss.

Passing quickly through Customs, they emerged, blinking in strong sunlight, Margarita scanning the line of waiting vehicles until she spotted the old man waving to her as he set out towards them.

'*¡Hola, Paco!*' she called as he approached.

'*¿Qué tal?*' Hurriedly acknowledging Margot, he motioned them quickly into the car, frowning and talking rapidly in Spanish as he threw the suitcases into the boot and jumped into the driving seat. As they sped away, Margarita leaned forward, gripping the back of the seat as she took in the enormity of what he was telling her. Briefly, she relayed the gist of the situation to Margot, striving not to alarm her. There had been an attempted coup two weeks earlier on the 18th July by Nationalists against most of the major cities and fighting had been particularly savage in Barcelona. Though the rising had been crushed and the city remained in Republican hands, casualties on both sides had been very high and though life was slowly returning to normal, the realisation was setting in that Spain was now inevitably embroiled in civil war, with fear and uncertainty on all sides. Paco assured Margarita that her family was in no danger, having no expressed political allegiances, though her father was exhausted from long hours spent in treating the wounded. He shook his head sadly, close to tears as he recalled friends and acquaintances, young and old, victims of the bloodshed. Margarita patted his arm consolingly, then sat back, closing her eyes in contemplation of the implications, until she remembered her duties as a hostess and sat up, smiling brightly at Margot, pointing out landmarks as they neared their destination.

The house was about five miles outside Barcelona, built on a hillside and split into two levels. A long drive swept up from the road past terraces of olive trees, through an orchard to a paddock with stables and two horses. Her father and brother were keen horsemen, but neither Margarita nor her mother rode. The house itself was built round a courtyard, cool and elegant with a central fountain and shady plants. Deep purple bougainvillaea rambled profusely over the front wall, framing the doorway and huge terracotta pots of palm and lantana adorned the wide, tiled terrace. A long, low sitting room, dining room, music room and study all opened into the courtyard. From the kitchen a door led to a small wine cellar and a laundry and thence to a garden planted with trees and scented shrubs, a cool haven in the scorching summer heat. A marble staircase led from the entrance hall to the upper floor where there were six bedrooms and two bathrooms. Behind the house, reached by stone steps and screened by a large hedge, was Paco's pride and joy, a pool, fed from a natural spring, which, with the addition of a cistern, had been cleverly converted for bathing. The surrounding patio contained a shady area with a table and chairs. Also on this level was a barn which had been converted into two flats, one of which was occupied by Paco, the gardener/handyman and his wife, Maria, who cooked and kept the house in order with the help of a young local woman who came in for a few hours each morning to clean. The other had been empty since the death, two years ago, of the old nanny, an English lady who had looked after all three of the children and had become so much a part of the family that when her services were really no longer needed she had been allowed to remain in the flat for the rest of her life.

Paco and Maria had been with the family for ten years. He was sixty, but looked much older, small, bent and wiry, his thinning hair grizzled, his kindly brown face wrinkled and weather-beaten, his smile almost toothless. Maria, comfortably plump, constantly blessed her good fortune, often singing softly to herself as she went about her work. Her hair, hardly touched by grey, was drawn into a neat bun at the nape of her neck, framing a pale face which, though careworn, had clearly once been pretty and her dark eyes twinkled with humour. As a young man, Paco Vargas had been an agricultural worker with a growing family, struggling to earn a living. The work was hard, long hours and a pittance for pay amounting almost to slave labour. Like many such families, they were often on the edge of starvation. Most of the land in Catalonia was owned by powerful, wealthy landlords, who flaunted their riches while the workers became increasingly resentful. Industrial workers, too, were suffering appalling conditions while watching the factory owners making fortunes from exploiting their labours.

Politicians and church leaders did nothing to stop the oppression and hatred, particularly against the Church, spread rapidly among the working classes. Out of this desperate situation grew the labour unions, socialist and anarchist, and there were several minor uprisings, which were quickly and cruelly crushed. Paco was uncomfortably aware that the Church in Spain had scant regard for the poor and oppressed, but found it hard to overcome his deep rooted respect for the institution and had steadfastly refused to become involved. In 1909 there came his first real experience of bitter revolution, when, during the colonial war in Morocco, Riff tribesmen had attacked and massacred Spanish soldiers on their way to protect mining concessions bought by one of the king's advisers. The reserves were called up for military service and the poor, unable to afford to buy themselves out, knew that their families would starve if the men had to go. In Barcelona, the reaction was swift and terrible. In a week of tragic self-destruction, young men rioted, attacking property, burning churches, committing acts of violence and desecration. The army was sent in to restore order and Paco watched in shame as fellow workers were slaughtered or arrested. The cavalier brutality of the militia drove him into the arms of the union.

Throughout the next decade there were sporadic bouts of militancy, encouraged by the revolution in Russia, but the uprisings were crushed by employers and police hiring criminal gangs who murdered many of the union leaders. When, after Spain had suffered a swingeing defeat in Morocco, there was a universal outcry against the King, General Primo de Rivera seized power, appointing himself as dictator, but early hopes that he would reform the agricultural system came to nought. By this time, Paco's health was beginning to fail and he was unable to do a full day's work, though all but one of the children were now working and able to support themselves. Weary, often in great pain, he managed to carry on for a few more years until he was taking so much time off work that he lost his job and feared that they would also lose their home. The local doctor, a benevolent man who worked tirelessly, often with no hope of payment from his needy patients, could do nothing more for him and knew that, without surgery, he would die. Presuming on his acquaintance with the eminent heart surgeon, Dr Ramon Martinez, whose charitable work was well known, he summoned the courage to ask for his opinion. As result, a delicate operation was performed, free of charge, and after a lengthy period of convalescence, Paco found that he had been given a new lease of life. That was not all. Dr Martinez, impressed by the couple's dignity and sincerity in the face of so much adversity, offered them an apartment in the grounds of his house, rent free, plus a small wage, in exchange for some light domestic duties.

Maria was beside herself with delight. The little apartment was bright and clean with everything she could wish for and she established an instant rapport with the children's nanny, who lived in the adjoining apartment. It was a pleasure to be able to work in the big house for such a lovely lady as Senora Martinez, who made her feel welcome and treated her as an equal. Paco, whose love of nature had not been dimmed by the hard life he had led on the land, realised his dream that one day he would have a garden. The doctor agreed that he could work in the garden, provided that he did not attempt anything too strenuous and, before long, it had become his own domain under the light hand of the Señora, who allowed him almost a free rein. The horses were an added bonus and he enjoyed grooming them, patiently showing the Martinez children how to do it properly and directing them in cleaning out the stalls. Seeing him washing the family car, running his hands lovingly over the gleaming bodywork, Dr Martinez had stopped to chat and found that, though he knew a lot about the mechanics of cars, Paco had never been able to afford to learn to drive, much less own a car. Driving tuition was arranged and he was able to run the odd errand or chauffeur the children, as well as having occasional use of the car for his own needs. Practical and good with his hands, he had time to experiment, his proudest achievement to date being the pool he had made at the back of the house. His health recovered and their financial worries over for the first time in their lives, Paco and Maria had never been happier. The debt of gratitude owed to the Martinez family was repaid in undying loyalty and affection. As the car drew up, the door of the house flew open and a small figure hurled itself into the arms of the emerging Margarita.

'Oh, Lallie!' she exclaimed, laughing as she extricated herself from the embrace of the child. 'My sister, Eulalia,' she explained, turning to

Margot, who felt a slight pang as she smiled at the bright face turned towards her. She would have loved to have had a sister. Eulalia was almost twelve years old, the age gap between her and Margarita signifying the loss of a boy born dead and hope dwindling until her appearance three years later. Adored by her parents and elder siblings, she had somehow managed to avoid being spoiled and loved people and animals unconditionally. Her short hair was light brown and curly, her eyes an unexpected dark brown against a pale complexion, her lips parted in a happy smile revealing even white teeth, this latent beauty hidden for the present in the dungarees and grubby shirt which were the habitual garb of the endearing tomboy. Without ceremony she took Margot's hand and led her into the house, where they were greeted by Senora Martinez, closely followed by Maria, who shooed off her grinning husband to unload the luggage. Again, there was the relaxed, unaffected welcome as she was ushered into the cool room where a table bearing sandwiches and a huge jug of iced lemonade awaited the travellers. A quick embrace for Margarita, a warm squeeze of the hand and a gentle word of condolence for Margot, then they were left to refresh themselves before going upstairs to unpack. Dinner was almost three hours away so there was plenty of time to explore.

Margot's bedroom was next to Margarita's, sharing the same lovely view over the hillside, so calm and peaceful it was difficult to imagine that such disturbing events as Paco had described had taken place only a few miles away. The room was cool in the heat of the afternoon, the windows open with light gauzy curtains pulled across to keep the sun out and a ceiling fan whirring softly, casting shadows on the dark wooden furniture. The bed, with its plump pillows and crisp white counterpane, was flanked on each side by a large red and black fringed Spanish rug. There was a clock on the bedside table and a little vase of fresh wild flowers, picked, as she later found out, by Lallie. The marble floor was cool and Margot gratefully slipped off her shoes as she began to unpack. Half an hour later, showered and in swimsuits, the girls slid blissfully into the swimming pool. Laughing and splashing, they raced up and down, until a loud whistle announced the arrival of Lallie, who had come to tell them it was time to get ready for dinner. Margot thanked her for the flowers and accepted her offer to show her where they grew.

Teresa Martinez was already in the dining room when the girls arrived, explaining that her husband would be along shortly, having arrived home late from the hospital. She was simply dressed in a pale green linen dress which accentuated her slim figure and showed off her hazel eyes and honey blonde chignon to perfection. She wore little make-up; her only jewellery, apart from a thin gold chain around her neck, was an emerald ring above her wedding ring. The strong, beautifully manicured hands were those of a musician, which indeed she was, and every movement, assured and graceful, languid almost, gave an impression of calm serenity as she motioned them to be seated and poured iced water into glasses.

Maria bustled in with a large tureen of chilled gazpacho soup and was just about to serve it as Dr Martinez arrived. Smilingly apologetic, he kissed his daughters and shook hands with Margot, who felt suddenly shy, unused as she was to a masculine presence in the house.

'You are most welcome,' he told her. 'Please treat this house as your own and stay as long as you wish.' She stammered her thanks, as Margarita turned to her father to ask about the situation in the city. Meeting his wife's eyes, he acknowledged her unspoken plea to avoid alarming the girls. 'For forty-eight hours it was very bad. We tried to contact you to stop you coming, but there was so much chaos the postal services and transport stopped. Things are already getting back to normal in the city, buses are running, shops are open. You will find that there have been some changes, but, provided that you do not become involved in any political way you will be safe, at least during the day. It is not safe to go into the city at night, however, unless you are accompanied and go direct to and from your destination.'

The conversation turned to more cheerful subjects and as the meal came to an end, Eulalia asked, 'Mamma, will you play for Margot tonight?' The suggestion was unanimously accepted and they withdrew to take coffee in the music room, where Senora Martinez seated herself at the beautiful grand piano.

Margot sat entranced as the music filled the room, now soft, slow, romantic, now tortured, sad, then lively, the skilled, sensitive hands drawing it into life. Teresa had been studying music in London and, when her family decided to emigrate to America, she remained in order to complete her course at the Academy, sharing a flat with some fellow-students and accepting engagements to play in recitals and at private functions. At a party following one of these occasions she had been introduced to a young Spanish doctor, in England to study developments in cardiac surgery techniques. When her course ended she went, not to America, but to Spain, where she married him. Both were sociable, attractive and charming, with a social conscience which demanded that they use their wealth and position to benefit others. Their three children were given love, education and respect for their individuality, but were not over-indulged. It was a disappointment to Teresa that none of her children had inherited her talent, but at least they all had an innate appreciation of music. When she finished playing, disarmingly acknowledging Margot's effusive thanks, she announced a further treat for them all. A Russian ballet company, which had been touring in Spain before the fighting began, was being allowed to give two performances of 'Swan Lake' in Barcelona the next week and she would take all the girls to see it. So, on a note of excitement and delight, ended Margot's first day in Spain.

Chapter Four

DR RAMON MARTINEZ was dedicated to his work as a consultant surgeon, leading the field in cardiac treatments. Apart from his private practice, he spent many hours at the hospital giving his services free to those who could not afford to pay, making no discrimination in his care for rich and poor alike. He had inherited considerable wealth from family holdings in South America and could have pursued a life of idle pleasure had he so wished, but he disliked ostentation and was driven by a need to use his talents for the benefit of others as well as for his own scientific prowess. Now forty-six years old, he was a tall, well built, strikingly handsome man with a full head of black, wavy hair, slightly greying at the temples, and dark expressive eyes which reflected humour, compassion, pain, as he dealt sensitively with his patients. He had no political allegiance and was deeply shocked and saddened by the behaviour of his compatriots during the recent horrific events as he struggled to pick up the pieces of shattered humanity presented to him for repair. He would never forget the night of the 19th July. On the previous day, following risings all over the country, there had been rumblings of an expected invasion by Nationalist troops, but demands for weapons by the anarchist defenders had at first been refused by the Republican Government. Fearing attack, the workers decided to help themselves and that night the city was stripped bare of everything that could possibly be utilised as weaponry. Ships in the harbour were plundered for dynamite and guns, cars and lorries were requisitioned and painted with the initials of the dockers' union, CNT and others.

The centre of Barcelona teemed with people and loudspeakers attached to the trees crackled with the latest news of progress on the arming of the workers. Very early next morning, fascist soldiers moved out of their barracks and set off for the city centre, joined by small contingents of other right wing supporters. Sirens all over the city sounded the alarm and fierce fighting broke out. Bursts of gunfire spat from snipers on rooftops, home-made bombs were hurled, barricades faced the soldiers at every turn and lorries loaded with explosives ripped suicidally into detachments trying to enter the city. Churches occupied by soldiers were set on fire. Buildings which had been seized by the rebels were soon all besieged as the determined workers gained ground and vicious hand to hand fighting raged, producing horrendous casualties. The injection of 4000 civil guards brought cheers from the workers and as defections from the invaders swelled their ranks, it became clear that the rebel forces had failed. The surrender of General Goded, who was made to broadcast a message over the radio telling his troops to give up their arms and save further bloodshed, brought an end to the fighting in the city, but did not prevent an anarchist assault next day on the Nationalist barracks near the port, which resulted in a sickening, almost mindless, slaughter and an increase in casualties on both sides.

The hospitals had been inundated from the start with the injured and dying. Doctors and nurses, working round the clock, coped as best they could, pooling their skills and experience regardless of specialisation or status. Calls went out to anyone with past medical or nursing training and makeshift operating theatres were set up in hotels and office buildings to handle shattered bodies, extracting bullets and shrapnel, amputating limbs, stitching gashes. Blood supplies soon ran out and water and food had to be channelled to where it was needed. The population rose to the occasion, local organisers from workers' commit-tees manned lorries to carry supplies and commandeered hotels to set up food kitchens. Dr Martinez had not left the hospital for three days, operating through the nights with just a couple of hours snatched here and there for sleep. He was shocked and saddened by the numbers and severity of the injuries, but mostly he felt anger that the lives of a whole generation of young men, many still in their teens, would be ruined because of political idealism. Heroes today, but what of the future? Limbless, eyeless, uneducated, would the society they had fought to protect care for them, employ them, years from now? This was not a normal war. It was Spaniard against Spaniard and though there had always been the chance of an occasional flare-up, he could not believe that people he had known as decent, responsible citizens could behave so callously towards each other. Not content with the carnage in the streets, some of the militiamen had burst into another hospital and shot dead in their beds patients they suspected of being fascist sympathisers.

Two priests had had their throats cut and one was crucified by being nailed to the door of his church. In his own hospital, he had bent to minister to a man with a severed arm who had raised his shattered stump, splattering the doctor with blood as, face contorted with hatred, he cried, '*No Paseran!*', before falling back dead.

For days afterwards there was chaos. People disappeared, relatives were afraid to ask for news in case of reprisals on their families, shots rang out through the night and trucks piled high with corpses ferried their grisly burdens to be thrown unceremoniously into pits. Fear pervaded the city. No-one with right-wing sympathies or connections with the church, professions or management who had not declared for the left could walk safely in the streets, so many had fled or gone into hiding. The Martinez family was safe because, apart from the esteem in which the doctor was held, his wife helped set up the food kitchens, comforted widows and the wives of the injured and organised play groups to distract the children and keep them out of trouble while the schools were shut. It was known, of course, that their son was away training for the priesthood, but out of sight out of mind and this was not held against them.

Only in the privacy of their own home and even then, careful not to upset Eulalia, could they give way to their desperate fear for Rafael. Valladolid had fallen to the fascists, but there had been fierce fighting there and they had not heard from their son since the rising. Ramon had always cherished the hope that Rafael would follow him into the medical profession, but from an early age the boy's heart had been set on the Church and his parents had accepted that. Any hope that Margarita would take on the mantle had long ago dissolved in her firm assertions that she was not prepared to spend long years in training in order to help people in whom she had not the slightest interest. Eulalia, though, already showed an inclination towards a medical career. Inquisitive, compassionate and unfazed by the sight of blood, she poked and prodded at dead animals, asked intelligent questions and loved looking at her father's medical books. He had been faintly worried by her composure when she related how she and her friend had watched as a man who had crawled into a house, blood spurting from his badly injured arm, had a belt applied as a tourniquet, but was proud of the clinical coolness and the accuracy of her description.

It was unfortunate that he had been unable to get a message to Margarita before she and her friend left England, but the situation appeared to be calmer now with the workers' committees desperately trying to show their ability to organise and restore services. The atmosphere was still heady, with anti-fascist banners and slogans abounding and talk of setting up armament factories in preparation for future war, but the wholesale killings had ceased and foreigners were welcomed with open arms, so Margot should not feel threatened. He knew that some of Margarita's old friends were heavily involved with the CNT and was concerned that she might get carried away by their political fervour, but for the moment it would be no bad thing for her to help with welfare work and the presence of her friend would no doubt impose some restraint.

Next morning he was up before the rest of the household and was making himself coffee and toast when he was surprised by Margarita.

'Pappa, please tell me what happened. I couldn't ask last night when Margot and Lallie were there, but ... what about Rafael? He can't come home now, can he?' She looked strained after a sleepless night and he shook his head as he put an arm about her shoulders and gave her a little shake.

'*Querida*, we must be strong. I would rather spare you the details but this was no minor skirmish. It was war at its most depraving level and I fear it is by no means over. We must be extremely vigilant and try to help those who have lost so much, but stay out of trouble. We have not heard from Rafael and your mother is distraught, but we dare not try to contact him in case we endanger his life. He will know not to come home – we must be patient and wait for news.'

Margarita shivered. She told him about the young men on the journey and he nodded. 'There will be many. The Communists have money and weapons from Russia and idealists from all over Europe, who know nothing about the situation, are being recruited, thinking they are helping to save Spain.' He spread his hands in a gesture of bemused resignation.

'But, Pappa, isn't that preferable to Fascism? In England people are talking about the threat to freedom from Germany and ...'

Frowning, her father put a finger on her lips. 'Margarita, you must be careful. As far as I can see, both would be equally disastrous for Spain. We do not know what is going to happen and it is better that you do not commit yourself to either. If you had seen what people did to each other three weeks ago just because they voted for the opposition, you would understand the danger. Do what you can to help, be friendly and polite, but for heaven's sake, stay out of politics.' He glanced at the clock and, dropping a kiss on her head, departed for the hospital.

Margarita sat quietly, hunched over the table, until a patter of quick footsteps announced the arrival of Eulalia. Amid sisterly banter they made fresh coffee, warmed some croissants and prepared breakfast trays as a treat for their mother and Margot.

'*Buenos dias!*' called Margarita cheerfully as she tapped on the door of Margot's room. 'Don't expect this every day!' she added as she whirled in with the tray.

'*Buenos dias!*' laughed Margot, who was sitting up in bed studying her Spanish textbook. 'You see, I'm learning already.'

The sun was already warm, the temperature climbing, and Margarita outlined her plans for the day. Eulalia wanted to show Margot her favourite walk in the hills and it would be better to go before the heat became oppressive. Mamma was going into the city at lunchtime to help at the food kitchen and would give them a lift in the car if they wished. Eulalia was going with Maria to her daughter's house to see Carla, Maria's granddaughter, who was a school friend. It was settled.

Breakfasted, bathed and dressed, the three girls grabbed sunhats and a bottle of water and set off from the back of the house up the winding track into the hills. Fig trees on each side of the path afforded partial shade at the beginning of the walk, but soon petered out into shrubs and rocky outcrops. The scent of rosemary hung heavily in the air from clumps of bushes growing haphazardly among the undergrowth, where Tusan palms stood out stiffly among soft grasses. The faint tinkle of bells prepared them for the sudden appearance, minutes later, of goats, leaping on to rocks high above them as their footsteps startled the animals out of their grazing haunts. They stopped to watch the graceful creatures, all differently coloured and beautifully marked, tan, grey, creamy white with splashes of brown and a particularly striking one, Eulalia's favourite, chocolate with a white blaze on its back.

Passing through a wood of sessile oaks, Eulalia pointed out a circle of stones and gravel and an old charcoal burner's hut, long since deserted and derelict. They pushed open the creaking door to show Margot the decaying mattress in the corner and the fireplace, still cluttered with rusting pots as it had been, undisturbed, for many years. Reaching a promontory, they perched on slabs of stone, sharing the bottle of water and watching the birds, rock martins, Eulalia informed them, bobbing in and out of thousands of holes in the sheer rock face across the valley. High above, a vulture hung on the thermals, looking for prey. So peaceful, thought Margarita, dreading what she knew would be a very different picture in a few hours time.

Back at the house, they changed their shoes, heeding the warning not to dress smartly, and helped to load the car with a large pan of soup Maria had made and some old blankets for refugees who were fleeing from towns and cities captured by the Nationalists. As they neared the city, they could hear music, interspersed with news bulletins, from loudspeakers attached to trees on the Ramblas. Party banners hung from buildings like bunting at a festival. Teresa drew up in front of the Ritz Hotel which sported the banners of the anarchist trade union, CNT and the socialist union, UGT and they unloaded the car. Curious, the girls followed her into the huge kitchens which had been transformed into a public canteen for anyone in need. The place was a hive of activity, women bustling around preparing food and accepting tins and parcels from people anxious to make a contribution, men bringing in supplies from wherever they could get them. Teresa, winding a kerchief about her head, shooed the girls out, telling them to be back by four o'clock when she would be ready to go home.

Outside, tramcars painted in the red and black of the CNT-FAI operated normally. Shops were open, some under new management where the owner had fled, many displaying a reduced range of goods as shortages of materials and erratic delivery services began to bite. Otherwise, everything seemed incredibly normal. Cafés and bars were serving customers, people were going about their business or sitting around on the benches chatting, with no apparent sign of the chaos which had reigned a few short weeks ago. Margarita led the way down a side street to a bar where a group of young people sat at tables on the pavement drinking coffee. Inside, the buzz of lively chatter rose above the whirring of ceiling fans as they pushed their way to the bar to order tapas and wine. Small wooden tables covered by clean but somewhat threadbare red and white cloths and surrounded by an assortment of chairs and stools were crammed tightly into the small room, where a pale youth in black trousers and an overlarge white shirt edged his way past lounging bodies and outstretched limbs to collect glasses and dirty plates or empty the thick brown earthenware ashtrays. Dried hams, loops of sobrasada sausages, strings of onions and garlic and a variety of gourds hung from the ceiling, yellowed from years of cigarette smoke and on one wall the once-resplendent cloak of a long-dead matador hung limp and faded under the horns of a bull. The whole of one wall was taken up by a long glass counter, behind which sweated the proprietors, two brothers, almost identical in appearance, short, rotund, bald, with thin moustaches, white shirts splashed with samples of the day's menu and red aprons tied over black trousers round ample waistlines. Shelves on the wall held a bewildering array of spirits and liqueurs and earthenware jugs, in the same brown glaze as the ashtrays, were filled with wine from little brass taps on two barrels which stood at one end of the counter and dispensed by a buxom young woman whose dark eyes flashed an unmistakable warning to anyone contemplating a touch or a comment as she squeezed her way between the tables. When the food was ready, the table number was called out and customers struggled to the bar to collect and pay for it. Though it looked chaotic, the system worked, the popularity of the place testimony to the fact.

Margot was fascinated, her appetite tempted by the delicious aromas emanating from the pots and pans behind the counter, as she tried to make up her mind, steered through the menu by Margarita. Served, they looked around for somewhere to sit and Margarita heard her name called by a girl dressed all in black who was waving from a table at the back of the room. Chairs scraped back and belongings were flung on to the floor as the occupants of the table made room for the newcomers. Greetings were exchanged and introductions made. Conchita, small, black-haired, vibrant, Lola, tall, thin, sad-looking and Pilar, sultry, generously proportioned, wearing a blouse a couple of sizes too small in Margot's estimation. All were old school friends of Margarita and there was much to tell each other after her absence and the events of recent weeks. Margot could not follow the rapid Spanish speech and Margarita did her best to summarise, with eager interruptions in halting English from the others, amid unselfconscious laughter when mistakes were made.

Margot felt at ease and was encouraged to try out her growing Spanish vocabulary, her efforts clearly appreciated by the uncritical audience. The girls admired her fair hair, already slightly bleached by the sun, and Pilar offered to show her how to keep it that way permanently, while Lola advised on creams to protect her skin. None of them had seen the actual fighting, but their faces became grave as they related the experiences of neighbours and Lola shivered as she told how her father had been stopped on his way home from visiting his mother in hospital and had his car 'requisitioned' at gun point. Most of the young men in their age-group had been made to declare their allegiance to Republican groups and some had disappeared into training camps or into the new agricultural collectives which were being established in villages outside the city. Nobody seemed to know exactly what was going on; there were committees everywhere, some running businesses from which their former bosses had been ousted or killed, others maintaining services such as water, gas, electricity and transport. Things seemed to be under control, though there were disputes and shortages in some areas.

Margot, trying to follow the conversation, spilled her drink as someone jostled her elbow in passing. Turning, she met the apologetic smile of a young man, tall, blond, tanned and muscular, who blushed as he stammered his regrets 'I, er, *no Español*, er ...'

Margot, aware of the girls' appreciative stares, smiled at his embarrassment. 'I am English. You speak English?'

He grinned, relieved. 'A little. I am from Sweden. My name is Sven.'

'Margot,' she replied, turning to introduce the others, but a chorus of hoots and whistles from his companions on another table brought the conversation to an end and he withdrew, red-faced.

'Mmm,' commented Margarita. 'Did you see those muscles? Who are those men?'

Pilar explained that they were athletes. There was to have been a 'Popular Olympiad' which had been organised as a boycott of the Olympic Games held in Nazi Germany, but the rising had taken place on the eve of the opening and the event had been abandoned. Several hundred athletes were stranded in their hotels and some had joined with the workers in the fighting next day. Most of them had gone home now, but some had stayed and joined the militia. Sven and his friends were regulars at the café, drinking and flirting with girls. She quite fancied one of them, the dark one with his hair falling over his eyes, but he had not made any attempt to speak to her and it would not be right for her to make the first move. Her prim expression drew derisive laughter from the others. Conchita looked at her watch and jumped up quickly, saying that she had arranged to meet Juan-Manuel. Margarita asked if she had any news of Vicente and Conchita wrinkled her nose as she replied that he was far too grand to bother with the old crowd since he had been promoted in the United Socialist Youth and was busy recruiting communists.

As she left, she called over her shoulder to remind the others of a meeting of the '*Mujeres Libres*'. Lola hastened to explain. They had all been involved in the Socialist Youth movement and espoused its feminist aims, but the '*Mujeres Libres*', an anarchist organisation, was taking positive steps towards equality for women. They demanded equal pay, equal opportunities in jobs and political status and had even raised a women's battalion in Madrid. Margarita grimaced at the idea of being involved in fighting, but laughed when Pilar interjected to tell how the *Mujeres* had plastered posters across the dubious areas of the city trying to persuade prostitutes to give up their way of life and stop being degraded by men. They ran training courses for ex-prostitutes to learn skilled work and earn a respectable living. Pimps who tried to interfere were shot.

Apparently '*Mujeres*' meetings were highly entertaining and, in the absence of their usual haunts, clubs and cinemas, which had still not reopened, the girls had taken to attending. They urged Margarita to come to the next one in three days' time, but, smiling, she shook her head and stood up, her hand on Margot's shoulder, as she declared it was time to go.

The car was unbearably stuffy after standing in the sun and Teresa, hot and sticky from her labours in the kitchen, suggested a dip in the pool. Lowering their bodies into the blissfully cool water, the three exchanged reports of the afternoon's activities. Teresa remarked how well–behaved and patient people were in the food queues when supplies ran out and they had to make do with whatever was available. She feared that things would get worse and it would be difficult to keep the soup kitchens running if they could not rely on regular transport from the collectives, especially as people were beginning to come into the city as refugees from the fascist areas. She frowned when Margarita relayed the stories of the '*Mujeres Libres*' and begged her not to get involved with any of the extremist factions, all of whom had enemies among the Republican allies, as well as the fascists, who would not hesitate to exact revenge if they achieved supremacy. Margot hurriedly reassured her that Margarita had already declined an invitation to attend a meeting and turned the conversation to the more pleasant topic of music, asking about a classical guitar concert she had seen advertised on a poster in the Ramblas.

When Teresa returned to the house to see about dinner, Margot asked about the girls in the café.

'Conchita is studying at Madrid University. She wants to be a pharmacist. Boring! Her fiancé, Juan-Manuel is a mechanic and she can only see him during the vacation because he can't get away from work to visit her. Pilar is a hairdresser, but the salon she worked in closed after the rising. She doesn't know what happened to the owner. Lola left school about two years ago and had a few jobs in shops, but she really wants to look after children. Some women are starting a nursery for poor children so that their mothers can work in the collectives or factories and she is hoping to start there. I suppose what she really wants is to get married and have her own children, but there's not much chance of that in the present situation.' She paused, reflecting.

'And what about you, Margarita?' asked Margot. 'What shall you do?'

Margarita shrugged. 'I don't know. I could be a journalist and be famous like Martha Gellhorn or someone.'

'Oh, yes? Why not a film star or a fashion model at Chanel?'

'Don't think so – I'd have to go blonde and lose weight and –' Both girls burst into peals of laughter, splashing each other furiously as they emerged from the pool. As they strolled towards the house, towelling their hair, Margarita said pensively, 'You know, what I would really like would be to do something, influence things, make things happen – politics!'

'Marry the President, you mean?' Margarita flicked her towel. 'Ever heard of La Pasionaria? You're right, though. There aren't many women like that. Vicente will be important someday, so maybe ... Oh, who knows? Come on, I'm hungry!'

Still no sign of Vicente, thought Margot, as she dressed, but his shadow hovered uncomfortably at the back of her mind and she wondered when the reality would intrude on the peaceful family scene.

Chapter Five

AUGUST TURNED TO September with no break from the baking sun as the temperature rose on the battlefronts. Foreign volunteers, mainly anarchists, were flooding into Barcelona from all over Europe, the United States and Latin America, swelling the ranks of the Militia. Unsuccessful attempts to dislodge the Nationalists from Majorca and Saragossa highlighted an urgent need for better organisation and training and the Communists began to take the upper hand in the struggle for power in the Republican army. Their officers were young, aggressive and fired either with ideology or the ruthlessness of ambition. Such a one was Vicente Alvarez. The son of an academic, he was clever, personable and articulate. While studying Economics and Social History at Madrid University, it had amused him to exercise his debating talents as a student spokesman, graduating seamlessly into the Socialist Youth Party and now, at the age of twenty-one, having dropped out of the academic scene, he had joined the Communist Party, where he anticipated there were glittering prizes to be had.

He had already attracted the attention of Dolores Ibarruri, the legendary La Pasionaria, the fiery, influential Communist leader whose wrath could strike terror into the hearts of those she hated while inspiring love and loyalty in those who won her approval. The Militia adored her. The stout middle-aged lady's piercing eyes had softened and her stern face was wreathed in smiles as she welcomed the young man at the military base in Madrid. It was said that she had an eye for an attractive lad and Vicente was flattered to have her full attention for half an hour while she congratulated him on his recruitment activities and explained her vision for Spain. Power, she said, would be the reward of those who worked to free it from the Nationalists and her hand lingered for a moment on his arm as she rose to leave. This endorsement would not go unnoticed by the military commanders. He felt drunk with inspiration and pride. This was his destiny and nothing was going to stand in his way.

It would have been nice to be able to write to tell his parents of his success, but there was no point. His father, a classicist, had already shaken his head in disapproval and reminded him of the fate of Icarus, who flew too close to the sun. His mother, with tears in her eyes, had reproached him for wasting his abilities and not finishing his education. His friends, such as they were, had no ambitions of their own beyond eking out a living and indulging a few modest pleasures and he had outgrown them. There was Margarita, of course. She would be home now and it was time he had a bit of female company. Wasn't she bringing an English friend to stay? Could be interesting. He had some leave due next weekend and might just pop over to Barcelona.

Antonio Alvarez and Ramon Martinez had been friends since their university days and they still met regularly to play chess and enjoy conversation. The families had remained close, the children going to school together and playing together until secondary education channelled them in different directions. Rafael's increasing commitment to the Church exasperated Vicente, whose taste for adventure and more earthy pleasures demanded lighter company. In the long summer before he went up to university, the old crowd had still hung around together and he had realised that Rafael's sister was no longer a gawky schoolgirl, but an attractive and spirited young woman. It had amused him to toy with her developing emotions and he teased and flattered, sighed and reproached, until he was sure of her infatuation. She was still very young, however, and he was aware of the danger of allowing the situation to get out of hand. Besides, like a good wine, it would be worth waiting for. They had agreed to keep in touch and wrote regularly until, alarmed by reports of his political activities and rumours of amorous adventures involving a chambermaid and the wife of one of his tutors (quite untrue, he had assured Margarita), her parents had packed her off to England. Contrary to their intentions, this added spice to the relationship and Margarita's romantic fantasy was fed by the excitement of secret correspondence. On his part, Vicente found it agreeable to have an outlet for his thoughts and aspirations which would not arouse jealousy or opposition. And so the relationship continued.

The telephone was ringing persistently and Margarita groaned as she rose from her chair in the cool garden, where they were lazing the hot afternoon away reading film magazines in the alleged interest of improving Margot's Spanish. 'Better answer it. It might be something important for Pappa'.

She was gone for some time, returning pink and excited. 'It was Vicente. He's in Madrid but he's coming over next weekend ... I can't wait for you to meet him! Oh!' She clapped her hand to her mouth. 'Don't say anything to Mamma and Pappa, will you? They don't like him and they don't know that I have kept in touch with him.'

Margot shook her head, but felt a twinge of panic at the thought of potential clashes ahead and the line she might have to tread between loyalty to her friend and betrayal of her hosts' hospitality. She stood up, brushing the creases from her skirt. 'I'll get some drinks. You had better tell me what I ought to know about him.'

In the kitchen she poured lemonade into the glasses and composed herself before going back into the garden, determined to keep an open mind. The rest of the week passed quickly. The city was full of young foreign men pouring in daily on lorries from the Atarazanas barracks near the docks, which had been hurriedly made ready for the newly recruited International Brigades. Wearing an assortment of 'uniforms', speaking a bewildering mixture of foreign tongues, but full of enthusiasm and high spirits, to say nothing of the cheap local wine, they sang and saluted in response to the cheers of the children. The atmosphere was heady, more like a fiesta than the preparation for war, while the Nationalist danger crept closer.

Talavera de la Reina, Irun, San Sebastian and Toledo fell as General Franco's Army of Africa, backed by the Luftwaffe and the Italian air force, advanced towards Madrid, leaving destruction and chaos in their wake.

Eulalia's school had reopened and she was collected daily by a battered old bus at the bottom of the hill. The children gave up their playtime to help the war effort, planting potatoes, rolling bandages and knitting scarves and socks for soldiers to wear in the coming winter. Each evening after dinner Lallie dutifully brought out her knitting needles, smiling patiently at the family's jocular guesses at what the article might be as the shapeless white tube lengthened slowly. 'Stump socks!' she declared triumphantly and grinned at their startled expressions. 'They are for men who have lost a leg and need to wear thick socks to keep their wooden leg from rubbing on the stump. We shall need lots and lots!'

There was a stunned silence, then Ramon stood up and hugged his daughter. 'Well done, child,' he said quietly. 'You are quite right.' Margarita and Margot both offered to help and after rummaging unsuccessfully for knitting needles and wool, Teresa remembered that Nanny had been very fond of knitting and there would probably still be some in the apartment. It was time to clear the place out, anyway. Next morning, armed with buckets, mops and dusters, they began the task of sorting through drawers and wardrobes which had not been touched since the old lady's death. No-one had had the heart to do it, though Maria had seen that the rooms were dusted and aired at least once a month. Teresa smiled sadly as they exclaimed at the neatness and order of the wardrobes and drawers, before placing the clothes in bags to be taken for the needy. They found knitting needles, balls of wool in abundance and a beautiful mahogany sewing box, inlaid with ivory, the inside lined with red satin and fitted with thimbles, needles and threads and a little pair of silver scissors. On top lay an exquisitely embroidered bookmark made from stiffened silk with the name Eulalia inscribed in the centre.

'She meant her to have it,' breathed Margarita, closing the lid. The child rarely spoke of Nanny, but they all knew that she still grieved for her. It would mean a great deal to her to have this personal memento. Margot shivered slightly as the memory of going through Aunt Janey's things brought back her own sense of loss and she fingered the little silver pendant which had belonged to her aunt. They finished the cleaning and returned to the house, where Maria had prepared a simple lunch. In the shade of the garden the girls sorted out needles and wool and began to knit.

Eulalia came into Margot's room holding the box and Margot smiled as she reached out her hand to the tearful girl. 'I miss her dreadfully. She was so wise and kind and she never laughed at me whatever I said.'

'I know, dear. My Aunt Janey was like that.' She showed the pendant on its silver chain around her neck. 'This was hers and whenever I feel sad or upset about anything, I look at it and somehow it makes me feel better. Your box will be like that for you. Your Nanny died, but she had a very happy life and she would not want you to be sad. And remember, you are not alone. You have a wonderful family who care for you very much.'

'Oh, Margot! How thoughtless of me. You have lost so much and here am I feeling sorry for myself when I should be thankful.' Margot shook her head and the girl said, shyly,

'I know it can't be the same as having your own family, but we all love you and want you to feel that you are part of ours. I would like to be your sister.'

Holding back the tears, Margot kissed her gently on the forehead. 'That is the nicest thing anyone has ever said to me! I can't think of anything in the world that I would rather have.'

The next morning Margarita went with her mother to deliver the clothing from Nanny's house to the committee at the Ritz, while Margot, who had got into the habit of helping Eulalia with the horses, went off into the stables to do some grooming. After an hour of vigorous soaping and rubbing down the patient, unjustly named Diablo, she straightened her aching back and looked round, startled, as a shadow fell across the doorway. He was leaning against the post, arms folded, a lazy smile on his lips, his insolent gaze slowly travelling over her from head to foot. Flushed with anger and embarrassment, she picked up the bucket of soapy water and moved towards him. He raised his hand, laughing. 'My name is Vicente. You, I guess, are Margot?'

She put down the bucket, wiping her hands on her slacks as he advanced.

'*Encantado!*' he murmured huskily as he took her hand and bent to kiss it, keeping his eyes on her face.

'Margarita has gone into the city with her mother. She was not expecting you until tomorrow.'

'I came early. I have business at the barracks. If I do not see her at the café at lunchtime I will meet her tomorrow at noon. She knows where.' He stepped closer, put his hand under her chin. 'You have a smudge,' he said, stroking her cheek gently with his thumb. '*Hasta la vista!*', then he was gone, laughing, as she stood, open-mouthed, shaking with indignation at the arrogance and presumption of this unwelcome intruder.

Turning back to her task she lathered the luckless mare, Pepita, until the animal squealed in alarm. Patting her apologetically, she gave her some sugar, telling herself firmly that she must not make hasty judgements, but she could not shake off a sense of foreboding. She quickly finished her work, tidied everything away and went into the house, where she made a sandwich, poured a glass of lemonade and took them, with her knitting and a Spanish grammar, into the garden. By the time Eulalia returned from school she was calm and relaxed and together they walked down to the paddock to exercise the horses. Margarita and Teresa arrived with news that the Nationalists were advancing on Madrid. Barcelona was full of foreign journalists who were interviewing volunteers who had come to help the Republican cause. It seemed that the whole world was now watching Spain's agony.

At dinner that night Ramon Martinez shook his head sadly. 'There will be no victors. This is just a rehearsal for something much more sinister. There will be no safe place in Europe.'

Before gloom descended, Teresa interjected. 'Speaking of rehearsals, we go to the ballet tomorrow! It's "The Nutcracker".'

The young faces turned towards her in excitement and, darting a warning glance at her husband, she answered their questions about the dancers and the music.

Later, as they made coffee in the kitchen, Margot passed on the message from Vicente, shaking her head as Margarita demanded to know what she thought of him. 'Really, I don't know! He was only here for few moments. Seriously, though, don't you think it's dangerous for him to come here? Your parents could have seen him.'

Margarita sighed. 'I am over eighteen, but you are right. I don't want to upset Papa. He has enough to worry about at the moment. I want to see Vicente and you can help by covering for me, so that nobody will need to know.'

Margot had no option but to agree and they arranged to go into the city together next day.

Chapter Six

THE BUS WAS LATE and it was almost noon when they reached the Ramblas. They had arranged to meet at the café at 3.30 to travel home together and it was too early for lunch, so Margot went to the art gallery and spent an hour in almost solitary contemplation of the paintings and sculpture. She had visited galleries in Paris and Milan with Aunt Janey and gazed in wonder at the rich variety of style and talent. Over the years she had developed a taste for modern art and in the long school holidays she would sometimes go into London on her own to visit the Tate or the National Gallery before meeting her aunt for lunch. In Barcelona she had been delighted to find so many Picasso paintings as well as other interesting Spanish artists with whose work she was unfamiliar and, on her first visit to the gallery, one of the curators, seeing her absorption in one of the pictures, had taken the trouble to explain the history and tell her about the artist. Since then, she had been several times, once with Margarita, who was also fond of art, but more usually, alone. The tourist trade had disappeared as a result of the rising and the galleries were quiet havens of peace, where one could sit and contemplate, shutting out the problems of the world outside.

Margarita hastened to her rendezvous with Vicente in a café on the other side of the Ramblas which had been taken over by the Communists for vetting their new recruits to the International Brigades. He was waiting at the door and, kissing her quickly, led her to a table in the corner, calling to the waiter to bring coffee and cognac as he settled her into a chair. Taking her hand, he told her how much he had missed her and had been desperate to see her. She was even more beautiful than he remembered and he was lucky that she had not found someone else and decided to stay in England. Margarita, charmed, protested her undying faithfulness and the next few minutes passed in pleasant dalliance until they were interrupted by the arrival of their coffee. Vicente told her of his elevation in the Party and revealed that he had a surprise for her. He was being transferred to Barcelona to train foreign volunteers for the International Brigades and would be able to spend some time with her.

Could she get away? She could, but it would mean taking Margot into her confidence. He raised an eyebrow. 'Your plain little friend? She seems nice enough. Perhaps we can find her an *amigo* to keep her occupied!' He laughed, then gazed intently into her eyes. 'I need you, Margarita. Don't leave me again.'

As she walked towards the cafe, Margot, ready for lunch now, caught up with Lola and the two girls went in together. Pilar was already there and Margot explained their friend's absence. They did not share Margarita's admiration of Vicente, but it was her choice. They had been to another meeting of the '*Mujeres Libres*' and recounted laughingly how Pilar had been propositioned by a woman dressed as a man and both had been badgered to join a women's battalion in the militia. They would be looking elsewhere for their entertainment in future. Lola had some good news. She was to start work at the new nursery next week, so she would not be joining them at the café. Pilar, looking over her shoulder, remarked that 'the boys' had come in and Margot turned as Sven approached their table.

'Pardon, there are just two of us, may we join you?' he asked and they made room for him and his friend, a stocky, red-haired Dutch lad with a cheerful grin. The others, he explained, had joined a regiment and were already at the Madrid front. He and Dolf wanted to fight on the Republican side, but, not being communists, were waiting to join a mixed Brigade, probably in the next two weeks. They still had enough money to pay for their accommodation for a while and could afford to wait for the right opportunity. Taking a piece of paper from his pocket, he offered it to Margot, who opened it hesitantly to reveal a remarkably observed drawing of herself, which he had done in the café after they had met. She thanked him, blushing, as her companions exclaimed on the likeness and demanded that he do the same for them.

'Maybe,' he temporised, then changed the subject to talk about American films, for which they all had great enthusiasm. Dolf, it transpired, was training as a sound recordist and hoped eventually to work at a film studio where his uncle was a producer. He could converse in both Spanish and English and amused them with back-stage stories until Margarita appeared and it was time to go. As Margot rose, Sven leaped up and asked if she would meet him somewhere. She hesitated, then nodded and said she would see him in the Ramblas at three o'clock in two days' time.

On the bus Margarita was dreamily quiet, but smiled her approval as Margot showed her the drawing and announced her intention of meeting

Sven. She told her of Vicente's transfer and hoped they could work out some way of leaving and returning at the same time, though Margot warned her that she would probably not be seeing Sven regularly. Eulalia met them at the bottom of the drive and they walked up together. They were to have an early meal before going to the theatre and there was just enough time to exercise the horses, so she and Margot stopped at the stables while Margarita went into the house to help Maria. Pappa was busy at the hospital and would not be home until after nine o'clock, so they would leave a cold meal for him.

It was a delightful evening. The packed theatre buzzed with anticipation until the curtain rose and the beautiful music flooded the auditorium. The young Russian dancers performed exquisitely, the principals taking five curtain calls before the audience would let them go. There must have been tension for the artistes touring a country ravaged and embittered, where sudden outbreaks of disorganised fighting threatened the lives of the innocent, as well as the participants, but there was no sign of it in their performance and the citizens of Barcelona showed their appreciation. Margot was captivated. She had never seen a professional ballet and her eyes shone as she hugged Teresa, thanking her profusely for the treat. Eulalia adored the Sugar Plum Fairy and they bought a picture postcard of the ballerina so that she could show Margarita, who had stayed at home with a headache, what she had missed.

Margot had a moment of apprehension as they approached the house, but relaxed as Ramon greeted them with a smile, telling an excited Eulalia to speak softly because her sister had a headache. Margarita appeared in a dressing gown, looking suitably pale, but saying that she felt much better and demanding to know all the details. The three needed no encouragement to relive the performance and each recaptured her favourite moments until Eulalia, attempting to illustrate the delicate steps of the Sugar Plum Fairy, overbalanced and fell on to a sofa to boos and catcalls from her unsympathetic family.

Later, Margot slipped into Margarita's room to check that all was well and was not surprised to learn that the headache had been a ruse to give her an opportunity to see Vicente. She was horrified to learn that he had been to the house and scolded Margarita for taking such a risk. What if her father had caught them?

Margarita was defiant. 'He didn't. Vicente had gone half an hour before Pappa came home and, anyway, we were in the stables, not in the house, so I would have had time to make up an excuse for being out.'

Margot shook her head in disbelief, remarking tartly that she did not look as if she had spent an enjoyable evening and asking how they had passed the time in such an uncomfortable place.

'Talking,' was the reply, then, forlornly, 'You wouldn't understand!' How could she explain her elation at Vicente's words of love, his gentle caresses as he described the future they would share when the battle for the Republic was won, the unease as his voice thickened and his embraces became more urgent and his kisses rough and demanding? When she resisted, he had pleaded and cajoled, reproached her for treating him so cruelly when he had waited so long for her, dreaming only of the day when they would be together. Why did she not trust him? She could not love him as she claimed. And afterwards, the flat, silent feeling of revulsion, tears pricking at her eyelids as she wiped herself with her handkerchief, trying not to show alarm at the spots of blood on the white cotton. Vicente, gentle again, had cradled her in his arms.

'It will be better next time,' he murmured, as they adjusted their clothes and brushed straw from their hair. She pulled herself together. 'You must go. Pappa will be home soon.' He hesitated, looking anxiously at her drawn face and she reassured him, agreeing to meet for coffee next day, as she pushed him towards the door. By the time her father arrived, she was bathed and in her dressing gown, the headache no longer a fiction.

Margot, breaking the silence, asked what was wrong. Had they quarrelled? No, nothing like that, Margarita assured her. It was just that she realised the trouble it would have caused if her father had seen Vicente. It would not happen again. Margot, looking keenly at the contrite face, kissed her and returned, not wholly convinced, to her own room. As the door closed behind her, Margarita felt a stab of guilt at not having confided fully in her friend. They had always told each other everything. Was it because Margot could not possibly understand something of which she had no experience, or was it because she was ashamed of what she had done? Certainly she could not have related the incident with enthusiasm. It had not been the romantic consummation of her dreams, nurtured by books and films, but rather a clumsy, messy, business, embarrassing, to say the least. She realised, gloomily, that Vicente would now expect to carry on in this way. Well, maybe it would, as he had said, be better next time. Pulling the sheet up under her chin, she huddled down in the bed and tried to sleep. There was rain in the night, but they awoke to the sunshine of a beautiful autumn day. Margarita was bright and cheerful, with only the merest suggestion of dark circles beneath her eyes. It was Saturday, so Eulalia was not at school and Margot had promised to go for a ride with her. Surprisingly, Margarita decided to accompany them, walking, and they set off slowly up the winding trail into the hills, breathing in the fresh smell of pine trees after the rain as the horses brushed against the overhanging branches. They stopped to pick some rosemary, the horses snuffling and chomping at sparse clumps of grass.

'It will be winter soon,' sighed Eulalia. 'Do you think we shall have enough to eat?' The others looked at her uncomprehendingly. 'Carla's pappa says they will run out of food in Madrid in the winter because of the fighting and having to feed the soldiers. He says they will kill horses and cats and eat them. And now soldiers are coming here and I don't want them to eat Diablo and Pepita.'

Margarita put an arm round her sister 'Oh, Lallie dear, you must not worry about that. Madrid is the capital and that is why it keeps being attacked. It is true that it might become difficult to get food into the city, but most of the food comes from this area, so we are not likely to have problems. We have quite a lot of food in the house, you know. Remember the hams and sausages hanging in the cellar and the vegetables that you and Paco planted in the garden?'

The child's face brightened.

Margarita added hastily, 'It would be better if you didn't mention those things, though, in case people think we are preparing for trouble and being selfish. We don't want to start a panic, do we? Now come on, I thought we were here to get some exercise!' Taking Diablo's bridle, she patted the saddle and Eulalia mounted happily. Behind her, Margarita raised an eyebrow and smiled ruefully as she met Margot's quizzical glance.

After lunch, with no further mention of the conversation, Eulalia disappeared to find Paco, while Margot and Margarita took the bus into the city to keep their separate trysts. The bus was packed, inhibiting anything more than inconsequential chatter, and as they parted, they arranged to meet at six o'clock at the bus stop. Margot could see Sven's blond head among the crowds in the Ramblas and pushed her way towards him. He looked relieved, as if he had doubted that she would come.

'Drink?' he suggested.

Margot shook her head. 'No. It's such a lovely day, why not go for a walk?' They boarded a tram and were soon out in the countryside.

They talked about their homes and families, Margot feeling the familiar pang of isolation as Sven described with affection life on the farm, his loving, but rather unworldly parents and the antics of his four younger siblings. He was studying architecture and still had two years of his degree course to complete. His prowess at athletics earned him popularity and privileges at the University and his expenses to compete in the Popular Olympiad had been paid out of a special fund to encourage sporting achievement. Margot urged him to give up the idea of joining the Brigade and go home while he still had the chance, but he insisted that it was important to fight Fascism, not just for Spain, but because, unchecked, it would certainly spread and stifle the hopes and ambitions of ordinary young people everywhere. Why did Margot not go home? How long did she intend to stay? She did not know. Soon, perhaps, though she had no family now and rather dreaded the thought of taking up her life again. He asked if she had a boyfriend and she smiled wryly at the memory of a couple of disastrous dates with an embarrassed young man she had met at her aunt's office in the school holidays, who, eager to impress, had flung himself upon her in the back row of the cinema, covering her face with wet, inexpert kisses. Struggling for breath, she had exploded into uncontrollable giggles. End of romance. Attending an all girls' school gave little opportunity for meeting young men, she told him, so apart from the occasional mild flirtation on holiday or at a dance, there was no-one. Sven was incredulous, relationships between the sexes being much more open in Sweden, but hopeful that she might consider him a suitable applicant for the vacancy. Margot laughed, but would not commit herself, then, all too soon, it was time to go. They arranged to meet for lunch at the café in two days' time and planting a swift kiss on her cheek he was gone.

On the bus home, Margarita reported that the situation in Madrid was worse than they had been led to believe from radio broadcasts. Republican forces, retreating from Estremadura towards the capital, were under constant bombardment and some of the militia groups had deserted in chaos. The aerodrome at Getafe had been taken, but the arrival of Russian tanks and aircraft had turned certain defeat into hopes of victory as their fighter planes chased the Germans and Italians from the skies. Vicente had been euphoric about the upturn in Republican fortunes and she was afraid that he would ask to be sent back to the capital. In the meantime, she had arranged to spend the next day with him and wanted Margot to cover for her. Margot sighed. She hated the deception and anyway had no intention of intensifying her own relationship with Sven, so she would have to find some other way of spending the day without arousing suspicion about Margarita's absence.

At dinner that evening Eulalia provided the answer. The pile of woollen socks which she and the rest of the family had knitted had been increased by contributions from Maria's family and some of her friends at school and needed to be taken to the hospital. It was too much for one person to carry and she had to go to school, so please could the girls do it for her? Dr Martinez said they could go with him in the car and he would show them where to take the socks. They might like to have a look round the hospital while they were there. Margot said she would love to see the hospital. Margarita wrinkled her nose, saying she would rather stay at home and tidy her room if they didn't mind, as she hated the smell of disinfectant and seeing sick people depressed her. It was arranged that Margot would go and the problem of finding an excuse for spending the day apart was solved.

Chapter Seven

THE MORNING WAS CLOUDY, the sky heavy with threatened rain, but Margot, after a fitful night, felt a strange sense of excitement as she dressed and ran downstairs to the kitchen. He was already there and smiled, raising the teapot enquiringly as she appeared. She nodded and put sliced bread under the grill, now quite at ease with the man whose presence had originally over-awed her. The radio was on and suddenly a news bulletin announced that overnight the Government had packed up and left Madrid for Valencia. Convinced that the capital would fall, the Prime Minister was determined that legal leadership of the Republic must be maintained to avoid international recognition of a fascist regime if the cabinet was captured and deposed. A military junta would rule in Madrid. The voice of La Pasionaria harangued troops and citizens to resist to the death and defend their city against the rebels and the dreaded army of Moors which supported them.

Ramon switched off the radio and Margot waited anxiously until he said, 'There is nothing we can do but wait. This may be the end of it, maybe not. Whatever happens, there will be work to be done and we must carry on.'

Hurriedly, they finished breakfast, conversing desultorily about the weather and the garden, then loaded the car and set out for the hospital. The reception area was buzzing with the news and the doctor nodded and made reassuring noises as he steered Margot firmly past the knot of voluble staff anxious for his opinion. His room was surprisingly small, with just a couple of armchairs in front of the polished mahogany desk, which held a telephone and some letters which had been opened and placed on top of a pile of blue files. A bookcase crammed with medical books ran along one wall and there was a door in the opposite wall which, seeing Margot's puzzled glance, he opened to reveal an examination room with a screened couch, washbowl, scales and a variety of mysterious machines and instruments, the tools of his trade. A nurse, checking the contents of a drug cupboard, smilingly undertook to deliver Margot and the socks to the matron, with instructions to have her back in the office by one o'clock, so that they could go to lunch. The telephone rang and Ramon answered, waving a brief farewell before turning to speak rapidly into the instrument as work claimed his attention. The friendly young woman chatted animatedly as they walked down the long corridor and Margot permitted herself a little glow of satisfaction at being able to hold a conversation in Spanish without any difficulty.

Matron was delighted with the socks and Margot gave Eulalia full credit for the idea and the enthusiasm which had encouraged the rest of them to join in. The motherly lady, small and round with a neat bun of dark hair, slightly grey at the temples and a serene expression in her hazel eyes, laughed gently and said she was not surprised. She knew Eulalia and predicted a brilliant future for such an agile young mind. Elena, the nurse who had escorted Margot, was sure that she could persuade some of her friends to start knitting and departed with a pair of the socks as a pattern to show what was needed. Tea was brought in and they were joined by the Assistant Matron, Maria Calhoun. Maria, tall and thin with a mane of red, curly hair and heavily freckled skin, looked totally out of place among her Latin colleagues. Saved from plainness by a pair of sparkling blue eyes, she was the image of her Irish father, who, while training as a chef at a London hotel, had become besotted with the visiting sister of his Spanish colleague, married her and returned with her to Spain, where they opened a small restaurant.

The business prospered and, after the heartbreak of several miscarriages, produced Maria, their only child, the pride and joy of both her parents. Nursing was her vocation and she had trained in Madrid and at St Thomas' Hospital in London, gaining impeccable qualifications. Only thirty years old, she was already near the top of her profession and totally content, with no desire for marriage or children. She readily undertook to show Margot round the hospital and they passed an engrossing morning as she carried out her daily inspection with the English girl in tow.

The wards were sparsely furnished, but spacious and very clean, with long rows of beds, almost all of which were occupied. A few seriously ill patients lay in small rooms outside the main wards and there was an operating theatre on each of the three floors of the hospital. Most of the patients were men, many clearly victims of war, but there was a small ward for women and a maternity ward, where Margot watched fascinated as tiny babies in incubators were fed through tubes. A proud mother thrust a baby boy into her arms and Margot, who had never seen a newborn child before, overcame her nervousness and gazed spellbound at the silky eyelashes, dimpled fists and tiny, perfect fingernails of the sleeping infant. Maria laughed and told her that all the nurses liked working on this ward best, because most of the time there was no bad news. In no time at all, the morning was over and as they walked back to Dr Martinez's office, Maria asked if she would like to come into the hospital for an hour or two sometimes to talk with two or three English-speaking foreign patients, injured in the fighting, who could not speak Spanish and might like help to write home or just have a chat with someone who spoke their language. Margot, flattered, accepted happily.

Dr Martinez was waiting and after exchanging a few pleasantries with Maria, they set out for the tapas bar opposite the hospital. It was raining and, as they ran for shelter, he put a hand on Margot's elbow to steer her across the road. She felt a shiver of excitement at the light touch and when they arrived, laughing and gasping as they pushed through the door, shaking the rain from their jackets, she was acutely aware of his physical closeness. Pretending to study the menu, she watched him covertly as he went to hang up the jackets, stopping for a moment to exchange a quick word with a colleague, acknowledging the proprietor's greeting, then returning to sit opposite her, enquiring solicitously what she would like to eat. She felt proud, possessive, of this handsome, distinguished man who treated her as a mature woman. Restraining an urge to push back a strand of wet hair from his forehead, she affected to puzzle over the menu, unable to make up her mind, and he suggested they share a selection of tapas if she cared to allow him to choose. While they waited, the proprietor brought bread, olives and wine and she sipped slowly, glowing as she described her morning. He was charmingly atten-tive, heaping morsels of food on to her plate from the little dishes, offering wine, telling amusing anecdotes of hospital life and expressing pleasure at her plan to visit patients. She could happily have sat all day, but regretfully, he had to return to work. She did not want to spoil the moment and, rather than return to wait for him at the hospital, she announced her intention of walking into the city to do some shopping before taking the bus back to the house. It had stopped raining and she thanked him earnestly for lunch and for introducing her to the hospital. With a slight bow of acknowledgement, he smiled and was gone. Walking along the damp streets in a glow of happiness, she luxuriated in the memory of that stolen hour, then almost laughed out loud at herself for her silliness. Of course it had meant nothing to him beyond being kind to his daughter's friend and she was acting like a schoolgirl with a crush on a film star. But she could dream, couldn't she? Young men like Sven seemed gauche in comparison she mused, nice enough as friends, but hardly inspiring romantically. She bought writing paper and envelopes in preparation for her next visit to the hospital and strolled for a while in the fitful sunshine before joining the queue at the bus stop. Margarita had waited until the house was empty before hurriedly changing her clothes and running down the hill to the main road, just a few moments before an old black Chevrolet sped into view, barely stopping as Vicente leaned over to open the door for her to jump in. Settling into the comfortable leather seat, she asked whose it was.

'Mine!' He laughed, jubilant at the symbol of recognition of his importance to the Party. Apparently the car had been taken from one of the foreign Embassies in Madrid, whose occupants were fleeing the city and, along with other such acquisitions, had been delivered to Barcelona for the use of key personnel. He needed to be mobile in order to check progress at all the barracks in the area and report back to the ruling Communist Committee, of which he was now a member. As the car approached the dock gates, two sentries armed with machine guns stepped out and flagged it down, then stepped back saluting as they recognised Vicente. Margarita found herself propelled past tanks and Scottish Ambulance vehicles, through a large shed where men and women in blue overalls were sorting through piles of uniforms and into a small brick building where Vicente had his office. The large room on the ground floor boasted a sofa and three leather armchairs, a small wooden table, two dining chairs and a desk, littered with papers. In one corner was a sink, on which reposed a collection of unwashed plates and mugs and, next to it, a paraffin stove with two rings. A partition running almost the length of the room from the door to the window screened the cramped sleeping area which consisted of a single bed and a chest of drawers.

A telephone on the desk shrilled urgently and Margarita flopped down on the sofa as Vicente answered it. She watched his lean body tense as he reached across the desk, his eyes narrowing as he listened, then, with a shout of laughter, he put down the receiver, and charged across the room, pulling her to her feet and dancing her round the room. The call was from Madrid. Fascist orders had been found on the body of a dead Nationalist officer showing a change of plan and, as a consequence, the bulk of the Republican forces were being switched to defend the University area in anticipation of a Nationalist attack next morning. The first of the International Brigades was going in to reinforce the army units and local militias already in position. Margarita stared at him dumbly, afraid that he was about to leave her and dash off to Madrid, until, seeing her dismay, he cupped his hands under her chin and kissed the tip of her nose, laughing softly as he reassured her.

'Did you think I could bear to leave my beautiful Margarita now that I know she loves me?' His kisses, passionate, demanding, melted her anxiety and she abandoned herself with an unbounded enthusiasm which surprised them both.

As they drove back, her head leaning on his shoulder, he told her that it might be difficult to see her in the next few days depending on the outcome of tomorrow's battle, but he would telephone. She pouted, demanding to know why she could not see him at the barracks if he was not going to Madrid, but he refused to be drawn, saying that it was top secret and she must be patient. He dropped her at the bottom of the drive, blowing a kiss as he roared off up the hill. She walked slowly up the drive and entered the house, noting with relief that she was the first one home.

Over the next week sporadic reports of the battle for Madrid were broadcast on the radio throughout the day as the citizens grimly dug themselves in and fought for their lives. Groups of workers, railwaymen, teachers, barbers, formed themselves into battalions, backed by an assortment of willing, but untrained, volunteers including refugees who had fled from previous Nationalist attacks. Women and children dug trenches, gathered stones and set up barricades, while buildings were converted into canteens and emergency hospitals where doctors and nurses from the Scottish Ambulance Unit and the Red Cross prepared as best they could to cope with casualties. Two International Brigades, under Communist command, fought bravely, but failed to check the Nationalist advance and an Anarchist Brigade, arriving from the Aragon front, led by Buenaventuro Durruti, who had spearheaded the attack on the Atarazanas barracks during the July rising in Barcelona, was forced to retreat when the promised air and artillery support failed to materialise. During a fierce battle in which the University was lost to the Nationalists, Durruti was wounded accidentally by one of his own men and died a few days later. There was total chaos as German and Italian bombers kept up a merciless bombing campaign, reducing vast areas of the city to rubble and cutting off food supplies, while Franco threatened to destroy the capital rather than concede.

The Martinez household tried to focus on its daily routine, but, like everyone else, could not avoid returning to the implications of the situation. Durruti's body was brought back to Barcelona, where it seemed that the whole population turned out to mourn at his funeral. Margarita and Margot went with Paco and Maria, but the streets were so packed that they could see nothing and were buffeted along as the shouts and wails of the crowd reached fever pitch. Holding hands and clinging to a street lamp, they managed to stay together. A man behind them asserted repeatedly that Durruti had died because the Communists, jealous of the Anarchist hero, had deliberately withheld reinforcements. Margarita, furious, turned to challenge him, but was stopped by a sharp dig in the ribs from Margot, frowning and shaking her head. Later, at the barracks, she told Vicente what was being said, but he merely shrugged, saying the Anarchists were a liability and should all be shot.

Margot had established a routine of going to the hospital in the afternoon on two days a week, delivering more socks and spending an hour with two boys who were recovering from operations. Billy, a Londoner, had been injured in a training accident at the barracks, badly damaging his hand, and the other, a Scot called Hamish, had been rushed in with a burst appendix. Neither could speak Spanish and Margot helped by giving them the news, writing letters and doing little errands for them such as buying sweets and stamps. Both were determined to return to the Brigade, though Hamish took a lugubrious delight in telling his voluble little companion that, with half a hand he would be 'Nae mair use than a chocolate teapot!' Sometimes she stopped for a cup of coffee with Matron or Maria Calhoun. Occasionally she caught sight of Ramon as he went about his work, but, apart from a wave as he passed, there was no contact. The day after the funeral, she went to the cafe with Margarita to meet Pilar for lunch before going on to the hospital. Conchita was there too, having left Madrid hurriedly when it became clear that the University was the focal point of the grim struggle. She had been terrified by being stopped and questioned several times a day by police and militia men searching for spies and shells ripping through buildings and tram tracks only yards away. Things had calmed down now and people were claiming that the capital had been saved, but there were still air raids and bomb explosions and she would not go back. Juan-Manuel was relieved and at least they could see each other. Pilar told them excitedly that a new hairdressing salon had opened. She had been offered a job and was due to start work there the following week. She would not have much time for lunch on most days, but hoped to see them, perhaps once a week at least. They could meet in the Ramblas for a chat, she suggested. The girls were delighted for her and promised to support her by booking appointments for themselves. Margot asked eagerly if she could lighten her fair hair. Bleached by the summer sun, the effect had been flattering, but it had faded now and she was eager to have Pilar restore the brightness and show her how to do it for herself. Pilar promised to do it, though she cautioned against going too obviously blonde, which would spoil the effect. Was Margot still seeing Sven? Margot confirmed that she was, but denied romance, saying it was not certain whether he would suddenly disappear into a Brigade. There was nowhere to see him in private and it was not safe to come into the city in the evening to go to the cinema, for instance, because the soldiers from the barracks were roaming the streets, often the worse for drink. The others laughed at her prim denial, saying love would always find a way, slyly suggesting nooks and crannies off the beaten track where lovers could find shelter from prying eyes. She joined in the good-humoured banter, but her thoughts were elsewhere.

Chapter Eight

CHRISTMAS PASSED without any religious celebration to arouse left-wing anger and suspicion, but many families did their best to make a festival of the New Year. The weather was cold, damp and foggy and the Martinez family made themselves as comfortable as possible with a meal of chicken roasted slowly in the pot with garlic, lentils and herbs and warm bread straight from the oven. There were oranges and dried figs to follow and a hot punch spiced with cinnamon. Paco and Maria were spending the day with their daughter's family, so Teresa and the two older girls had prepared the meal while Eulalia kept her father company. There had been no word from Rafael apart from a message delivered to Ramon at the hospital a month earlier by a doctor passing through on his way to Madrid to say that he was safe. At breakfast they had said a prayer for him, Margarita hiding her anti-religious principles in deference to her parents.

After the meal came the exchange of presents. Eulalia, flushed and giggling from excitement rather than the small glass of punch she had been allowed, gave out lumpy packages to everyone. A woollen scarf for Pappa, mittens for Mamma and long, striped knitted stockings for Margarita and Margot, lovingly made by her own industrious hands.

'You can wear them under your slacks to keep warm,' she explained as Margot held them up for inspection and pronounced them perfect. She squealed with delight as she saw the shiny leather riding boots, a joint present from Margarita and Margot, and loved the carved olive wood horse her father gave her. Mamma's gift of a book about ballet completed her happiness. Margot shyly presented her gifts. A pretty marquetry box inlaid with ivory for Teresa, a filmy scarf for Margarita and a silver tiepin for Ramon. Margarita had soft leather gloves for her mother, an engraved glass paperweight for her father and a lovely Spanish mantilla with combs for Margot. Teresa had managed to procure French perfume for both the older girls, while Ramon gave them books, *Don Quixote* for Margarita, a collection of Spanish poetry for Margot. All pronounced themselves delighted with their presents as they retired to the music room for an evening of piano music and singing. As they drank a toast to the New Year, Margot felt that she had never been happier.

The weather continued cold and wet throughout the month. Both girls fell into a routine of helping Teresa at the soup kitchen on two days a week, after which Margarita dashed off to the barracks to see Vicente while Margot continued her visits to the hospital. Hamish had returned to the barracks and Billy had been spirited away by the Scottish Ambulance Unit to Valencia to be transported home on a British ship, but there was a steady stream of casualties from the International Brigades to take their place. She still saw Sven, who had not yet made a decision whether to join a Brigade, though the weather was too bad to go anywhere apart from the café or a cinema matinee. Civilian travel to and from Spain had ceased and it was no longer possible to leave without consular authority and a permit from the local workers' committee to board a foreign ship. Even then, there was no chance of a passage to Sweden and he would have to make his way from Marseilles or Gibraltar with very little money left in his pocket. Time was running out. Heavy rain and fog hampered both sides in their objective of taking the capital, though air attacks and fierce hand to hand fighting were reported daily over the radio as the Nationalist forces crept up the coast from Marbella culminating in the shock defeat of the Republicans at Málaga following heavy naval bombardment. Civilians and militiamen were slaughtered as they fled or were rounded up and put up against a wall and shot. Meanwhile, an offensive designed to cross the river Jarama and cut off the road between Madrid and Valencia resulted in stalemate with appalling casualties on both sides and hunger adding to the misery as supplies failed to get through. Newly formed International Brigades, hastily pushed out after minimal training, were thrown into suicidal attempts to hold the sector and a British battalion was practically wiped out.

Vicente was moody, raging against the incompetence of the Government, whose lack of co-ordination and failure to supply ammunition had almost caused the collapse of the whole Republican sector at Pozuelo and again at Malaga. Fleeing militiamen, many without weapons or ammunition and with no battle experience, had died of cold and starvation or been shot as deserters. Morale was low and he was impatient to see the various militia groups organised into a disciplined army under communist control. Tight-lipped, he paced up and down, paying little attention to Margarita, apart from perfunctory acts of lovemaking, leaving her bored and resentful.

The battle for control continued to beset the Government, who were powerless to stop communist infiltration of the police, the assault troops and the Brigades. As a result of pressure from the Russian ambassador, Rosenberg, the Prime Minister was forced into sacking the War Minister, General Asensio, who had demanded an investigation into irregularities in a communist regiment's accounts and objected to their efforts to win over the paramilitary organisations. Furious at seeing his authority slipping away, the Prime Minister, Largo Caballero, complained to Moscow. On the 21st of February Rosenberg was recalled, but the spread of communism continued under his successor.

A few days later, Vicente was called to Madrid and returned exultant, having been appointed as a commissar to Brigade Headquarters with responsibility for supervising the commanders. Margarita's pride was tinged with jealousy because his elevation meant that he would have less time for her. She was also concerned for his safety, knowing that his activities in furthering communist infiltration of the Brigades would make him a target for anarchists still rankling over the death of Durruti. He laughed, ruffling her hair and pulling her to him, eyes narrowed, voice thick with lust as he told her that, for now, the only target he was interested in was her. At the hospital, Margot went straight to Maria Calhoun's room to check the ward list and was greeted with relief.

'I am so glad to see you today. We have a very sick boy in a state of shock, probably a deserter from one of the fronts, and we are so busy I have no time to spend with him. He doesn't speak, but I think he may be English. Will you try to talk to him, very gently, and see if you can help? If he is a deserter he will be in great danger and we may have to get him away.'

She led Margot to a small room, away from the ward, where a small figure sat hunched and motionless, wrapped in a blanket. He had been found that morning, barely alive, in a ditch on the Valencia road, fortunately by a doctor from the Scottish Ambulance on his way back to Barcelona. Filthy, encrusted with dried vomit and faeces, cold and starving, he had been carefully warmed back to consciousness, bathed and deloused and his injuries tended. He was covered in bruises, and had a broken leg and a festering flesh wound, probably from a gunshot, on his back. Throughout the painful handling and treatment he had shown no reaction, made no sound, his eyes fixed dully on some nameless horror. They had managed to force a couple of spoonfuls of thin chicken soup between his cracked and swollen lips before he started to retch, but that was all. It would be some time before he could take food normally. Maria nodded to Margot and left.

Pulling up a chair, Margot sat by the bed.

'Hello,' she said, softly. 'Are you English? Don't be afraid, you are safe now.' There was no response. He hardly seemed to be breathing. His hands were clenched, gripping the blanket, his eyes lifeless, staring straight ahead. She talked very slowly, gently, about anything, home, childhood, favourite film stars, but there was not a flicker to show that he had registered her presence. Feeling helpless, she went into the corridor and asked a passing nurse whether he had any belongings which might at least give a clue to his nationality. His clothes had been burned; the nurse thought there were some bits and pieces, but doubted whether there was anything which would identify him. Margot followed her to an office where she produced a bag containing a pencil, a cheap little St Christopher medal and, of all things, a flute, battered and rather bent. Nothing to show who he was, but, if the flute was his and not just something he had stolen to sell, music might be the key to gaining his attention. She asked if she could take the instrument home to see if it could be mended.

Back home, she showed it to Paco, who was sure he could do something with it and bore it off to his shed. Two hours later he returned, proudly bearing a clean and shiny instrument, having scoured it, straightened the mouthpiece and beaten out most of the dents. 'The reed looks to be intact. I think it will play,' he said, as Margot hugged him in delight. He asked no questions and Margot, conscious of the need to move swiftly without arousing undue interest, dashed off back to the hospital before anyone else returned home. The boy still sat, immobile, expressionless. She held the flute in front of him, but he gave no sign of recognition, his eyes unblinking as she pleaded with him to look at it. In desperation she grabbed his hands, clamping his fingers on the instrument, holding them in place to prevent rejection. Suddenly she realised that he was holding it and took her hands away. As she stepped back, a tear rolled down his face, splashing on his hand, though he made no movement and his eyes remained fixed, staring into space. The nurse appeared, with a doctor who had come to check his injuries, and Margot excitedly pointed to the boy's face, now wet with tears. The doctor nodded approvingly and turned back the blanket, exposing the short bowed legs and Margot gasped.

'Rickets,' said the doctor, 'caused by malnutrition in infancy. It's a wonder he managed to walk so far in his condition.'

Margot, remembering the ferry crossing, exclaimed excitedly, 'No, I mean I think I have seen him before. He is English and they were coming to join an International Brigade.' She racked her brain for the name, trying to connect this broken waif with the perky, bright-eyed youngster on the boat. 'Jimmy, yes, I'm sure it was Jimmy. From Tyneside. He had what looked like a clarinet case. It must have been the flute.'

The nurse ran to fetch Maria Calhoun as the doctor finished his examination. Margot had a sudden inspiration and began to sing, softly, 'The Bladen Races'.

The eyes flickered as she paused, saying, 'Why ay, man. Come on, Jimmy, give us a tune.' The fingers moved along the flute and he raised it to his lips, but winced at the touch of the mouthpiece. He turned to Margot, the dead eyes alive and anguished now, and began to sob, 'Mam, Ah want me Mam,' as she took him in her arms, saying, 'Hush, Jimmy, you're safe now. We'll get you home.' Maria rustled in, carrying fresh clothes, followed by the nurse with soup and bread. He must have deserted in the rout at Malaga nearly three weeks ago. God knew how he had survived, but they must get him out before he was discovered. There was an escape route, but Margot must go now and not ask questions or mention anything to anyone about this boy or his life could be in danger. Obediently, Margot went.

As she left the hospital, she heard her name called and saw Ramon Martinez hurrying towards her. She had not realised it was so late, she told him, as he escorted her to his car, she had been trying to help someone write a letter. 'Yes, I know,' he smiled. 'Maria will see that it is posted.' She glanced at him sharply, but he made no further comment, turning the conversation to a discussion about art. During the evening she could not help wondering about poor Jimmy and had to concentrate hard, busying herself with her knitting to conceal her inattention. 'Had a tiff with Sven,' she told Margarita, who had remarked on her unsociability, immediately regretting it as her friend withdrew, satisfied, with a knowing smile.

It was two days before she returned to the hospital. Maria Calhoun greeted her with the news that all had gone well. Jimmy had been transported overnight to Valencia by the Scottish Ambulance and embarked on a British ship which sailed a few hours later. Margot knew better than to ask for details and the realisation of the danger they all faced was brought home to her when Maria told her quietly that two militiamen had visited the hospital the previous day, inspecting the patients and asking questions about their political affinities. Maria had told them angrily that she was a nurse, interested only in treating sick people whoever they were. Having found nothing suspicious, they had departed satisfied.

Sven had at last made up his mind to join the Brigade and he duly presented himself at the barracks, only to be told that he would first be sent to Albacete for induction before being assigned to a battalion. He would be leaving in a few days' time and did not know whether he would return to Barcelona. Margot received the news with mixed feelings. Her fear of his being injured in battle was mitigated by relief that he had enlisted, because there was an increasing danger that young foreign men who had not committed themselves to the cause might be seen as spies and shot. She would miss him, for she liked him and he was fun to be with, but her own emotions were confused. She loved a man who was quite unattainable. She could not reveal her feelings to him or, indeed, to anyone else and, even if there was a remote possibility that he might return her affection, the betrayal of the kindness shown to her by his family was beyond contemplation. It was idiotic to think that a romantic relationship with Sven would mean being unfaithful to Ramon, but was it fair to Sven to allow him to believe that she cared for him? On the other hand, the future for everyone now seemed so uncertain, why should they not just have fun? And she was curious. The other girls all seemed to have had more experience with boys than she had and Margarita's relationship with Vicente certainly involved more than a few stolen kisses. Maybe it was time for her to find out for herself what it was all about. Her silence troubled him.

'Margot?'

'I'm sorry, Sven,' she said, collecting herself. 'I know you have to do this. I just don't want you to get hurt.' They agreed to spend as much time together as possible in the few days left.

Chapter Nine

AT LAST THE WINTER WAS OVER and the sweet scent of blossom filled the air. The Ramblas teemed with people, cafés and shop fronts were painted and spruced up, young lovers strolled in parks and gardens. Madrid was still under siege and, while there was little outward sign of conflict in Barcelona, people were becoming less tolerant, the heady days of the July revolution fading as the bread queues lengthened and people hoarded, instead of sharing, supplies. The communist-controlled council had disbanded the food distribution committees and the black market flourished, supplying nightclubs and expensive restaurants. The atmosphere was uneasy, fear palpable in the growing awareness of danger ahead.

When she was not at the hospital, Margot spent most of the soft spring days with Sven. Like carefree tourists, they walked around the city, marvelling at Gaudi's spectacular Church of the Holy Family, still unfinished since building began in 1883. The famous architect had imprinted his flamboyant Art Nouveau style all over Barcelona and Sven, an ardent admirer, insisted on seeing everything. Margot, too, admitted to being impressed, but drew the line at the apartment block built to resemble a wave, which she considered to be quite ugly. She steered him round the art galleries, where they visited an exhibition of modern art and argued amicably about the relative merits of Picasso and Miró. They ran barefoot on the beach, where Sven wrote their names and drew pictures in the sand with a stick, until the stony stares of a little group of militia men reminded him that a young man out of uniform was an object of suspicion and hostility. Hurriedly he explained his embarrassment to Margot and they agreed that the beach should be avoided in future. Instead, they wandered happily down country roads, through olive groves, talking and laughing, with no mention of the war. They bought food and wine and picnicked among spring flowers, dabbling their fingers in the cool water of a stream or tossing breadcrumbs to the ducks. They held hands and kissed and when his lovemaking became more urgent, she did not resist. Margarita had settled into a pleasant routine, spending the mornings with Margot or helping her mother and the afternoons with Vicente, whose new responsibilities did not appear to be too onerous. On some evenings the girls washed their hair and played records on the gramophone in her room, giggling and exchanging confidences. She was glad that Margot had a steady beau, not only because it made her feel less guilty about neglecting her for Vicente, but because she genuinely felt that her friend needed someone of her own to care about. Sven would be away for several weeks, but she had already established, through Vicente, that he would be assigned to one of the Barcelona barracks. When Eulalia, seeing them whispering and laughing together, became curious about how they spent their days and asked whether they had boyfriends, they told her that they were meeting a group of girls and boys, including some young athletes who had not yet gone home, but that they were not seeing anyone in particular.

There was a new air of confidence about Margot, as she went about her duties at the hospital. Her friendship with Maria Calhoun had ripened through mutual respect since the 'Jimmy' episode and she often helped out in many ways when the hospital was under pressure, running messages, checking supplies, filling out patients' admission forms. Once or twice she had lunch with Ramon and the enchantment remained. It was strange, she mused, that she could contain her feelings at home when others were present, but come alive like this when she was alone with him. Talking, laughing, luxuriating in his undivided attention, she ached to touch his hand or stroke his face when concern furrowed his brow. If he suspected anything, he gave no sign, urbane and charming as always, to her and to everyone else.

On free afternoons, left to herself, she would take a book and walk a little way up the hill to sit in her favourite spot among the olive trees, breathing in the fresh scent of spring flowers and listening to the sweet sad song of hidden nightingales or the liquid bubbling notes of goldfinches. She delighted in the honeycombed limestone crags, millions of years old, stretching into the sky, pitted with caves and large dark holes and dotted with clumps of grass and plants which had seeded themselves in the rocks. Who knew what bird and insect life abounded among the stalactites and stalagmites and how many people, like her, had sat in wonderment imagining shapes and faces in the craggy rock face? The silence was awesome, the feeling of tranquillity something she had never before experienced.

One day she decided to walk further to watch the birds on a sheer wall of rock where they nested in the thousands of small holes. The afternoon sun warmed the huge stones scattered in the undergrowth and basking geckos scampered away as she approached. As she came out of the oak wood, within sight of the charcoal burner's hut, the door opened and a woman came out. Margot, shocked at seeing someone else in this lonely spot, quickly hid behind a tree. The woman turned back towards the door and a man appeared, taking her in his arms and kissing her. They clung together for a moment, then the woman pushed him away and ran down the hill, pulling a scarf over her hair. He did not watch her go, but withdrew into the cottage, closing the door. Margot, shrank back as the woman passed within a few feet of her hiding place. Then her mouth went dry, her heart beat rapidly and she thought she would faint as she recognised the woman dabbing tears from her face as she hurried unheedingly down the steep path. It was Teresa Martinez. Margot's head was whirling as she crept cautiously back to where she had left her book. There was no sign of Teresa, but who was the man? She had been too far away to see his face, but he was of medium height, slim, with dark wavy hair. It occurred to her that he would probably wait a few minutes, then come down the path and she decided to get back as quickly as possible, looking behind her every few yards to check that there was no-one behind her. She did not want Teresa to know that she had been there. It was not her business, she told herself, suppressing anxiety for Ramon, tinged with a guilty thrill of excitement as her imagination took flight. Back at the house, she sat in the garden for half an hour before wandering in through the back door. Teresa was in the kitchen washing lentils and smiled, noting the book.

'Oh, I didn't realise you were in the garden. I would have joined you. I'll make some tea.' Perfectly composed, she produced a sewing pattern and talked about a dress she was making for Eulalia, who was growing out of everything. It was as if nothing had happened and Margot resolved to put it out of her mind.

The next day was May Day, but the usual celebrations had been cancelled because of trouble between communists and anarchists which threatened public order. Margarita fretted because she could not find an excuse to go into the city to see Vicente. He had been preoccupied the previous day, pacing the floor and speaking curtly into the telephone, which rang incessantly. Hastily scribbled notes were handed to a procession of silent men who appeared at the door and her questions had met with a blank stare. Eventually she had flounced out, stung by his neglect and lack of trust. She was convinced that something important was about to happen and uneasy about his involvement. Trying to appear unconcerned, she twiddled the knobs on the radio, but there was no mention of anything other than the horrific reports of the destruction by German bombers of Guernica, leaving the shocked city a blazing inferno as flames devoured inhabitants, buildings and animals indiscriminately. The brave attempts by Republican battalions to hold back the Nationalists as they retreated towards Bilbao served only to heighten the growing bitterness at the government's failure to produce a unified defence strategy. Teresa busied herself with cutting out a dress for Eulalia, who was impatient to go for a ride and would not keep still, while Margot, having failed to interest Margarita in a walk, offered to accompany the child, consequent upon her co-operation in the fitting. Ramon had a full operating list at the hospital and would not be home until late, so dinner would be delayed. There was no chance for Margarita to escape her mother's eye, so, reluctantly, she resigned herself to helping with the sewing.

Wending their way up the path, the scrape of the horses' hooves on the rough stones echoing in the silence, the girls breathed in the soft woody smells and laughingly brushed spiders' webs from their faces as they passed under the trees. Lallie chattered happily and Margot, thinking about Sven, marvelled at the contrast between this place and the news they had heard on the radio. As they approached the charcoal burner's hut, she had a sudden feeling of apprehension, and was relieved when Lallie decided to stop and pick bluebells in the wood. Not that she expected anyone to be there, but it seemed prurient to pry into someone's love nest and, in the circumstances, she would prefer not to go there with Eulalia. The horses grazed quietly while they gathered the flowers and wrapped them carefully in paper bags salvaged from their lunch packs. The afternoon passed pleasantly and they made their way back bearing their bouquets for Teresa.

By the time Ramon arrived home, tired from a long day spent in complicated operations, the horses had been groomed, the dressmaking finished and tidied away and dinner almost ready. Margarita, pale and restless, disappeared after dinner to wash her hair and Margot followed, while the others retired to the music room to blot out the misery of the world outside. The spectre of Guernica, with its implications for their young men, haunted both girls and they shared their anxieties. Surely, Sven, untrained as yet, would not be sent to the front? Why was Vicente so secretive? Might he be preparing for action and leaving the barracks? The war was escalating, with new fronts opening up all over the country as outside forces joined in on both Republican and Nationalist sides. So far, Barcelona had escaped, but the fascists were gaining ground, launching air and marine attacks from Majorca and it could only be a matter of time before the Republican stronghold was broached. Margarita was devastated by the thought that she had unwittingly brought Margot into danger and begged her to consider going back to England while there was still time, but Margot assured her that she had never been happier and would not leave without her. Hugging each other tearfully, they decided to go to the barracks together next morning, hoping to reassure themselves.

At breakfast they proposed a shopping trip. Teresa had a committee meeting to attend and gave them a lift into the city, from where they took the tram to the barracks. All seemed normal and the sentry, used to seeing Margarita, waved them through the gate without comment. Vicente was not in his office, but a guard informed them that the Commissar was at the docks questioning a suspected deserter caught trying to stow away on a ship and would be back soon. He would not allow them to wait in the office, so they sat on a bench outside the building, ignoring the lascivious glances and crude remarks of passing soldiers, until, some twenty minutes later, Vicente appeared. He was flanked by two men in boiler suits, dragging between them a thin, bedraggled little man with a limp. There was blood in his matted beard and his hands were tied. At the sight of the girls, Vicente's face darkened with anger. He barked a command over his shoulder and the men disappeared with their prisoner into a shed. He walked past the bench, gesturing to them to follow and Margot looked tremulously at Margarita as they rose.

Margarita was in no mood for sulks and prepared to meet his displeasure with her own righteous indignation. As he held open the door of the office, however, he turned, smiling, and ushered them in, apologising for the lack of courtesy shown by his staff in making them wait outside. It made him angry, he said, that they had been subjected to the gaze of rough recruits. If he had known that they were coming he would have left instructions for their comfort. All charm now, he poured wine and handed round the glasses, pausing to drop a kiss on Margarita's hair before settling himself behind his desk. Margarita, mollified, but not deflected from her objective, told him of her fears that he might be about to be sent into danger and demanded to know what was happening. He put his feet up on the desk, leaned back in his chair and laughed, raising his glass to her as he declared, 'No, my sweet, I'm not going anywhere. I'm too important!' He had not meant to upset her the other day. It was simply that he had been busy, trying to arrange for the arrival of a large batch of recruits from training camp and being hampered by the inefficiency of the officers concerned. Everything was now ready and the troops were due that afternoon. Yes, he said, Sven Lindberg would be among them, but Margot must understand that he could not act as messenger and must wait for Sven to contact her. As they rose to leave, Margarita paused. 'What will happen to the prisoner?'

Vicente shrugged. 'He will be shot.'

Avoiding each other's eyes, they walked through the gate to the tram stop, where Margarita, fidgeting in her purse for pesetas, asked, 'Well, aren't you excited about Sven?' Margot shook her head slowly.

'I don't understand. Surely he was supposed to be in training longer than this? Why are they suddenly bringing extra troops here?' The same thought had occurred to Margarita, who was desperately trying to reconcile Vicente's performance as the charming host with that first malevolent glance and the cold, brutal way in which he casually dismissed the prisoner. She was uncomfortably aware of the swings in his attitude towards her, one moment the ardent lover, the next abrupt, dismissive, secretive. He had changed and she was no longer sure that she knew how his mind worked.

'You don't like Vicente, do you, Margot?'

Margot sighed. 'I hardly know him, but there is something about him ...' Her voice trailed off, then she said firmly, 'He probably has a lot on his mind at present and it is none of our business, but I know he upsets you sometimes and I hate to see you unhappy, that's all. Come on, let's have lunch.' She squeezed Margarita's arm affectionately and was rewarded with a grateful smile as they boarded the tram.

After lunch they sat in the Ramblas planning how Margot could see Sven. It seemed unlikely that he would get leave in his first few days, but if he did, he would certainly go to the café. She could look in there on her way to the hospital and leave a message for him. Margarita had decided to wait a few days before visiting Vicente at the barracks unless he telephoned her in the meantime. By then the recruits should have settled down and he would be less harassed. In a more optimistic frame of mind they pottered idly round the shops, buying some sweets for Lallie before going home.

Alighting from the bus they were surprised to see Ramon's car turning into the drive. It was at least two hours before his normal arrival and they looked at each other in alarm, quickening their pace to see what was wrong. Teresa, seated at the kitchen table, looked up as they entered and Margot felt faint as she saw tears in her eyes, then realised that she was smiling. Ramon, standing behind her, put his hand on his wife's shoulder and said quietly,

'I have some news, but it must not be repeated outside this room, not even to Paco or Maria and certainly not to Eulalia. Do you understand?' The girls nodded dumbly. Addressing Margarita, he continued, 'Your brother is safe. He has reached Majorca and is staying in the house of a priest.'

Margarita gasped in delight, throwing her arms round her mother, as he raised a warning hand. 'Be careful! I am sorry that we cannot tell Eulalia. She is a very sensible child, but still a child and such knowledge could put her life and that of all of us in danger. You know that the Church is regarded as fascist in this area and Rafael would certainly have been shot if he had been found on Republican soil. Your mother took the risk of meeting him a few days ago to provide him with suitable clothes and money and some very brave people arranged his escape. One day we will all be together again, but for now we must be patient.'

So that was it! The man in the charcoal burner's hut. Margot felt ashamed of her suspicions and shuddered at the thought of the risk Teresa had taken. She would never reveal that she had seen her at the hut. What if it had been someone else on the hill that day? She marvelled at the strain Teresa must have been under to maintain her composure, not knowing whether her son had reached safety. Drawing a deep breath, she joined in the general euphoria and went to put the kettle on for tea, prompting much merriment at the English response to occasions of great moment.

Chapter Ten

MAY DAY HAD PASSED, uneasily, but with only a few outbreaks of trouble in the city between small groups of youths, which had been quickly dispersed by the *asaltos*. Margarita went with her mother to the canteen, while Margot carried on to the hospital. There were no foreign patients for her to see, so she checked and sorted the laundry and rolled bandages for an hour, before she was disturbed by the sound of running feet and voices raised in excitement in the foyer below. Going down the stairs, she was met by one of the porters, breathing heavily, as he rushed up, accompanied by two militiamen, to find Matron. Following them, she deduced from their rapid bursts of information, that there had been an attack on the telephone exchange in the city centre. The exchange was being strongly defended by the anarchist committee who had been in control since the July revolution and it was thought that there would be many casualties.

Matron picked up the telephone receiver. The line was dead. Nurses were hastily summoned and word put round the hospital for doctors to come to her office. As they crowded in, the details emerged. At three o'clock, without warning, the communist police chief had arrived at the exchange with three truckloads of armed guards, who rushed into the building and attempted to take control. A fierce gun battle ensued and as the news spread, people all over the city came out of the woodwork, barricades were erected, weapons appeared as from nowhere, cars and buildings were set alight as political frustrations boiled over into wholesale war. It was unsafe for anyone to attempt to get through the city, but casualties were already mounting and emergency treatment centres would have to be set up. Ambulances stood by as medical staff hastily gathered instruments, drugs and dressings and prepared to go, leaving a small team to look after the patients, none of whom, mercifully, was seriously ill.

As Ramon Martinez climbed into the back of an ambulance, Margot seized a white overall and jumped in after him.

'I'm coming with you,' she insisted, despite his protest. 'I can't go home, so I might as well make myself useful.' Maria Calhoun nodded her approval.

'She will be all right. We need all the help we can get.' As the ambulance careered through the streets they passed gangs of youths throwing stones from behind hastily erected barricades or firing guns from balconies. Children were dragging sandbags across doorways and cars plastered with party initials, the paint not yet dry, were being driven at breakneck speed, some with guns firing from the windows in Hollywood style. There was panic everywhere with people caught in the crossfire as the violence escalated, apparently spontaneously, and old scores were settled. The ambulance screeched to a halt outside the Hotel Colon, where a Scottish Ambulance unit had already begun to set up an emergency clinic. Mattresses had been dragged out into ground floor rooms and volunteers rushed out to help unload supplies from the ambulances as they arrived. A makeshift operating theatre was quickly set up, as the ambulances moved off to recover casualties. Two other hospitals were making similar arrangements in other parts of the city. They just hoped it would not be as bad as the last time.

Margot helped Maria Calhoun to unpack surgical instruments and dressings and collected bowls from the kitchens for washing. They did not have long to wait. Maria was magnificent, coolly assessing the injuries, directing treatment, allocating the seriously wounded to doctors and firmly ejecting those whose treatment was complete or who hoped to remain in the comparative safety of the clinic longer than their condition warranted. Margot bathed wounds and bruises, and held instruments while Maria stitched gashes, and bandaged arms and legs and heads. The doctors worked flat out extracting bullets and pieces of home-made bombs, sometimes losing the battle to save the victims, who had to be laid out and tagged for identification later. There were soldiers as well as police and civilians and rumours were rife about a calculated plot. It was well into the night when two new nurses arrived and Maria and Margot were able to take a break. There was food and coffee in the kitchen and Maria insisted that they eat, then try to sleep for a couple of hours. More medical staff had been alerted and were on their way, so from now on they could take turns to rest.

Margot awoke from fitful sleep to see Maria already up and ready for duty. It was still dark outside as she sluiced her face with cold water and prepared for another stint. During the morning reports came over the radio that the Government was sending two destroyers with paramilitary forces from Valencia to quell the rising. They also heard that communists had seized the telephone exchanges in other towns and cities all over Catalonia, with the same anarchist resistance, forcing the Government to divert troops from the front at Jarama. Gloom descended on the clinic as they steeled themselves for a protracted siege. There was worse to come. Several bodies were brought in, shot in the back of the head. Some were prominent citizens known to be anti-communist and murmurs of cold-blooded execution fuelled the fear creeping over the city. Margot wondered where Margarita was and asked Ramon if he had managed to make contact with the family. He had not, but a message had been sent from the hospital, so they would know what was happening.

There was a flurry of activity, as a stretcher bearing a severely injured man was rushed into the operating room. Blood was spurting from a dreadful wound in his abdomen and he screamed as they lowered him on to the table.

'Chloroform, please, quickly,' called Ramon, as he washed his hands and reached for a mask. Another doctor hurried in and Maria Calhoun looked at Margot.

'Are you up to this?' Margot hesitated, then stepped towards the table and began cutting away the blood-soaked clothing. As she did so, fresh blood spurted out, splashing her chest, but she waved away help as she continued with her task. Fascinated, she watched as a further incision was made into the gaping wound and the intestine, pulsating, blue and slithering, was exposed. As the stench filled her nostrils she felt sour vomit rising in her throat and her knees buckled as she fought to stay conscious.

An arm grasped her round the waist and she was propelled swiftly to the door, Maria's voice in her ear whispering, 'You did very well, but there is nothing more for you to do now. Go and clean yourself up. Someone will find you something to change into.' The door closed behind her and she leaned against it, hot tears of shame and exhaustion pricking her eyelids.

'Margot?' She raised her eyes as he reached her, taking in her stained overall, her hair streaked with blood and sweat, her pale worn face.

'Are you hurt?' She shook her head, laughing weakly.

'Oh, Sven! What are you doing here. Don't look at me. I must go and wash.' He insisted on helping, found a bathroom for her on the next floor and disappeared in search of clean clothing. She ran the bath water, lukewarm, but it would do. Miraculously there was a small piece of soap and she lathered her hair as best she could, then lay soaking in the water, feeling her tiredness ebb and her senses return. A knock on the door told her that Sven had returned and she climbed out of the bath, wrapping herself in a towel as she slid back the lock. Triumphant, he held out a black dress, rather creased but clean and seizing another towel, began to rub her hair. She indicated the bath.

'It's almost cold, but you might as well take the opportunity,' she said and turned her back while he disrobed and got in. She sat on the toilet lid while he recounted what had happened. There were still three weeks of training to go when his group was suddenly ordered to Barcelona and told to prepare for action. At the barracks they were given a pep talk by the Commissar on the virtues of Communism, told that anyone who refused to join the Party would be regarded as a traitor, then provided with uniforms and guns. Next day the rioting started and the troops were split up into small commands and ordered to hold the positions captured from the anarchists. Some of his comrades had been badly injured and he had been detailed to help convey them to the emergency clinic. He was waiting for news of the man in the operating theatre when, to his astonishment, Margot came out. She threw him a towel, explaining how she came to be helping at the clinic, then suddenly, the towels were in a heap on the floor and they clung to each other, the fear and frustration of this insane place momentarily forgotten.

It seemed that an age passed before, dressed and composed, they tidied the bathroom and walked down the stairs. The door of the operating theatre was still closed and they sat down to wait. Sven was tense, his face dark with anger as he answered Margot's anxious question about the rumoured executions. Yes, it was true. Fortunately he had not been among those ordered to do it; it seemed to have been regarded as an honour to perform that obscene act on petrified, unarmed men who had been dragged from their homes and made to kneel as the gun was put to their heads. In fact, the Commissar had shot several of them himself. He seemed to be enjoying it! Margot's head whirled. Vicente? Praying for denial, she knew that it would not come. She wept silently for Margarita. And for Ramon.

The door opened and Sven rose to his feet as Maria came out. She told him quietly that his friend was alive, two bullets had been removed, but the operation had been delicate and he had lost a lot of blood. He was being transferred to the hospital, where he would have better care, but there was a strong chance of infection and it would be some days before his chances could be assessed. Sven could report back to his unit. He thanked her and smiled at Margot, blowing her a kiss as he turned to go.

'He is a friend,' she said in reply to Maria's quizzical look. They walked to the kitchen together in search of coffee, Maria eyeing the crumpled, oversized dress with amusement.

'Not exactly the height of fashion, but definitely preferable to your previous ensemble!' Margot apologised for her weakness in the theatre, but Maria laughed.

'I fainted the first time I watched an operation. Yes, really,' she said, as Margot raised her eyebrow in disbelief. 'We could make a very good nurse out of you if you wanted to do it. You have the right temperament.'

'No, thank you!' came the firm reply. 'I don't have the stomach for it!'

The kitchen was full of people. A detachment of doctors and nurses from a French Brigade had arrived to relieve them and two of their own doctors were already briefing them, while an ambulance was standing by to take the hospital staff home. Gratefully, they scrambled aboard, wedged like sardines as the ambulance bumped and swayed through the debris. Smoke drifted upwards from smouldering fires dampened by the light drizzle which had been falling all day and dirty banners fluttered dejectedly against walls covered in graffiti. They peered through the windows in silence broken only by shouts to the driver to stop as one by one the occupants reached their destination. Margot and Ramon were dropped at the bottom of the drive and he held out his arm to her as they walked wearily towards the house. She leaned thankfully against him, feeling the warmth of his body through her thin dress, the pressure of his thigh on her hip as they walked. She shivered and he looked anxiously at her, asking if she was cold.

'No,' she smiled. 'Just someone walking over my grave!'

They were greeted with a shriek of excitement from Lallie, who had spotted them as she returned from the stables and rushed to fling herself upon them. Soon the household was bustling with activity as baths were drawn and a pan of stew set on the stove. Over a leisurely meal Margot blushed at Ramon's flattering account of her efficiency and protested when he declared his intention of buying her a dress to replace the one ruined at the clinic. She was howled down in a chorus of approval and Margarita insisted that she should have the best dress in Barcelona to make up for having to wear that shapeless black sack in public. She knew the exact shop and would take her there as soon as the trouble in the city died down.

Later, propped up in bed, drowsily sipping hot chocolate, she recounted her escapade with Sven to an incredulous Margarita, carefully leaving out any mention of Vicente.

'You said I was taking chances! What if Pappa had caught you? 'Margot blushed, her imagination captured by a very different scenario than the one envisaged by her friend, then they dissolved in conspiratorial giggles. The family had not left the house since hearing the news on the radio about the uprising and seeing truckloads of soldiers passing on the road to the city, so Margarita had no news of Vicente. With nothing to do until the fighting stopped, she agreed to go with Margot to the hospital.

Chapter Eleven

COMING INTO THE KITCHEN, Dr Martinez was surprised to find both girls, breakfasted and dressed in slacks and sweaters, waiting to accompany him to the hospital in order to offer help wherever it was required, washing patients, distributing food, cleaning, taking messages or anything else that was required. The hospital was full to overflowing and the emergency clinic, now staffed mainly by the Red Cross, was also stretched to the limit with minor injuries and infections. Maria Calhoun greeted them with delight and promptly put them to work with mops, buckets and disinfectant to clean the floors of all the wards, releasing auxiliary workers to assist with the patients. Laughingly, they made a competition out of it, dividing the wards between them, to see who could work fastest. By mid-morning they had finished almost in a dead heat, despite stopping from time to time to exchange a few words with patients or write down messages to be delivered later. During coffee break with some of the nurses, a call came from the Red Cross for help at the clinic, where staff sickness was causing problems. A heavy operating schedule meant that many nurses were fully occupied in theatre and Matron pored anxiously over staff rotas with Maria to see whether anyone could be spared. None of the others wanted to go to the clinic, so Margot asked tentatively if she and Margarita would be of any use, since most of the duties were most likely to be auxiliary, rather than nursing tasks. The Red Cross ambulance was waiting at the door and, after checking that their assistance would relieve the situation, Matron gratefully accepted the girls' offer.

They were met by one of the young French doctors whom Margot had met briefly the previous day at the clinic and a young woman assistant. Armand Duclos had trained in France and on completion of two years hospital work had developed an urge to travel and see something of the world before committing himself to his career. The Red Cross had provided him with the ideal opportunity and he had worked for over a year in Africa before being drafted into Spain to help with casualties from the uprising. Boyishly handsome, with fair hair flopping casually over his face and light blue eyes accentuated by tanned skin, he grinned in recognition as Margot appeared, then stood gazing in frank admiration at Margarita as the introductions were made. '*Enchanté!*' he murmured, bending over her hand.

'*Encantada!*' she replied, lowering her eyes demurely before flashing a teasing smile at him as she withdrew her hand and turned to exchange greetings with his assistant, Suzanne. As the ambulance bowled down the narrow streets through a squalid area where burned-out vehicles and debris still littered the roads, they were forced to slow down by a small knot of people blocking the way. Peering from the windows of the ambulance as the driver drew to a halt, they were immediately besieged by anxious faces and a weeping woman, pointing to a building which had been badly damaged with part of the wall broken down and a hole in the pavement where masonry had collapsed and fallen through, presumably into a cellar. The driver got out and after a few moments surveying the scene and talking to the onlookers, established that a little boy, Tomas, had somehow got into the hole and had disappeared from view. They had heard faint cries and thought he must be injured, but attempts to reach him had failed and they had no equipment such as ropes or ladders. The wall appeared to be unsafe and they were afraid of causing him greater danger.

The driver and the doctor looked down the hole, but could see nothing apart from dust and rubble, though there appeared to be a small opening at one side. A child's cries could be heard faintly, but there was no response to the mother's frantic appeals to him to say whether he was hurt. Having satisfied themselves that there was no access from inside the building, they began to work out how to reach the child and winch him up, possibly on a stretcher. There was a drop of about ten feet and, although the opening was wide enough at the top, it narrowed towards the bottom, making it unlikely that a man, let alone a stretcher, could get through. It would have to be widened, dangerous though that would be. While Margot attempted to comfort the mother, Margarita walked round the hole, peering into it.

'I think I could get down there if we could fix a rope,' she said. The others protested. There was a rope in the ambulance, but it was too dangerous to allow her to do it. They should call the militia. This set up a further panic among the onlookers, who were clearly frightened at the thought of the militia being involved. Margarita quietly pointed out that, if the child had been injured, delay could be fatal. If the driver could manoeuvre the vehicle nearer to the hole they could anchor the rope to the tail bar and she could let herself down. She had climbed ropes at school in gymnastics often enough, she assured them, looking at Margot, who confirmed that it was so and that Margarita had always been athletic, though she warned that this was a difficult situation with more masonry likely to fall at any moment.

Margarita insisted on trying and the men, unable to produce a better solution, did as she asked. The stout rope was long enough and as soon as it was secure, Margarita lowered herself carefully into the hole. It was fairly tight at the bottom and she scraped her arms on the sides as she attempted to bend to examine the situation. She called up that there was a sort of narrow tunnel, but it was too dark to see anything. The ambulance driver produced a torch and threw it down to her. Through the dust she could just see the child. He was about six feet inside and there seemed to be a block of stone or wood trapping him. She called his name softly, telling him not to be afraid, she would get him out, but though he was whimpering, she could not establish whether he was hurt. He was only three years old and could not understand what was happening. She would just have to feel her way and hope that she could pull him clear without causing him any further distress. Inching along the narrow passage on her stomach she was conscious of the jagged stones just above her head and knew she had to keep her movements to a minimum to avoid any disturbance which might cause them to collapse. The boy could see her now and became excited, crying and reaching out towards her, bringing down a shower of dust over his head. Praying that he would keep still, she put out her hand and touched him, feeling carefully round the broken stone between them. Mercifully it was not touching him and did not appear to be supporting the roof of the tunnel. If she could move it just a few inches, she should be able to pull him through. It was heavy and resisted her attempt to pull it away. Carefully, keeping her head down, she pulled up first one knee and then the other, trying to get into a kneeling position in order to get a better hold on it. A vicious cramp seized her foot and she could feel the sweat trickling down her body as she gripped the stone, rocking it gently until she managed to shift it a few inches to one side, enough, she reckoned, to allow the child through. He was quiet now and did as she told him, lying down with his legs pointing towards her, so that she was able to grasp him by the hips and drag him under her own body.

The watchers waited anxiously. Margot bit her lip as the minutes ticked by with no sound apart from a steady scraping noise. The boy's mother had stopped crying and sat with her head in her hands, rocking to and fro in silent prayer. Ten minutes seemed like an hour, when Margarita reappeared, feet first, backing cautiously out of the tunnel. They held their breath as she heaved herself up stiffly to a standing position and cried out with relief as they saw the small figure clasped to her chest.

'He's bruised and scared, but I think he is all right,' she gasped. The driver threw down a blanket and she wrapped the child tightly in it, then tied the rope around him so that they could haul him up. In a short time both child and rescuer, covered in dust, were on the surface. The doctor signalled to Margot to keep the child's mother away until he had examined him. Apart from severe bruising all down one side and some cuts and bruises, there appeared to be no serious injury, but he was badly shaken and the doctor wanted to take him to the clinic for a more thorough examination and observation. The mother became agitated. She could not afford to pay for treatment and pleaded to take him home and nurse him herself. Gently the doctor insisted. There would be no charge and she could go with him to the clinic. She looked round nervously at her neighbours, who nodded approval and urged her towards the ambulance. Throwing her arms around Margarita, she poured out tearful thanks and prayers of gratitude. Margarita, dusty and bleeding slightly from cuts on her face and hands, disentangled herself, disclaiming heroism and assuring her that she was just pleased to have been able to help. In the ambulance the small boy sat quietly, a beautiful child, thin and light as a bird, with large dark eyes in an elfin face. A perfect teardrop hung glistening on improbably long thick lashes, then rolled down a dirt-streaked face and off his chin. His gaze fixed on Margarita's face, he murmured shyly something incoherent and she leaned forward to hear, then laughed.

'Oh, Margot, I promised him sweeties if he kept still so that I could get him out. There are some in the pocket of my jacket.' His reward clinched, the little face lit up and he sucked blissfully and noisily for the rest of the journey.

Inside the clinic, Margarita brushed off the dust from her clothes and hair as best she could and washed her hands and face. Armand Duclos insisted on tending the cuts and grazes on her arms and face himself, much to her embarrassment and Margot's amusement. Margot found a chair for Tomas's mother, then swept up the child into her arms and carried him off to a bathroom, where she carefully sponged and dried the little bruised body. Painfully thin, he looked as if he had not had a decent meal for weeks, perhaps months. He was filthy and smelt of urine, having wet himself during his ordeal, so she washed out his clothes and put them to dry over a towel rail, wrapping him in a soft hospital gown. Throughout the procedure he made no protest, not even when she washed his hair and combed the tangled curls, though his eyes, wide with apprehension, never left her face and he did not reply when she spoke to him. There was no bed available, but she managed to find a cot, which she pulled into a corner away from the other patients, and placed him in it. His mother sat by his side, smiling and speaking softly to him, while Margot went to the kitchen in search of food. When she returned, with bowls of thick soup and chunks of bread for mother and child, Margarita had come back and was deep in conversation with the woman, Juanita, who, though more relaxed now, still looked anxiously around from time to time as if expecting trouble. She was younger than she had first appeared to be, small and slight with light brown hair and a face that would have been pretty but for the hollows in her cheeks and dark shadows under her eyes. Her hands were clasped and twisted restlessly in her lap or wandered nervously to her throat, where she fingered a thin gold chain, which looked as if might once have held a cross. She took the food gratefully and ate quickly, while Margarita fed Tomas from a spoon. They were obviously very poor and Margarita, treading carefully to avoid injuring her pride, spoke of the soup kitchen, where they could get a hot meal almost every day. She asked if there were other children and Juanita's eyes filled with tears. She had lost a baby daughter from the fever a year ago. Her husband? She froze and looked round quickly before replying, in a hoarse whisper, that he had been taken away in the night by the militia after the July rising and had not been seen since. She did not know why. He had done nothing; there were others to whom the same thing had happened, but no one dared ask questions and she was afraid that they might come back and take her son. There was no money, no work for the families of the disappeared and she had sold almost everything she possessed in order to buy food. The two girls listened with growing dismay. They had known, of course, about the atrocities and the disappearances, but it was the first time they had encountered at first hand the plight of the families involved. They wanted to help, but how, without making the situation worse? Juanita confirmed that several of her neighbours were in a similar situation, not knowing who to trust and afraid to ask for help in case they attracted the attention of the militia. Two red spots of anger burned in Margarita's cheeks as she dwelled on the inhumanity of her fellow citizens and Margot placed a restraining hand on her arm, anticipating an outburst. Any further discussion would have to wait, however, as Doctor Duclos was approaching to examine his patient. Fed and sleepy now, Tomas submitted patiently to the examination. There was no lasting damage, but he would wake up stiff and sore the next day and would need plenty of rest and feeding up. They would keep him in overnight and his mother could collect him in the afternoon. Smiling as he acknowledged Juanita's thanks, the doctor left and Margarita followed to tell him of the family situation. Margot bent over the cot to kiss the angelic little face, his eyelids drooping, the heavy lashes fluttering like dark moths on his pale cheeks as he smiled and snuggled deeper into the blanket. Turning to Juanita, she fished in her pocket and produced a handful of pesetas which she thrust into her hand, deaf to her protests, then hurried away before tears got the better of her.

The girls spent the rest of the afternoon changing bedclothes and cleaning, with no time to speak to each other. It had been a very long day when, at last, they clambered thankfully into the ambulance to go back to the hospital. This time they were the only passengers and Margot, with an impish grin, began to sing in a low voice, 'Lady of Spain I adore you, Right from the night I first saw you ...'

'What on earth ...?' began Margarita, as her friend burst out laughing at her puzzled face. 'Oh, come now! Don't tell me you haven't noticed the handsome French doctor falling at your feet? He never took his eyes off you, described you as "*magnifique*" and asked me if you had a regular beau! I was discreet, of course. Told him I didn't know.' Margarita sighed. Armand had been very attentive, she admitted. He was nice and it was flattering, but Margot knew very well that she was committed to Vicente, so there was no point in speculating. Incidentally, she said, she had talked to him about Juanita's problems and he was hopeful that the Red Cross would be able to find a way of helping unobtrusively. In bleak silence they looked at each other, contemplating the horrors that so many innocent people were suffering in a struggle for power beyond their comprehension. Margot could not help thinking of Vicente and wondered grimly whether it had crossed Margarita's mind to ask herself whether he and his fellow activists knew or cared about the lives they had ruined.

Back at the hospital, Margarita went straight to her father's office, while Margot retailed the day's events to an incredulous Maria Calhoun.

'The two of you certainly seem to attract adventure!' she commented.

'Not to mention romance!' was the rejoinder, 'Margarita made a conquest!' She told of Armand Duclos' fascination with Margarita and her friend's refusal to accept his attentions. Her face clouded as she opined how simple life would be if only people could fall in love with someone suitable who loved them in return. Maria looked thoughtfully at her. Her sharp eyes had not missed the way Margot looked at Ramon Martinez and she was uneasily aware that her young friend's infatuation could prove disastrous to her and to the family which had befriended her. Over the years she had seen many women glance in his direction, but to no avail. The man was a saint. Totally dedicated to his work and content with his family life, he was oblivious of the fluttering he aroused in female hearts. It would not occur to him that, in this girl who had grown up without a father, the flattering attention of a charming older man might fuel a romantic notion difficult for either of them to handle. She wondered about that attractive young soldier at the clinic. He was clearly smitten and Margot was obviously at ease with him, so might he break the spell? She sighed. How long could a soldier expect to remain in any one place in these uncertain times?

'Have you ever been in love, Maria?' The older woman smiled slowly.

'I have thought so, once or twice when I was younger, but never enough to let it stand in the way of my work. You seem to be doing well enough, though. That young soldier I saw you with seemed very fond of you.'

Margot frowned. 'But I am not sure. I like him, but it is not the same feeling as – well, how do you know whether you really love someone or whether it's just making do with second best because you can't have the one you really want?' Maria took a deep breath.

'Well, I am hardly the voice of experience, but I think that you have to use your head as well as your heart if you want to avoid disillusionment. Physical attraction is not enough and nor is fantasy.'

'Fantasy?' queried Margot.

'Yes. When you are young, it is easy to build a dream round someone, a film star, perhaps, or an older man who appears more sophisticated and successful than boys of your own age, weaving a fairytale romance in your imagination. If it stays there, fine, but any attempt to turn it into reality is likely to end in tears. When I was seventeen, training in London, there was a professor, married and more than twenty years older than I was. He was handsome, brilliant, magnetic and I adored him, mooning after him on ward rounds like a lovesick calf, clutching at any smile or word of praise as a sign that he had special feelings for me. If I made a mistake and he rebuked me or made fun of me, I was devastated and cried myself to sleep. I would dream up imaginary scenes, where we dined by candlelight or danced beneath the stars, while he told me I was the girl of his dreams. There was never any sexual content in those dreams, apart from the sort of romantic kisses you see in films. That would have spoiled everything, because the essence of such attachments is that they are idealistic and above the sordid realities of life. Oh, why am I telling you all this?' She laughed, but Margot put a hand on her arm, saying quickly, 'No, do go on. What happened?'

Maria shrugged. 'Nothing, of course. Oh, I got over it. I became aware that there were attractive young men who were available and who took me out dancing and made me laugh.'

'And the professor? Have you seen him since?' She sighed, ruefully.

'No. He must be in his fifties now and the last time I heard of him he had lost most of his hair, his wife had run off with a younger man and he had the gout!' Their eyes met, held for a fraction of a second, before Margot giggled and they collapsed, spluttering with laughter.

They had barely recovered their composure when Margarita returned, accompanied by her father, ready to go home. Dr Martinez, though proud of his daughter's bravery, felt that both girls needed to rest and decreed that they should spend a day at home before resuming work at the clinic. Maria agreed, despite their protests, saying that it was in everyone's interests that they should not overtire themselves and she would inform the clinic. As they left the room, Margot paused and turned back.

'Thanks!' she said simply, as Maria inclined her head in acknowledgement.

Chapter Twelve

Margarita sank thankfully into a hot bath, gingerly soaping the scratches and bruises all over her body, wincing as the water stung patches where the skin had been badly grazed on knees and elbows. The cut on her face was superficial and did not look too bad when she had sponged off the dried blood. By the time she had finished and washed her hair, the water was filthy with dust and grit, which she cleaned carefully away before patting herself dry with a soft towel and snuggling into her dressing gown. Exhausted, she sat on a stool, rubbing her hair dry and reliving the day's activities. All in all, it had been satisfactory, she concluded. In fact, considering that she had not been particularly enthusiastic about going to help at the hospital and had only done so because she had nothing better to do, she had to admit that she had enjoyed every minute. There had been no hesitation in going to the aid of the child. She had weighed up the situation and felt confident that she could do it, any fear of danger to herself being offset by the challenge of adventure. The mother's gratitude and the admiration of Margot and the others had boosted her self-esteem, which of late had been somewhat lacking, and it felt good to have done something to help someone. She smiled, recalling the little boy's face when she gave him the sweets, then reflected miserably on the family situation. Such an adorable child, such a loving mother, but how long could they survive in this callous society torn apart by envy and hatred? According to Vicente, this sort of thing would not happen under a communist regime. Vicente! A shadow of doubt crossed her mind. It would be prudent not to mention the incident to him, at least for the present time. Her mother's voice outside the door roused her from her reverie. 'Just coming!' she replied, hastily brushing her hair before going down to supper.

When she opened her eyes next morning, the early sun was streaming in through the window and she groaned as she turned over in bed, stiff and aching all over. Painfully she struggled to her feet and began cautiously to stretch her arms and legs, turning her head from side to side to ease the stiffness in her neck.

'Ouch!' she exclaimed, as she overbalanced and accidentally bumped a tender spot on her knee, just as the door opened and Margot came in, grinning.

'Ah, the price of heroism!' she commented, as she dodged a pillow flung at her head.

'I don't feel very heroic this morning. Shut up and run me a bath,' ordered Margarita. 'I have to get moving if we are going out with Lallie.' Eulalia had been flatteringly impressed by her sister's bravery and in a weak moment Margarita had agreed that the three of them should spend their free day together. They could not go far in case further hostilities broke out, but a ramble and a picnic in the hills was safe enough. When they went down to breakfast, Eulalia was already assembling bread, cheese and fruit in a basket and pouring lemonade into a flask. She greeted them happily and Margarita felt a rush of affection for her little sister, her aches and pains almost forgotten as she watched her making preparations for the promised treat.

The air was fresh and pleasantly cool as they wandered up the track, Eulalia chattering excitedly as she darted about, pointing out new rabbit holes and looking for caterpillars, which she brought, curled up in her palm, for their inspection, to Margarita's disgust. She wanted to hear all over again about their adventure of the previous day and their work at the clinic. They were questioned about injuries and treatments and the abilities of the Red Cross doctors and nurses.

'I wish I could come with you,' she sighed. 'I could help to clean and push the trolleys and I am very good at bandaging.'

'I'm sure you are, darling,' laughed Margarita, 'but you are too young and the patients would think it very strange. And it can be very unpleasant, you know, lots of blood and dirt and smells, not at all like reading medical books!'

Eulalia sniffed. If Margarita could stand it, she certainly could. It wasn't fair! Margot, admiring the sense of responsibility in one so young, felt a tinge of sadness that, in this scarred society, children had to face early the realities of injury and death. She put an arm round the girl's shoulder.

'Lallie, dear, I am sure that one day you will do much more than just help with cleaning and bandaging, but today is our day off and we would like to talk about nicer things. I would love to see where the birds are nesting and you haven't told us what happened to the baby rabbit you and Carla rescued last week.'

'The rabbit? Oh, Paco said its leg was only bruised and he cleaned the cut on its neck. I put a bandage on it, but it kept pulling at it with its paw and getting tangled up. Carla's pappa made a hutch for it and we have been giving it lettuce and cabbage leaves. It is almost well again now and I think we should put it back where we found it, but Carla wants to keep it. What do you think?' she asked, turning a worried face towards Margot, who said she thought it might be lonely away from its brothers and sisters and that it was not fair to keep it caged up, but Margarita said that its family might not recognise it and if the girls had been cuddling it, they might reject it or attack it, because it would smell of human beings. Eulalia said that they had not touched it except to scratch its ears through the wire netting, because Paco had told them not to and they all agreed that she should persuade Carla to let the little creature go free.

The rest of the day was spent exploring the burgeoning life of plants and animals in the woods, challenging each other to guess the origins of leaves and feathers and sharing fragments of knowledge and folklore about the mountains. Time passed quickly and they returned home relaxed and grubby, in time to share a pot of tea with Teresa in the garden. When Eulalia went off to see the horses, her mother thanked them for giving up their day to her and hoped it had not been too tiring after the strain of the last two days. Both girls replied immediately that they had enjoyed every minute and Margarita announced that she was fully recovered and intended to return to the clinic next day. Ramon, back from an exhausting day at the hospital, confirmed that the clinic was still in need of help, which the hospital could not supply, and accepted gratefully their offer to continue for as long as necessary.

Armand Duclos was delighted to see them and relieved that Margarita had suffered no ill effects. Margot took bowls and towels and made her way round the beds, sponging hands and faces, arranging pillows and trying to make patients more comfortable, while Margarita talked to those needing reassurance or wrote down messages to pass on to families. There were only two doctors and they spent most of their time in the operating room, though most of the more serious cases had by now been dealt with or passed on to various hospitals. The nurses changed dressings, cleaned and stitched wounds and administered such medicines as were available, though supplies were becoming alarmingly low and they were hoping desperately for another delivery in the next two days. Sometimes it was difficult to get patients to leave when they were considered fit to do so. They felt secure in the calm, clinical atmosphere and some had nowhere else to go. There were places of refuge run by the Red Cross and local voluntary workers, but priority was given to women and children and, in the present climate of hostility between communists and anarchists, who were supposed to be on the same side, they were wary of young men who might start trouble.

An ambulance arrived with a young woman on a stretcher and Margot, rushing forward to help, recognised the attendant, Suzanne, who had been with them when they stopped to help little Tomas. As they lifted the patient on to a bed, the French girl told her that she had just spoken to a Red Cross worker who had visited him and his mother the previous day and they were both well. Neighbours, shaken by the child's narrow escape, were friendly now and had persuaded the woman to go with them to the food kitchen. Grinning, the girl asked how Armand was getting on with Margarita. Before she could answer, the doctor himself came out to examine the patient and Suzanne, after giving him a quick assessment of the her condition, disappeared on her next call. There was a head injury, a bad gash which must have been sustained two or three days earlier and had been roughly bandaged without being cleaned. Blood was still oozing through the matted hair and infection had set in. The woman was feverish, nauseous and moaning and had bruising on her chest and abdomen. And she was pregnant and about to miscarry. A nurse began to cut away the hair round the head wound as Armand and his colleague debated whether she could safely be given chloroform if an operation proved necessary, then she began to haemorrhage and was wheeled quickly into the operating theatre. An hour passed before Armand came out and Margot, seeing him lean wearily against the door, hovered anxiously until he looked up and smiled briefly.

'She will be all right,' he said, before she could ask the question, 'but we could not save the baby. There is no fracture to the skull and we have cleaned the wound and given her a sulphonamide, so I am hopeful that the infection will clear up. Her bruises will fade, but I doubt if the mental scars will heal so quickly. She has been badly beaten.' He had been unable to establish exactly what had happened. She had tried to tell him, but she spoke rapidly and almost inaudibly and though, like Margot, he could now converse reasonably well in Spanish, he had been unable to make much sense of it.

Margot passed on the information to Margarita, who, when the woman was comfortably settled in bed, took her a cup of coffee and stayed to talk to her. Margot busied herself with changing bed linen, emptying bedpans and returning trays to the kitchen, until Margarita appeared, agitated and angry. The woman, Inez, had told her that, on the day the telephone exchange was stormed, her husband had been dragged from their house in front of her and their two children and taken to where several other men were already lined up, kneeling, with their hands tied behind their backs. She had run after him, screaming, but she could not stop them and she had watched in horror as a young officer put a gun to his head and shot him. She had thrown herself across her husband's body and soldiers hauled her off, jeering and saying that all anarchists should be shot, then beaten and kicked her until she was unconscious. Friends had picked her up and taken her to safety, but she was too frightened to leave her children to let them take her to the hospital. Now she had lost her baby, but perhaps that was for the best, as she did not know how she could manage to keep herself and the other children, without having to worry about another mouth to feed. 'Oh, Margot, how could they do this? Those men must have been from Vicente's barracks. He must be told about this!' Margot, sick with apprehension, could not reveal what Sven had told her, but suggested that she should say nothing to Vicente until things had calmed down. It would only make things worse. Margarita retorted that things could not possibly be worse and went off to tell Armand Duclos about her conversation with his patient.

The two of them sat huddled over cups of coffee in the kitchen, reflecting gloomily on the situation and the unlikely prospect of an early end to the conflict. She felt guilty about having unwittingly brought Margot into danger from which it was now too late to escape back to England. Armand remarked bitterly that he doubted whether England or any other European country would remain safe for long. Had she not heard of Hitler? Anyway, from what Margot had told him, she was happier here than she would ever have been at home, despite the dangers. Margarita asked when he intended to return to France and he shrugged his shoulders, saying he was committed to the Red Cross for another year at least and had only a limited choice as to where he was posted. He would like to have seen more of Africa and maybe India, before returning to a medical career in France, but it depended on where help was needed and life tended to be fairly exciting anywhere with the Red Cross. He told her of his work in Gabon and Nigeria, where drought and disease claimed more lives than wars. In many areas there was little money for food and shelter, let alone hospitals and medical supplies and foreign aid from international organisations like the Red Cross was often their only hope. She listened in silence, her head bowed, a slight frown furrowing her brow.

'I'm sorry. I should not be rambling on like this, he said, slapping his knee in exasperation. I get carried away!'

'No, really. I am interested', she protested. 'Gabon. Isn't that where Albert Schweitzer has his hospital?'

Yes, he said, he had visited Lambarene and had actually talked with the great man. It was very impressive, but he would not wish to work there, because he did not have the religious zeal on which it was founded. Religion and politics! He had no time for either. It seemed to him that these were responsible for most of the troubles in this world and that, wherever there was conflict, no matter which side triumphed, it was always the poor who paid the price. He was just applying skill and knowledge to repair physical damage as best he could and wanted no part in converting people to causes.

Margarita sighed. 'You are lucky. You know exactly what you want to do with your life and you are making it happen. I have no idea what I want to do, but I would like to feel that I could do something useful to change things, make a difference to people's lives.'

He looked at her, half-mocking, 'You could start by making a difference to mine,' he suggested, lightly touching the back of her hand with his finger. She looked pensive, then withdrew her hand.

'It's too late, I'm afraid, Armand,' she said, wearily. 'It's just too late.' She rose and went back to the ward, where Margot pounced on her, demanding eagerly to know what had kept her for so long. 'You like him, don't you?' she persisted, but Margarita, after a moment's hesitation, said firmly that she could forget any idea of matchmaking.

Chapter Thirteen

OVER THE NEXT TWO WEEKS there was a fragile ceasefire with accusations on both sides of provocation and sabotage. People were bewildered by press and radio reports heavily censored by the communists seeking to discredit the local Trotskyist party, the POUM. Questions about the executions remained unasked and rumours of secret arrests and correction camps spread fear in the community. As a result of the events in Barcelona the coalition government broke down and the communists' choice, Juan Negrin, replaced Largo Caballero as Prime Minister. The scene was set for a communist coup.

Margot and Margarita spent several afternoons at the hospital, where they made themselves useful, fetching and carrying for the nurses or talking with patients. Margarita was surprised to find that she actually enjoyed feeling needed and proved adept at gaining patients' confidence and calming their fears. She flirted mildly with old and young alike, restoring their self-esteem and bringing smiles to their faces. Her father was gratified by her newfound sense of responsibility and began to hope that her wayward days were over. Maria Calhoun was glad to see her and hoped that her continued presence in the hospital would help to keep Margot's feet on the ground, though after their last conversation, she had a feeling that the infatuation was fading. Staffing levels had improved and there was no need for the girls to help out at the clinic. There had been flowers and messages for Margarita from Armand Duclos, but despite encouragement from Margot and Maria, she refused even to see him. At home, as if by common consent, there was no talk of the crisis. They went through their wardrobes, sorting out discarded clothes for Teresa's charities, altering, mending and planning. Margot would have to wait for the promised new dress, but it was something to look forward to when life returned to normal. Eulalia's school was open, though some of the parents kept their children at home, fearing further trouble, and homework was suspended so that teachers and pupils could spend time helping to clear debris and repair damage to property. She spent time with the horses, but was forbidden to take them outside the grounds and bored, she hovered around her elders until Margot had the bright idea of making toys for little Tomas and others like him. Paco found them wood and paint and glue and the three of them enjoyed painstaking hours of trial and error, competing with each other to produce simple little boats, windmills and brightly painted building blocks. Teresa spent most days at the soup kitchen or at meetings of local charity groups, but Saturday afternoons were devoted to the Music Circle, where she and a group of fellow musicians and aficionados met to entertain each other and indulge their love of music. There had been no meeting for two weeks because of the crisis, but now she was excited by the prospect of a special performance. Senora Garcia's sister, Luisa, was a dance teacher in Madrid. With her husband, Fernando, she had toured South America the previous year, performing Flamenco and Latin American dance exhibitions, winning great acclaim and a coveted competition award. They were staying with Senora García and had generously agreed to perform a paso doble for the Music Circle.

'Luisa Fuentes?' breathed Margarita. 'Oh, Mamma, could we possibly come too?' Teresa considered.

'I am sure that can be arranged,' she smiled. 'You will love it, Margot. It is the bullfight. The man is the matador, the woman is the cape he uses to entice the bull.' The room was packed and, after a short piano recital and an elegant performance on the harp by a pretty, willowy young woman, the Chairman announced to the rapt audience that Luisa and Fernando Fuentes would perform their celebrated version of the paso doble. The dancers, dramatically poised, stood motionless, Luisa slim and dark, in black and scarlet, Fernando, all in black, tall, dark, brooding. The music began. Arrogant, challenging, he circled and stamped, drawing her towards him, she bold, seductive, as she stepped across him, then away, her beautiful arms almost caressing, her olive skin gleaming, the flash of scarlet skirt echoing the fluid rhythm of her limbs. As the music swelled and the pace quickened, the movements became more intense, the steps more intricate. The dancers, bodies arched, elegant, supple, moved in perfect unison until they seemed almost to blend into one another. Then the climax, challenge, defeat and death for the bull. The matador struck the ground with is heel, head flung back proudly, one arm raised in triumph, the other holding the cape as she floated gracefully to the floor at his feet. There was a split second of silence, then the audience roared its approval as the dancers bowed and acknowledged the applause. Margot's eyes shone.

'It is so beautiful. I couldn't bear to watch a real bullfight, because the bull always dies and that is unfair, but I can appreciate the grace and the drama.'

Teresa smiled. 'It is also dangerous for the matador,' she remarked. 'Many of them suffer terrible injuries and even death in a short career. As for being unfair, well, life is not always fair. To me, in a way, the bullfight mirrors life. It is often beautiful, but there is an ugly side as well. Like the bull, we are tempted, thwarted and enraged as we try to achieve what we perceive as our goals. We may be defeated prematurely or struggle for many years in the pursuit of happiness, but in the end, however successful we may appear to have been, inevitably, we are all cut down to size. It is about survival.'

The girls looked at her in astonishment, then Margarita laughed. 'Oh, Mamma, that is far too profound after such wonderful entertainment.' She turned to Margot. 'What did you think of Luisa? Isn't she just beautiful?' The talk turned back to the dance and they mingled happily with the other guests, sharing their pleasure until the time came to go home.

The emergency clinic closed, the telephone exchange reopened and life began to return to the city, though a pall of gloom persisted as people went about their business, tight-lipped, wary, the presence of soldiers on the streets no longer a sign of security and republican solidarity. Between stints at the hospital the girls ventured back to the cafe, but there was no sign of Sven and Margarita had still not heard from Vicente. At the barracks they were informed by a sentry that the soldiers were under strict training and all leave was cancelled. Margarita fumed and fretted. She tried telephoning, but the Commissar was out or busy, would she leave a message? She rejected Margot's excuse that he must be under a lot of pressure with the concentrated training programme and began to question his involvement in the attack on the telephone exchange.

'He must have known!' she expostulated. 'All those secret calls and messages while we were there the day before. Why did those recruits arrive here so conveniently in time to back the communists? For all he knew, we could have been in the city when it happened and been killed, but he didn't bother to warn us. What sort of man is that? Just wait until I see him!'

Margot felt a knot of fear tightening in her stomach. The man was dangerous, psychopathic even, and nothing and no-one would stand in the way of his ambition. She could not tell what she knew about the executions, but Margarita must be warned against confronting him.

'I'm not saying you're wrong,' she said firmly, 'but we have no proof and he is not likely to admit it. He is a communist with enough power to cause trouble, particularly for your father. Please don't even think of accusing him. Just be patient and think before you do anything hasty!'

Margarita began to cry softly, but she nodded, taking the proffered handkerchief, and Margot put her arms around her. 'Try to sleep. You will feel better in the morning.'

She did not feel better. It was imperative that she saw Vicente and, as luck would have it, her mother had a headache, so, Margot having left for the hospital, she was able to take the car and set off for the barracks. Knowing that she was unlikely to be allowed in, she parked where she could see the gate and waited until, after about an hour, she saw Vicente's car glide through the gate, heading towards the docks. She noticed that there was no guard on the gate and, pulse racing, she followed at a discreet distance. He would be unlikely to recognise the car and would certainly not expect to see her driving. Instead of going to the dock office or the customs shed he parked the car on the approach road and walked over to one of the bars. Ten minutes later he reappeared. He was not alone. His arm encircled the slim waist of a pretty girl with long black hair and flashing eyes, who walked with the lithe, arrogant sway of a gypsy dancer and he whispered in her ear as she tossed her head, laughing. He did not notice the car that parked behind his and the eyes that followed them to a small hut used as a storehouse and when the girl left half an hour later, he was startled, as he struggled to pull on his trousers, to see the door fly open to reveal a furious Margarita. Smiling ruefully, he held up his hands in submission, then shrugged as she raged at his infidelity. 'I saw you with that tart! How could you? You said you loved me!'

'I do love you,' he said silkily, as he leaned back against a table, his hands resting on the edge, 'but not exclusively. I do not question what you do when I am not around and I do not expect to have to account to you. Free love is part of the revolutionary philosophy!'

She felt sick, shaking, betrayed, her mouth dry and her voice hoarse as she gasped, 'But, but ... I'm pregnant!'

He stood up, calm, his eyes cold, his lip curled in a sneer. 'Tough! Not my problem!'

She could not believe that this was the man who had beguiled her with his endearments and promises into believing that they had a future together. 'How can you say that? It's your child too, your flesh and blood!'

He laughed, brutally 'So you say! Get rid of it. I'm sure you can find one of your father's pals to do the job!'

A red haze swam before her eyes as she sobbed, reaching towards him, pleading. He pushed her aside impatiently. 'You are beginning to bore me.'

Her head reeled as she backed towards the door, every movement seeming to be in slow motion, every detail etched in her brain. She saw his jacket lying where he had slung it, carelessly, on a chair, the revolver sticking out underneath it. She saw her hand reach down, the barrel of the gun gleaming as her fingers curled round the trigger. The look of incredulity on his face turning to fear as the bullets ripped into his chest, lifting and twisting his body, then dropping him, crumpled, on the floor.

She stood in silence, staring down at his lifeless body, the gun still in her hand, her dress clinging to her body with sweat, as reality returned. Then panic. She threw the gun down and turned to the door, listening before opening it cautiously and peering out to see if anyone had heard. There was no one around. Down on the quay she could see a little knot of people gathered round a sailor with a monkey, laughing at its antics. Otherwise, the road outside was deserted. She had to get to the car, only about a hundred yards away, but it seemed like a mile. She closed the door quietly and crept along the side of the building, past the bar and collapsed into the car, all the time looking over her shoulder to see if there was anyone watching. There was no one. Shaking, she reversed, trying not to look at his car, turned the wheel and drove swiftly away along the dock road, past the barracks, towards the city.

She could not remember the rest of the journey, but somehow she reached home. Turning into the drive, she realised that she had no idea what time it was and prayed that the house would be empty. Margot had heard the crunch of wheels on the drive and saw her stricken face from the window as she got out and leaned against the car, eyes closed. She ran down the stairs, taking her by the shoulders and shaking her, 'Margarita, what is it? Have you had an accident?' She peered anxiously at the car but there was no sign of damage. The blank eyes looked at her.

'He's dead! I killed him,' she said, flatly.

'Vicente?'

Margarita nodded. Margot's head swam. This was a dream, a nightmare. It could not be happening. She pulled her into the house.

'Are you sure. Couldn't you be mistaken? I mean, if you hit him, he may just ...' Margarita waved her aside, 'He's dead. I shot him.' The full implication of what she was hearing hit Margot like a blow. There would be no mercy for the killer of a commissar and there might be reprisals against the family and beyond. She had to get Margarita away as far and as soon as possible.

'Where is he? Did anyone see you?' Margarita passed a weary hand across her forehead.

'There was nobody around. He's in an old storage shed, but they will find him. I don't think I was seen, but I can't be sure.'

Margot grasped her arm and led her into the house, thinking quickly. They must pack some things, essentials only and passports, money. She found a holdall and stuffed clothes into it. Her passport and personal papers were all together in a drawer with house keys and money and she gathered them up, found Margarita's passport and other personal items and thrust them all into a large canvas bag. Telling her to gather what money she could, she ran down to the kitchen and collected dried fruit and bread which she put into the pockets of a raincoat.

'Come on,' she said, pushing Margarita towards the car. 'You will have to drive.'

'Where to?'

'The hospital.' Margarita recoiled in horror. She could not face Pappa. Margot insisted. They were not going to see her father, but there was someone there who might be able to help. It was their only chance.

Chapter Fourteen

MARIA CALHOUN LISTENED QUIETLY as Margot explained. She did not know the full details of how and why it had happened, but she understood that the dead man had influential friends and there would be a witch-hunt when his body was found. Was there anywhere Margarita could go for safety until it blew over and avoid involving her family? Maria considered. It would be dangerous to try to reach Valencia or Alicante; the road would be swarming with police by the time they were ready. She needed to get out of Republican Spain. There was a chance of getting them to Majorca by sea, but it was risky. There could be air raids and the coastguards were vigilant, but if they kept their heads and could put up with the discomfort, it was possible. They must understand that other lives, as well as their own, would be at risk, so they must have no contact with anyone, leave no messages and, above all, do exactly as they were told. Glancing at Margarita, whose colour was slowly returning, Margot agreed. Maria picked up the telephone, spoke briefly and rapidly about 'supplies', then looked into the corridor, beckoning the girls to follow. She unlocked a door, ushering them into a small room containing a bed, a chair and a small washbasin. Impressing on them the need to be quiet, she withdrew, locking the door behind her.

Hours ticked by before they heard footsteps on the corridor and the key in the lock. The door opened to reveal a large red haired man with the same startling blue eyes as his daughter. Michael Calhoun quietly handed them each a woollen hat to cover their hair and a pair of large woollen socks to put over their shoes to deaden the sound of footsteps. He checked that they had passports and money and pulled out an oilskin pouch to wrap them in. There was a lot of water around boats, he reminded them wryly and it might be difficult to keep them dry. They were to lie down on the floor of his van, covered by blankets, and remain motionless until they heard three taps on the side of the van, then be guided down the steps to a fishing boat. There had been no news so far about Vicente's death, but that did not mean that he had not been found. They could not assume that Margarita had not been seen and must expect extra vigilance at the docks, so it was vital that they followed his instructions to the letter. If they were found in his van, he would deny all knowledge of them. Did they understand? They nodded their agreement. He picked up their bags and, as they prepared to leave, Margarita suddenly remembered her mother's car, parked at the back of the hospital. It had been taken care of, he told her. Maria had driven it back and would explain the situation to her parents. If questioned, they would say that the girls had gone back to England to complete their education. He warned that there must be no attempt to contact the Martinez family.

They crept along the dimly lit corridor, down an emergency stairway and out into a goods delivery yard where an old black van was parked. Lying flat on the floor they felt every jolt as it rattled at speed through the empty streets to the docks, where it stopped and they heard cheerful greetings being exchanged between Michael and the guards.

'Are they not in yet, then?' asked Michael, looking out to sea.

'Not yet. Looks like a good night for fish. They might be late.' Their hearts beat rapidly as the doors at the back of the van were opened. The van was obviously empty, apart from a little pile of empty fish boxes and a blanket. There was a pause and the sound of coughing as cigarettes were lit up.

'Time for a drink then?' It was two o'clock in the morning and the dock was deserted. The banter continued as they strolled across the road to a bar. Minutes later came the three taps on the side of the van and they slid silently out. The van was parked at an angle, covering them from view as they descended a flight of stone steps leading down to the quay. Several boats creaked and bumped gently against the side as they bobbed on the water. Their guide hurried them into a rowing boat and, hugging the shoreline, took them round the headland where they were transferred to a waiting fishing boat and installed in a small dark hold reeking of stale fish. As they put out to sea, the skipper brought them a steaming mug of soup, telling them it would be at least an hour before they reached the next stage of their journey.

Huddled under a blanket to keep out the night chill, they tried to sleep, but the rolling of the boat made them feel sick and they were relieved when at last the clanking of the anchor chain and the sound of voices, low and hoarse across the dark water, jerked them into consciousness. A large motor launch stood by, engine throbbing, its lights switched off. Strong hands helped them scramble over the side and into the other vessel, which immediately roared into life in a cloud of spray, as they waved goodbye to the fishing boat. To their surprise, the skipper was English, a jocular middle-aged man, bald with a trim white beard. His wife appeared from the locker with bread and a plate of cheese and cold ham. Their son piloted the boat. Dawn was breaking as the engine died and they slipped quietly into the harbour, mooring the launch on a long jetty where several other craft were berthed.

'Here we are – Palma.'

They had taken off the hats and socks, washed their faces and made themselves as presentable as possible. Just an eccentric English family taking a couple of nieces for a spin if anyone asked. No one did. They strolled off the jetty with not a soul in sight and, as the sun rose, they piled into their little car and drove along the palm-fringed coast road. The cathedral shone magnificent in the early morning light and Margarita made a silent vow to visit it and make her confession. She thought of her brother, but dared not hope to see him or bring her shame upon him.

The car turned off the promenade into the city, down narrow streets lined with high buildings from which hung tiny balconies above heavy, uninviting wooden doors, eventually drawing up outside an iron grille, through which an open doorway revealed a large, cool courtyard. A slim, middle-aged lady, elegantly dressed in black, appeared when they pulled the bell at the side of the gate and admitted them.

'We are expecting you,' she said in perfect English, smiling kindly at the two girls. Their rescuers waved aside their profuse thanks, wished them luck and sped away, while Dona Mercedes motioned them to follow her through the courtyard. A narrow stairway led from the tiled hallway to a spacious sitting room, where, still unsteady from the rolling of the boat, they collapsed gratefully onto a sofa. The tantalising aroma of hot coffee heralded the arrival of a trolley laden with croissants and rolls and, as they breakfasted, their hostess explained what was to happen. They would be safe here for a few days, but must use that time to make arrangements to move on. It would be difficult to explain their presence any longer than that and even more difficult for them to find work to support themselves. Majorca was under fascist control at present, but there were spies every-where and it was, of course, a military base, so there was a danger of reprisal bombing from the mainland. Several foreign ships were watching the coastline under an international non-interventionist agreement and there were other foreign merchantmen and traders in the bay. It should be possible to arrange a passage on one of these, provided their papers were in order, at least as far as Gibraltar or Marseilles.

She looked at their weary faces. 'Come, now. You must sleep'. She led them up a steep staircase to a large bedroom with gauzy white curtains fluttering gently at the open window and two beds, the covers turned back to reveal invitingly cool, immaculate starched white sheets. 'The bathroom is next door and there is hot water. I will see you when you are rested.'

Bathed and relaxed, they fell gratefully into bed, too tired to talk. Hours later, refreshed by dreamless sleep, the reality of the situation dawned and they felt humbled by the thought of the risks taken by so many brave people, most of them strangers, on their behalf. Margarita was horrified at having involved her friend.

'You could have stayed, but you put yourself in danger for my sake and you don't even know the full story,' she moaned in self disgust.

Margot put up her hands in protest. 'When I needed someone, you were there. You and your family showed me more love and kindness than I could ever repay. We will get through this. Don't worry!'

Margarita shook her head miserably. 'You don't understand. I didn't tell you everything. I'm pregnant!' She recounted the fatal confrontation with Vicente and waited for her friend's shocked reaction.

Margot sat silently, looking down at her hands.

'Say something! Oh, I know what a fool I've been, a selfish, wicked fool. My poor Mamma and Pappa. How could I do this to them? I can't ...'

Margot stopped her. 'I know,' she said quietly. 'It seems we are both in the same boat. I can't face your parents either. I feel that I have betrayed their trust.'

'You mean – Sven? Oh, Margot,' she exclaimed, as the other nodded. 'Does he know?'

Margot shook her head.

'What's the point? His regiment will be posted to the front soon and he will have enough to worry about. Besides,' she shivered, 'he is better off without me. I know it sounds awful, but I was not really in love with him, I just – oh, what does it matter now?'

'How long have you known?' asked Margarita.

'Oh, about two weeks. I couldn't say anything and I kept hoping, well, so much was happening, I tried to convince myself that it was just stress that was causing everything to go haywire. What about you?'

'Nearly a month.'

'Oh, Margot, what fools we have been. We thought we were being so smart, but we knew nothing, just two silly schoolgirls!' They looked at each other in dismay, then Margarita said tentatively, 'You wouldn't do anything silly, would you? I mean, you will keep it?'

Margot looked down at her clenched hands, then said quietly, 'Oh, yes. I feel,' she paused, searching for the right word, 'elated, in a way, that I will have someone who really belongs to me. But I am scared, too. Everyone close to me seems to die, my parents, Aunt Janey. I seem to put a jinx on people I love. Oh Margarita! I don't want my baby to die. Maybe you would be better off without me, too.' She looked so miserable, Margarita threw her arms around her.

'That's nonsense. What happened to them had nothing to do with you. You have just been desperately unlucky, whereas I,' she stopped and sighed heavily.

'Nothing is going to happen to these babies. We must stop feeling sorry for ourselves and make plans.' Margot recovered her composure. They must get to England as soon as possible. At least there would be time to sell Aunt Janey's house before her condition became obvious. She could not have her aunt's neighbours see her like that. They could move to another area and make a fresh start. Between them they should be able to earn enough to support themselves and bring up the children decently. In a more positive mood, they dressed and descended the stairs.

Dona Mercedes was not alone and they hesitated as two young boys turned to look at them, 'It is all right. Come and meet my grandson, Antonio, and his friend, Karl-Heinz.'

The boys, both aged about thirteen or fourteen, stood up and bowed gravely. Dona Mercedes was the widow of a diplomat and her son, also a diplomat, was a friend of the German Consul, Karl-Heinz's father. The boys often visited her after school to look at her late husband's butterfly collection or play chess with the beautiful carved ivory pieces. They were quite used to hearing talk of passports and papers and understood the necessity for discretion. Over tea, they talked of school and hobbies and were shown the butterfly collection. Karl-Heinz was eager to hear about England. His father was being recalled soon and he hoped his next posting would be to London. Dona Mercedes explained that she had arranged for Karl-Heinz to take Margot to see his father, who would provide them with papers authorising them to travel on a German ship. The boy's presence would allay any suspicions. She suggested that, once the exit permit had been obtained, Margarita should destroy her Spanish passport. She would travel as Margaret Martin and, if questioned, she was to say that her British passport had been lost. Better no papers at all than raise suspicion of a link with Republican Spain. It would also be a wise precaution to change her appearance just in case anyone was looking for her. She could bleach her hair and wear a pair of spectacles. Margarita agreed readily, both girls open-mouthed in admiration of this charming lady's attention to detail.

'It is what comes of reading detective stories,' laughed Dona Mercedes modestly.

'Shall we make a start?' Margot collected their documents and followed Karl-Heinz into the cool of the early evening. Walking along a lovely boulevard, El Borne, he pointed out buildings and places of historical interest. Margot was struck by the normality of the busy city, where people laughed and joked as they journeyed home from work or paused to dally with friends in the tree-lined avenues, unscarred by bombs and vandalism. The heavy presence of armed soldiers and civil guards was a grim reminder that the war was part of life here, too.

Italian and German planes based on the island regularly strafed the Republican mainland and Karl-Heinz's guileless face shone with pride as he told her of the Luftwaffe's destruction of the Basque region. No one paid any attention to the boy and his companion as they entered the Consulate. The meeting with the Consul was brief and after perusing the passports he duly signed two impressive looking official documents. Margarita's name had been anglicised and he repeated Dona Mercedes' instruction that her Spanish passport must be destroyed. It was unlikely that they would be challenged, but they should take no chances. They must be ready to go at short notice tomorrow or the day after, as soon as a suitable vessel was ready to sail. They were back in time for dinner and Margot went upstairs to find Margarita brushing her damp hair. She tied it back, put on a pair of wire-rimmed spectacles and the transformation was startling.

Next morning, very early, Dona Mercedes was persuaded to take Margarita to the cathedral, while Margot waited at the house. It was clearly important to the girl and she seemed to have had a weight removed from her shoulders when she made her confession. There was no news until late afternoon, when Karl-Heinz appeared in a chauffeur driven car to inform them that he was to accompany them to the docks. A merchantman bound for Morocco, would be putting in at Gibraltar, from where they would have no difficulty in finding a British ship to take them to London. At the docks, merchant ships and tramp steamers unloaded food and supplies, traders haggled and bargained and ragged children ran around, begging for scraps and pesetas.

Anchored further out in the bay were several military vessels, among them the German battleship the *Deutschland*, covetously regarded by Karl-Heinz, who would dearly have loved the chance to go aboard. The car, unchallenged, stopped at the foot of the gangway of the *Amadeus*, a merchant ship making ready to cast off, the captain loitering casually on the quayside. The boy grabbed the bags and, with the car partially obscuring them from view, led his charges up the gangway, followed by the captain. He clicked his heels and bowed solemnly as he accepted their fervent thanks and retreated quickly to the car, which sped off immediately. Installed in a small cabin, the girls listened as the gangway was hauled in and the throb of the engines rose to a roar. They held hands, smiling shakily at each other with relief. They were free. Slowly the ship drew out of the harbour making for the open sea. It was almost sunset.

Suddenly the sound of a siren shattered the air and people ran for cover as the hum of aircraft heralded a Republican raid. Panic reigned as the first bombs splattered in the water, hitting nothing, but causing small craft to break from their moorings and jostle helplessly against each other. Then the whine of the engines as they banked and dived was drowned by the noise of explosions as they found their targets. Smoke billowed from crippled hulls, twisted metal was hurled into the air and men fell into the sea as boats were hastily lowered from sinking vessels. Those already under way tried to make a run for it and the *Amadeus*, passing on the starboard side of the *Deutschland*, was covered by the destroyer's guns trained on the attackers.

'*Schnell!, schnell!*' The door of the cabin burst open, an officer urging the girls to take their belongings and get up on deck. Bewildered and frightened, they clung together as the lifeboats were lowered. The booming of the guns ceased abruptly with a direct hit on the *Deutschland*, then the sky turned orange as fire sparked an explosion in her ammunition store, blowing her apart and sending men screaming into the sea, alight with burning fuel. The shock from the explosion rocked the *Amadeus*, tossing her into the air and dropping her, bows first, into the swell. She began to break up, people and debris flung overboard as she sank, swiftly and silently, beneath the waves. The raiders departed as suddenly as they had arrived and people creeping cautiously back to the quayside gazed in horror at the scale of the destruction. Ambulances nudged their way through the dock and rescue craft were quickly mobilised, but the death toll was high. At the German Consulate the news of the destruction of the *Deutschland* and the sinking of the *Amadeus*, with no survivors, brought tears to the eyes of a young boy.

Chapter Fifteen

'MISS CHASE!' The voice was a long way off, muffled, but insistent in the darkness. Floating in space, her head, filled with thick cotton wool, seemed detached from her body, a red mist behind her eyelids. Something, someone, gripped her shoulder and she tried to scream, but no sound came from the cracked lips and the taste of salt on her swollen tongue made her vomit. She felt herself being lifted gently, her face sponged, the voice now insistent in her ear, telling her to wake up, telling her she was safe now. Safe? Where was she? Her eyelids flickered as she struggled to force them open over bursting eyeballs, slowly bringing into focus three faces peering anxiously into hers.

'She's coming round! Can you hear me, Miss Chase?' She stared at him blankly, her eyes, wide open now, taking in the uniform, the English accent, then nodded. She was on a ship. A ship! The fog began to lift from her brain and the nightmare returned. She began to shake, whimpering, as a cup was held to her mouth and a sweet liquid dribbled into her mouth.

'Drink this. It will help you sleep. I am a doctor and we'll soon have you on your feet again.' She awoke to find herself in a small bunk in a cabin. Her head ached and she was stiff all over. When she tried to move her arm, the pain made her wince and she saw that it was bandaged from her elbow to her wrist. Her clothes had been removed and she was dressed in a large white gown like the ones in the hospital. She remembered being thrown across the deck and falling, falling towards the churning waves, then searing pain and blackness. There was a knock on the door and the doctor entered, followed by a man carrying a tray of coffee and rolls. Feeling suddenly hungry, she dragged herself painfully into a sitting position. The doctor smiled sympathetically.

'Headache? I will give you some tablets. You must have taken quite a crack, but fortunately you seem to have got away with a mild concussion and a couple of days rest should do the trick. There was a nasty gash on your arm, but I have stitched it and it should not give you any trouble.' Hesitantly she asked how they had found her and how he knew who she was? The merchant vessel, having delivered its cargo, had been anchored a mile out from the bay and they had watched helplessly as the harbour was attacked. During the night, a sailor on watch had spotted a large crate floating on the water with what appeared to be a body on it. A boat was lowered and they were amazed to find a young woman, still alive. The doctor picked up the sodden canvas bag, 'This saved your life,' he said. 'You had it slung diagonally across your chest and the strap caught on the crate as you fell. You were lying face down with the bag underneath you, acting as a sort of cushion. The crate was carried out to sea by the current and here you are! Your passport was in the oilskin bag inside, so we guessed you were trying to get home.' They would be calling at Gibraltar, he told her, where she would be able to telephone or send a message to her people to let them know that she was safe and make arrangements to be picked up when the ship docked at Dover. She nodded and thanked him.

She closed her eyes, trying to avoid the dreaded question, reliving the desperation as they clung together, the horror as they were wrenched apart, their hands slipping, the gap between them widening, the sea on fire, then, nothing.

'Was anyone else saved?' she managed at last. He shook his head. 'I don't know, but from what I could see of the situation when the ship went down, I doubt it. You were thrown clear, but we found no-one else, though we searched the area.' She grieved inwardly, silently wishing that she, too, had perished. She was alone. No dear friend to share tears and laughter and help her face a judgmental world. Her hand rested briefly on her stomach as, dismally, she contemplated the future. There was a moment of panic as she wondered whether the doctor had noticed her condition. Presumably it was still there? He had said nothing and it was very early, only a few weeks, but ... Oh, what did it matter anyway, she concluded wearily. The steward arrived bearing her clothes, expertly washed and pressed, and she managed a smile of gratitude, ashamed of her negative thoughts in the face of the kindness her rescuers had shown her.

The captain refused to accept any payment for her passage and the crew took a benevolent interest in her welfare, seeming to regard her as a lucky mascot. They lent books, showed her pictures and carvings they had done to while away the hours at sea and one of them gave her a sweater he had been knitting for himself which had turned out too small. Another insisted that she choose a piece of cloth from a pile of gorgeously patterned cottons he had picked up in Morocco and she borrowed needles and cotton to make herself a skirt. She looked at photographs, listened to stories about their families, shared their hopes and fears. When the ship docked briefly in Gibraltar, she was able to buy a shirt and underwear and replace the overlarge deck shoes she had been wearing, her own having been ruined by the sea. She began to feel human again, warmed by the unquestioning friendship of strangers, a glimmer of hope and determination awakening in her heart. When the time came to say goodbye, it was with a mixture of relief that the ordeal had ended and sadness at parting with people who had given her the chance to make a fresh start. Now her thoughts must turn to practicalities.

It was ten o'clock in the morning when the taxi deposited her at the door of the house with a request to pick her up two hours later to take her into the town centre. She glanced anxiously around, but there was no-one in sight as she took a deep breath and turned the key in the lock. Inside, she leaned briefly against the door, her heart pounding, before going resolutely up the stairs. First, clothes. It was a hot, sunny day and she rummaged through drawers, selecting underwear, a navy blue cotton skirt and a white blouse, into which she changed, then sat on the bed to sort out what needed to be done. She must move to another area and find work before her condition became obvious, so the house had to be put up for sale immediately. She had some English money, thanks to the oilskin pouch and some pesetas which she could presumably change at the Bank. A search produced Bank statements, cheque book, the key to a deposit box and a copy of the Will and she stuffed them all into a large handbag. By the time the taxi returned she was ready, looking reasonably smart, despite the bandaged arm, a pair of sunglasses partially hiding the fading bruises on her face.

The estate agent was soon dealt with, an appointment made for the next day to value the property. At the Bank the assistant hardly glanced at her as she filled in the slip to exchange her pesetas and transfer the money into the account. Now for the solicitor. Among the letters lying behind the door, she had found a letter from the solicitor advising that Probate had been granted, but they needed her signature to transfer the house into her name. She found the office and produced the letter to the receptionist. Unfortunately Mr Brown was away. Could Miss Chase come back a few days later? Miss Chase thought not. She was going away again tomorrow. Could not someone else deal with it? After some hesitation and a murmured discussion on the telephone, she was asked to wait and a few moments later she was ushered into a room, where a young man, apologising for his senior's absence, took just a few moments to complete the business. Back in the street, she could hardly believe how smoothly everything had gone. The problem now was to find work. On the train on the way down, she had searched through the advertisements in the newspapers, but, outside London, there seemed to be few openings for a young woman, apart from shop assistant and waitress. She found the library and went into the reading room to look through the local papers, but there was nothing suitable. Standing up to leave, she caught the eye of the assistant at the desk, who smiled back at her. Encouraged, she approached and asked how one might go about getting job in a library, adding quickly that she had a Higher School Certificate. She was recovering from an accident, she explained, noting the lady's appraising glance. They chatted for a few moments about the work of a librarian, then, having established that she wanted to move to a different area, her informant produced an internal memo advertising vacancies in libraries all over the country. Currently there were three, one in London, the other two in the North of England. She copied down the details and addresses, gratefully accepting an offer to help her with information should she get an interview.

It was getting late and she had not eaten, apart from a sandwich and a cup of coffee in the town. There was no food in the house, so she did some shopping before boarding a bus, relying on the conductor to ensure that she did not go past her stop. She had almost reached her door, when, to her dismay, a woman coming towards her stopped, barring her way. 'You must be Margot! We never met, you being at school, but I knew Miss Chase well and she often talked about you. I just want to say how sorry I was when she died. She was a lovely lady. I saw you arrive this morning. Shall you be living here now, dear?' Thanking her, she stammered that she was at college and that the house was to be sold. She had just come down for a few days in her vacation to sort things out. The woman nodded sympathetically.

'Memories,' she said. 'It's best to get away if you can. Make a fresh start. Anyway, I must be going. Just wanted to pay my respects.' Then she was gone, no doubt to spread the news that the house was up for sale and start speculation as to how much it would fetch.

There was an old typewriter in the house and she laboriously typed out applications for both of the jobs in the North. She had unearthed the Higher School Certificate, but references might be a problem. Miss Gresham at Sevenacres School for one, but what if they wanted another? Time to worry about that when a job materialised. Miss Gresham! She grimaced at the thought of that estimable lady seeing her in what used to be called 'a delicate condition'. The estate agent seemed to think the house would sell quite quickly and suggested a most acceptable price. He undertook to send a man to tidy up the garden, which had been neglected for so long. After he had gone, she busied herself with clearing everything she could not take with her, ruthlessly discarding clothes which would soon be too tight, retaining smart simple garments, a few jumpers, a mackintosh and a warm winter coat. The rest she bundled into a bag to pass on to a church or charity organisation. Drawers were emptied, their contents consigned to the dustbin. Ornaments, furniture and household equipment would have to wait until she knew where she was going. Meanwhile, she continued to investigate work possibilities, schools, offices, hotels, prepared to consider anywhere so long as it was far enough away.

To her amazement, only a week later, she had a reply to her application from the library in a place called Barnard Castle in County Durham offering her an interview. She posted her acceptance and began to plan for the journey, which seemed fairly complicated, so she would need to be prepared to stay overnight. Examining herself critically in the mirror, she noted that her arm had healed and the bruising had almost disappeared, but her hair looked untidy. A visit to the hairdresser would boost her morale and she decided that the expense was justified. Wrapped in a large cape, she listened absently to the girl's constant chatter as she pressed in the waves and expertly wound curls round her fingers, securing them with crossed hairpins. 'I've done you a Ginger Rogers, Madam. It's all the rage and it'll suit you down to the ground, you'll see!' Her head covered with a hairnet, she was placed under the drier and given some magazines to read, mainly back numbers of *Picture Post* and *Picturegoer*. Flipping idly through the pages, she realised that she had missed the excitement of the Coronation and the wedding of the Duke of Windsor to Mrs Simpson and tried to memorise a few of the details for future reference in conversation. Then her eye fell on the dramatic pictures of the airship, the *Hindenburg*, as it blew up and burst into flames seconds before it reached the landing field in New Jersey. A wave of panic washed over her. She could smell the fumes and feel the heat and almost cried out as she had when the sea had tossed her to safety among that twisted wreckage. Hurriedly, she closed the magazine, shutting out the image, forcing herself to think of other things, the words of a Tennyson poem, half-remembered from school, dredged up to demand her concentration.

Released from the drier, her face red from the heat, she watched anxiously as the hairdresser brushed out the curls, smoothing the ends into a pageboy roll, primping and pulling until she was satisfied with her handiwork. Turning her head to see herself from all the angles as the girl held a mirror behind her head, she was pleasantly surprised. Miss Rogers was in no danger of being upstaged, she thought, but the shining blonde pageboy bob certainly looked smart. She parted happily with her two shillings and stepped out with a newfound confidence, stopping to buy a trial size Tattoo lipstick in pale pink. The interview was next day and she agonised over what to wear. It was too warm for the smart navy wool suit and she finally settled on a striped cotton frock, pink and white, with a white belt, wide-topped sleeves and a short skirt. The black patent leather court shoes were rather tight, but looked right with the handbag, so they would have to do. She stuffed them into her overnight bag along with a pair of clean white gloves, to be changed into at the last moment before the interview.

The train journey seemed to take forever, but, despite her anxiety, she had no difficulty in making the connections and arrived in Barnard Castle with over an hour to spare. Apart from a sandwich and a cup of coffee from a snack stall at one of the stations, she had not eaten, so she was glad to find a spotless tearoom where she had eggs on toast and a pot of tea. Her first impression was of a delightful old market town, the long steep high street with its stone houses, shops and taverns leading down to the river, bustling with life. The waitress had recommended a boarding house where she could spend the night and she booked in, changed her shoes, and, having ascertained where the library was, she set out, gloves in hand, fingers crossed.

Inside the building, she approached the desk and waited while a customer was served, then introduced herself. 'I'm Margot Chase. I have an appointment to see Mrs Pomfret.'

With a friendly smile, the girl took her arm and showed her to a door across the room. 'She's expecting you. Good luck!'

Margot returned the smile and knocked at the door, which opened immediately to reveal a pleasant, rather plump lady, with neat grey hair, wearing a black skirt and a crisp white blouse.

'Ah, Miss Chase. Come in, my dear. I do hope you had a reasonable journey. I forgot to mention that we will, of course, reimburse you for the expense.'

Margot, surprised, stammered her thanks. She felt an instant rapport with this motherly lady, whose shrewd questions quickly established that, despite her lack of experience, she had before her an intelligent, conscientious young woman who would, in her estimation 'eat the job'. The girl was clearly from a good background, well-educated, smartly dressed and beautifully spoken. She intimated her intention to offer her the post, adding that she could not understand why someone with her qualifications wanted to come to a place like this when she could surely do so much better in London.

A stab of conscience punctured Margot's resolve to cover up her situation. She looked despairingly at the kind face and blurted out, 'I'm two months pregnant.'

Mrs Pomfret's eyes rested briefly on Margot's left hand.

'I'm sorry. I should have told you, but I desperately need to work and I should be able to find someone to look after the baby, but I don't suppose you can give me the job now.'

'You are not married?'

The girl shook her head miserably. 'We were going to be married, but he was killed in an accident. He was a soldier.'

Mrs Pomfret felt her heart miss a beat as her mind flew back twenty years to the end of the war. Her youngest sister had been left in the same situation when the man she expected to marry was killed in the trenches less than a week after their farewell tryst. This girl seemed to have the strength of character to cope, unlike poor Joyce, who had taken her life rather than face the shame, but she would need more than that if her child was to have a decent chance in life. She thought quickly. Her instinct told her that she was making the right decision, as she said quietly, 'Let's talk it through. Perhaps we can make it work.'

Margot's head shot up in disbelief. 'You mean?'

Mrs Pomfret nodded, her eyes twinkling. 'We are fairly desperate and you have been straight with me. Now we need to sort out the details.'

Margot would need somewhere to live until the house was sold and she could find a place of her own. Mrs Pomfret was sure that would not be a problem. There were several respectable boarding houses in the town and she would find an affordable place for her. When could she start? Today was Wednesday and Margot said she could travel up on the following Monday. That would give her four or five months to work before the baby was due, plenty of time to arrange for someone to look after it when she was ready to return. She waved aside the girl's gratitude, reminding her that, in addition to her daily duties, she would have to study for examinations in librarianship if she wanted to improve her status as well as her pay. It would be in everyone's interest, she concluded, if Margot were to be introduced as a widow, calling herself Mrs Chase and wearing a wedding ring. Drawing on her gloves over the bare left hand, Margot agreed.

'Oh!' as she turned to go, 'One more thing. "Margot" sounds a bit posh for this part of the world. How about "Marge?"'

They both laughed as they shook hands.

Chapter Sixteen

FORTUNE SEEMED TO HAVE SMILED at last on the young widow, tragically left pregnant when her husband died so suddenly. She had been lucky to find a job and people had nodded approvingly when she bought a little semi-detached house on the new estate, presumably with the compensation for the accident. She was a nice young woman, always clean and neatly dressed and very pleasant to speak to. Such a shame that she had no relatives to help her cope with her grief, but at least now she would have the baby. In fact, the house in London had sold quickly and she was thankful that she had put the furniture into storage in the few days before taking up her new job, enabling her to move into a fully furnished house a month before the baby was due. A local solicitor had dealt with everything for her, so there was no need to travel back to London. There was more than enough money to pay for the house, leaving her with a comfortable nest egg.

Housekeeping was a new adventure for her and she learned by trial and error, unwilling to parade her ignorance by asking for advice. The school curriculum had been heavily committed to academic achievement, with barely a nod in the direction of domestic science or household management. After all, most of its pupils were unlikely ever to have to trouble themselves with such matters, hired help being easily affordable. She had picked up a little culinary knowledge in Spain from watching Maria and helping at the soup kitchen, but few of the familiar ingredients seemed to be available in Barnard Castle and she had no idea of what quantities to use. Apart from keeping her own room clean, she had never had to tackle a bathroom or clean windows and had no idea what to ask for in the shops, peering furtively at products on the shelves to read the labels. Mistakes cost money and, realising that common sense alone was not enough to produce the standards to which she was accustomed, she invested in a cookery book and pored over advertisements in magazines extolling the virtues of cleaning fluids. There were programmes on the wireless about household economy and a section in the library with books on the subject. She experimented and practised and it was not long before she felt confident enough to exchange recipes and offer her opinion on the quality of goods in the shops. The little house was soon clean and tidy and she had even managed to give the kitchen a fresh coat of paint. On that occasion she had hesitantly sought the help of the man at the ironmonger's shop, who had worked out the amount of paint she would need, explained how to prepare the walls and handle the paintbrush and had even given her a discount.

Violet Pomfret had reason to congratulate herself on her decision to take a chance on the plucky young woman who had appeared from nowhere with such a tragic tale. Margot Chase had proved to be hard-working and reliable, learning quickly and enrolling immediately for a correspondence course to begin her studies in Librarianship. Within weeks she had suggested and implemented improvements in the layout and organisation, pleasantly and tactfully, which had made life easier for everyone. Janet, the junior clerk, whose sweet nature did not entirely compensate for her slovenly attitude to dress and work, was enslaved by this elegant, friendly young woman, not that much older than herself, who talked posh, but always spared time to listen to her and give advice. Anxious to please her new role model, she got on with her work without having to be told and even volunteered to help in other areas. With her hair washed and combed, her blouse and skirt pressed and her shoes polished, she had smartened up considerably and glowed with pride when Marge said how nice she looked. Marge found that, apart from being grateful for the employment, she actually enjoyed the work. It was not onerous and with Violet and Janet ensuring between them that she did not have to stretch or carry anything heavy, she was able to carry on working until two weeks before the baby was due. She could hardly believe how easily she had been accepted in the community. Violet's endorsement had helped, of course, but she had also formed friendships with people she met in the library and, as her condition became obvious, some of the regulars would pause to chat as she stamped their books, giving advice or just wishing her well.

As December approached, the weather turned dark and dismal, with sleet spattering the pavements and the threat of snow in the air. It was not fit to go out and, having stocked up with food, she spent most of the day studying or reading. She was currently diverted by Georgette Heyer's historical novels, accurately portraying the Regency period, but light and amusing, just what she needed to distract her from the ordeal to come. Her friend, Sally, had been wonderfully supportive, telling her what to expect and helping her to prepare for the baby's arrival, but as the days went by, anxiety began to set in, the magnitude of her loss felt never more keenly than at this moment when, alone, she must assume responsibility for another living being. When she went into labour, two weeks before Christmas, Sally was with her and accompanied her to the hospital, promising to call in at the library to let Violet know. Her ordeal was relatively short and less painful than she had imagined and from the first fearful look at her baby girl, Marge was enchanted.

Rested, she looked around the large, busy ward, noisy from the chatter of nine other new mothers fussing over their offspring or exchanging their experiences. Her baby lay in a cot by the side of her bed, eyes open, struggling to focus as Marge bent over her, stroking the fuzz of downy fair hair on the little head.

'That will all come off!' laughed the nurse, as she approached with her temperature chart. 'You have had a couple of stitches, but you can get up now and walk about for a bit. I will be back in about half an hour to watch you feed her and check that all is well, then we take the babies away until visiting time to give you a chance to rest.'

Margot smiled and thanked her, then got out cautiously and went in search of the toilet. Two women, standing by the washbasins smoking cigarettes, stopped talking and looked at her as she entered the room. Smiling hesitantly, she passed them and went into a cubicle. After a few seconds they resumed their conversation. They were discussing birth control. Not much use to her, now, she thought wryly, nodding to them as she returned to the ward.

Visiting time came round and she felt conspicuous, acutely aware that all except herself and one other woman had a husband to admire the new arrival. The younger men, first-time fathers, most of them, looked proud and embarrassed, peering cautiously into the cots, trying hard to see the family resemblance claimed by their triumphant wives, their hearts sinking with apprehension as the bawling of infants threatened months of disturbed nights. Older fathers sat awkwardly, caps between their knees, making desultory conversation or answering questions about how they were coping at home, eyes constantly straying towards the clock as it ticked slowly on to the end of visiting time and their escape to the pub. She was relieved when Violet walked in, bearing a large bouquet of flowers and bringing messages of congratulation from several people to whom she had managed to pass on the news. The baby was duly admired and questions about her own health satisfied.

'Have you decided what to call her?' asked Violet.

Before the birth, she had been unable to make up her mind about a name for the child, other than to decide that it should not be a family name or have associations with anyone she knew. It should be truly a new beginning. While in the hospital, she had heard someone use the name 'Laura' and felt immediately that it conjured up an image of elegance and serenity. She had looked down at her baby, silently mouthing the name. It felt right and the decision was made.

After Violet had gone, she lay back, eyes closed, planning a routine in readiness for her return home in a few days' time.

'Want a cigarette?' She opened her eyes to see the young girl from the bed in the corner holding out a packet of Woodbines.

'Er, no thank you, I don't smoke,' she replied.

The girl had not had a visitor, she recalled.

'It was nice of you to offer, though.'

The girl looked into the cot. 'Girl is it? I got a girl.'

Marge smiled. 'It's a relief to get it over with, isn't it? My name is Marge. What's yours?'

'Sylvia,' she replied, perching on the edge of Marge's bed. 'You got no husband neither?'

Marge shook her head.

'I'm a widow,' she said carefully. 'He died soon after I became pregnant.' She waited. Sylvia sniffed, her arms folded tightly against her body. She looked very young.

'I'm not married,' she said. 'He cleared off when I told him.'

Marge put out a hand in sympathy. 'Do you live with your parents, then?'

There was a pause, then, 'Yes, but me mam won't have the kid. It'll have to be adopted.'

Marge was horrified. Was that what the girl wanted? Could she not find somewhere else to live and keep the baby? It appeared not. Sylvia was only sixteen and could not hope to find a job paying enough to support her and the baby and pay for child care. She liked the baby and it would have been all right if her mother had seen fit to take it in, but she would not want to stay in every night and have no fun. It would be better off somewhere else. She just wished they would take it away immediately instead of having to wait six weeks. Her mother would not have her at home during that time and had not even visited her in hospital. She was leaving the hospital in the morning and would go straight to a home for unmarried mothers, where she would stay for the required six weeks. Marge shuddered, shocked by the girl's plight, thankful for her own good fortune. A nurse came to collect the infants for the night and Sylvia retreated to her own bed.

The child was a delight and Marge was enchanted. She put out a tentative hand to touch the tiny fingers grasping hers as the little button of a nose nuzzled against her breast. The sweet smell of the sleeping infant, bathed and fed, made her dizzy with pride and happiness. She could hardly believe that this perfect little creature had come out of her body and could not refrain from tiptoeing to the cot every few minutes to watch her as she slept, looking for an excuse to pick her up and cuddle her, contrary to the instructions of the midwife at the hospital. There was no shortage of bootees and matinee coats and the child's progress was watched with a proprietary air by the local matrons. Few of the married women worked and there was no problem in finding someone to look after Laura when Marge was ready to return to work. Sally Woods, a placid, rosy-faced lass with a five-year-old girl who had just started school, was ideal. She loved children and would dearly have loved another baby, but it seemed it was not to be. Her little house was neat and clean and she had wondered how she would fill in her time now that Lucy was at school. When Marge asked if she could help, she was delighted. The two women had met in the library when Sally had requested a book that was not on the shelf. They had chatted and found they shared the same taste in books and music. It was Sally who had told her about the house on the estate, just round the corner from where she lived and, in the last weeks before her confinement, she had taken to spending an evening at Sally's house while Tom had his night out at the pub. He was a miner, who, through hard work and study, had already been made a Deputy at his colliery. Sally shared her pleasure in the new-born babe, so placid and content, and the two young women soon worked out a routine that would enable Marge to return to work as soon as she felt strong enough.

Violet had insisted that Marge should spend Christmas with her and sent her son-in-law, Harry to collect her in his car. She had given Marge a warm comfortable bedroom next to the bathroom and turned a large drawer into a makeshift cot for the infant. Her own daughter's twins were just over a year old and had just begun to walk, so the house was filled with the sound and smell of babies as the adults managed to swallow their turkey and mince pies while keeping a watchful eye on the new generation. The talk was almost exclusively of babies and Marge felt as if she had joined a club, part, at last, of a community, establishing her new identity as a mother. Four weeks later, though winter was not yet over and flurries of snow still fell on the bleak landscape, she decided that she must go back to work. Violet and Janet had been so kind to her, covering her duties and unable to take any time off themselves, she must relieve them as soon as possible. It was a wrench to leave Laura, but she could not put it off forever and the child would be in good hands. They were delighted and relieved when she returned and she was soon back in her routine, enjoying the companionship and touched by the genuine interest of local people in her baby's welfare. Often, weather permitting, Sally would wheel Laura's pram round to the library at lunchtime, so that Marge could see her and show her off. Evenings belonged to the baby; household tasks set aside until she had been settled for the night. There were times when her thoughts dwelt sorrowfully on what might have been, but, at last, she had begun to live again through this tiny being who belonged to her alone.

The library was very busy, people clamouring for detective stories and thrillers, particularly by Margery Allingham and Dornford Yates, who had lists of readers waiting for their books to be returned. The reading room was nearly always full in the cold, wet weather, people drifting in for an hour or so of warmth to browse through reference books or flick through the newspapers. Each morning, Marge skimmed through the papers as she set them out, looking anxiously for snippets about the Spanish Civil War and noting the growing crisis in Czechoslovakia, where Sudetan Germans, industrial workers living near the frontiers, unsettled by the economic depression, were demanding concessions from the Government and expressing a desire for repatriation into the German Reich. The Czech president sought British and French help to stop Hitler gaining control of his country, but they were unwilling to commit themselves to policies which might, in public opinion, run too great a risk of war. Throughout the next few months, the papers reported on the comings and goings of various heads of State, meeting to debate the unpalatable options, until, in May, the Czech military reserve was called up and the frontier posts manned with armed guards. The danger of war loomed large, as Hitler alleged provocation, leading Britain and France to put pressure on the Czech president, forcing him to agree to talks with the Sudetan leaders, at which he agreed to all their demands, ostensibly removing their grievances. At the end of the summer, the British Prime Minister, Neville Chamberlain, flew to Germany to meet Hitler face to face and thought he had brokered a deal under which the Sudetan lands would be ceded to Germany, leaving the rest of Czechoslovakia independent and guaranteeing peace. It did not satisfy Hitler, however, and he appeared to be set on obtaining control of Czechoslovakia. The British public, through their newspapers, newsreels and wirelesses, watched events with growing unease, as it became clear that the British Government was preparing for the eventuality of war. Anti-aircraft guns appeared, sirens were being tested and gas masks tried on. The sight of trenches being dug and an emergency scheme set up for evacuating children from London caused concern and indignation, even in Barnard Castle and Marge, mindful of the prophecies voiced in some quarters in Barcelona, listened with sorrow and anger to the arguments for aggression and appeasement. It would not stop with Czechoslovakia, whatever agreements the politicians made. When, in September, the Munich Agreement was signed, partitioning Czechoslovakia to the detriment of the Czechs, Chamberlain returned home, claiming that peace with honour had been achieved. He was greeted by rapturous crowds and most of the newspapers applauded, though there were dissenters who felt that the threat had not been removed and that there would be a war sooner or later. They were right, thought Marge gloomily, refusing to join in the excited conjectures of friends and customers.

Chapter Seventeen

IT WAS A WARM BRIGHT SUNDAY MORNING. Marge Chase stood at the kitchen sink peeling vegetables for lunch. The door was open so that she could keep an eye on little Laura playing in the garden. and she smiled to herself as she listened to the happy toddler mangling the words of nursery rhymes as she sang to her teddy bear. The wireless was on and suddenly the voice of the Prime Minister, speaking slowly and deliberately, was delivering the words that the whole country had awaited with dread for so long.

'This morning the British Ambassador in Berlin handed the German Government a final note stating that, unless the British Government heard from them by 11 o'clock that they were prepared at once to withdraw their troops from Poland, a state of war would exist between us. I have to tell you that no such undertaking has been received, and that consequently this country is at war with Germany.'

She stood still, a wave of nausea sweeping over her as the memory of the nightmare days in Spain hammered in her brain. Now the terror was spreading until there was nowhere safe for innocent children to live. Would people never learn?

She ran out into the garden, scooping up the child and hugging her to her breast until she squealed indignantly.

The woman next door called over the fence, 'Did you hear that?' and she boxed the ears of her children, who had been running round the garden blowing rude noises through the gas masks. 'Put those away, they're not toys. The Germans are coming!'

Everywhere people talked of nothing else. It was a relief, in a way, that the uncertainty of the past few months had come to an end. Air raid shelters had been put up, piles of sandbags deposited round public buildings, searchlights manoeuvred into place, blackout practised and volunteers trained for civil defence, but to most people it had all seemed like some sort of game. Not to Marge. Behind the sandbags she saw the hard, defiant faces of children, aged beyond their years by hatred and deprivation, hurling stones. The shelters might provide some initial protection, but people had no idea of the devastation and heartbreak caused by relentless bombardment, reducing homes to rubble and lives to dust. She must remain silent, keeping her worries to herself. Her life appeared to be serene and peaceful, but there were moments of over-whelming sadness when the pain in her eyes was interpreted as the widow's grief for the dead husband who could not share her hopes and fears for their child. She had listened with sick horror to reports on the wireless of the intensive bombing of Barcelona throughout the spring, avidly scouring the newspapers in the reading room for details, unable to talk of her fears for those dear ones she could not expect to see again. By May it was all over. Franco's triumphal march through Madrid meant little to the inhabitants of Barnard Castle as they went about their daily lives, but she knew that the reports of hundreds of executions and trials of thousands of Republicans in revenge for anti-fascist activities were not exaggerated. Most of all, she grieved for her alter ego, torn from her grasp by the cruel waves and lying cold at the bottom of the sea and that child, unborn, who should have been her daughter's companion. Their lives had been inextricably bound and she had taken a silent vow to live for both of them the life they had planned together. Sometimes, when the sense of loss was almost unbearable, that presence seemed to invade, vibrant, encouraging, comforting, and she would draw strength from it, until she almost felt she was that other self. It was odd, she smiled ruefully to herself, how even the change of Christian name, prompted by a stranger, could have been used by either of them. Life went on. She had been given a second chance and must take it with both hands for the sake of the child whose unquestioning love warmed her grieving heart.

The town was already filling up with young soldiers on their initial training. A large purpose-built Army camp was being erected at Deerbolt, a few miles away, but it would be some time before it was ready, so troops were being billeted in the Drill Hall and other large buildings in the town. Some were billeted with private householders, who received an allowance of sixpence per man per day. It was good news for the local economy, bringing increased trade and jobs such as altering and repairing uniforms. Public houses did a roaring trade at the weekend and, apart from the odd scuffle after a night of excess, soldiers and civilians got along amicably. It was not long before some of the churches and the Mothers' Union got together to organise entertainment for the boys so far from home and Violet Pomfret, who was on the committee, placed a collection box in the library to help raise funds for a Christmas party.

Marge Chase, who felt privately that she had seen more than enough of soldiers, produced artistic posters as her contribution and agreed, with Sally's help, to make decorations and crackers for the event. Over the next few months the reality of war began to bite. On the first day of war, the liner *Athenia*, carrying passengers from Liverpool to the United States, was torpedoed and sunk off the Hebrides. Thereafter, newspapers and newsreels increasingly carried reports of a trawler sunk in the English Channel, German bombers spotted over Scotland or the south coast, driven off by the RAF ... the sinking of the German battleship, *Graf Spee*. The streets were dark, air raid wardens patrolling to ensure that the blackout was enforced and anyone showing a chink of light would get a knock on the door and an order to put it out. Coal was rationed on the first of October and Marge was thankful that she had stocked up over the summer, thanks to Sally's warning that it was bound to happen.

As Christmas approached, the mood in the town lightened and people made their normal preparations for the festivities, grumbling gently about shortages which were already becoming a normal feature and joking about the latest outrageous broadcast in English from Hamburg by 'Lord Haw-Haw', intended to break their morale. Little Laura was excited. She had her second birthday two weeks before Christmas and there was a tea party attended by Sally, with Lucy whom she adored, Mrs Pomfret and Jean Walker, Mrs Pomfret's daughter, with her three year old twins, Peter and Penny. There was a cake with two candles and her eyes shone as she blew them out. She did not really understand who Father Christmas was, but clapped her hands when Mummy pointed him out in her book and said he would bring chocolate and a dolly if she was a good girl. The day of the soldiers' Christmas party arrived and the ladies spent the whole morning decorating the Church Hall, while their husbands gave up their precious Sunday to carry chairs and set up tables. Violet Pomfret had stationed Marge and Sally in the small kitchen, where they sorted out the mountains of sandwiches, cakes, pies and jellies arriving in a constant stream as the local housewives rose to the occasion. By one o'clock, the big room looked splendidly festive, the tables groaning with food and jugs of lemonade and a tea urn stood ready on a trolley filled with thick white cups. A trio, hired to play dance music, was practising round the piano and some of the young local girls who had been invited were beginning to arrive. Marge longed to go home, but Violet had arranged for Jean to have Laura for the day and Sally's Tom had taken Lucy to see her grandparents, so there was no escape. Sally thought it might be fun, though she hoped there would be some volunteers for the washing up afterwards, so Marge put on a smile and resolved to make the best of it.

The party went with a swing, food disappearing like magic as the hum of conversation and laughter rose and the lads' initial shyness wore off. They came from all over the country and all walks of life, into a harsh regime among strangers, missing their mothers and miserable at the thought of their first Christmas away from friends and family. After the meal, the tables were pushed back to make room for dancing and the trio struck up with 'Sweet and Lovely'. It wasn't Geraldo, but competent enough to dance to and soon the place was filled with couples as the soldiers lost their shyness and vied with each other to display their varying degrees of prowess on the dance floor. Marge and Sally withdrew to the kitchen to help with the washing up, but were quickly expelled by a battery of redoubtable matrons urging them to 'Go and have some fun!' They looked at each other resignedly and drifted back into the room where 'The Lambeth Walk' was in full swing with nearly everyone on their feet, laughing and bumping into each other as they shouted 'Oy' at the top of their voices. Sally spied some empty chairs in the corner of the room and they sprinted over to occupy them. When the music stopped, they were joined by Mrs Pomfret, flushed and gasping from her exertions, with four young men in tow.

'Dear me!' she cried, fanning herself with a lace handkerchief. 'I am much too old for this sort of thing. Let me introduce you to some younger ladies.' Chairs were duly shuffled and the lads sat down shyly. Conversation was difficult over the music, but the girls managed to keep the talk flowing, Sally's knowledge of the area being particularly appreciated.

The foursome seemed an ill-assorted bunch, but they had met during their initial training and had stuck together. Jack, from London, did most of the talking. A bit older than the others, perhaps twenty-five or so, tall, with dark wavy hair slicked back with hair cream and a predatory look in his blue eyes, he clearly fancied himself as a ladies' man. As a party trick he drew amusing cartoons of his companions and claimed to have been working in the art department of the *Daily Mirror*, though the exact nature of his job was not specified. His mate, Mick, a sharp-eyed, ginger-haired youth from Liverpool, barely eighteen, hung on his every word, laughing at his jokes, learning the chat. The Army was a great adventure for Mick, who had never left his home town, had no job and little education and hoped to sign on as a regular when his National Service was over. Bill, from Eastbourne, was twenty-two, tall, quietly spoken and shy. He was studying accountancy and was keen to get his National Service over with and obtain his qualifications. The last member of the quartet, Andy, another Londoner, had just started a job in the Civil Service when he was called up, so had no worries about finding work on his return to Civvy Street. Short and thickset, with blond curly hair and clear blue eyes, he looked younger than his nineteen years. He had an encyclopaedic knowledge of films and film stars, volunteering a wealth of information whenever a Hollywood name was mentioned. As the afternoon drew to a close, the trio played 'Here's to the Next Time' to great applause and people began to drift away. The light was fading and men were waiting to pull down the blackout blinds and lock up the hall. Mrs Pomfret thanked the girls for their help, telling them there was no need for them to stay, the Committee would finish the clearing up. Jack jumped up immediately, offering to see Marge home. When she declined, saying that she and Sally lived close by and were walking home together, he gallantly declared that he would be delighted to escort both ladies. Gently but firmly they assured him that they had no need of an escort and that they must dash as they had things to do. They said their goodbyes, adding that they hoped they would all meet again and left to the sound of his companions laughing at his discomfiture. Outside, they dissolved into giggles.

'What a nerve! Obviously a wedding ring doesn't put him off,' said Marge indignantly.

'Probably thinks it's a safer option!' laughed Sally. 'He seems quite nice, though. Seriously, Marge, technically you are single and it is nearly three years now. You're young and attractive and there's no reason why you should spend the rest of your life alone.'

Marge stood silent for a moment, then replied, slowly, 'I'm not ready yet. And I don't feel alone. I have Laura.'

Sally squeezed her hand 'I know. I'm sorry. But don't close the door. One of these days you might meet someone and it would be good for Laura to have a Daddy. Come on, let's go before they come out!'

Laughing, they hurried off down the darkening street, as young couples began to spill out from the hall to continue their new-found romances elsewhere.

Chapter Eighteen

CHRISTMAS DAY DAWNED bright and cold. There was ice on the inside of the windows and the net curtain in the bedroom had stuck where it touched the pane. Marge shivered as she scraped at a patch of ice with her nail to reveal a perfect Christmas scene. Snow sparkled on all the rooftops and lay like a soft white blanket on the ground, unsullied as yet by footprints or car tyres. Hedges and bushes were hidden beneath drifts, forming mysterious shapes with icicles dripping like candles from branches and frosted spiders' webs shimmering delicately in the gaps between. So beautiful, but so treacherous. Her thoughts strayed inevitably to that other Christmas when, despite the danger, she had been surrounded by love and peace in the security of a happy family. It seemed so long ago, so far away, that family now wrenched apart, dead for all she knew, dead to her forever, as she was to them. The patter of little feet broke her reverie and she turned as Laura, rubbing her eyes, ran into the room. She scooped up the child, pointing to the snow and breathing on the window to melt the frost. Laura wriggled with excitement.

'Out!' she said.

'No, darling, not yet. Shall we see if Father Christmas has been?'

Leaving Laura in bed opening her presents, she went downstairs and set about lighting the fire, putting a match to the screwed-up paper under the firewood over which she had placed a few pieces of coal. She stood a shovel upright on the grate in front of the fire and put a sheet of newspaper across it to draw the flames up the chimney, waiting until the paper began to turn brown before snatching it away, then scattering half a shovelful of slack on the cheerful blaze to keep it low and save her best coal. Satisfied that the fire would stay in, she put up the fireguard and returned to find a blissful Laura cuddling her new celluloid baby doll, gazing into its wide painted blue eyes and examining the little pink dress with matching bonnet and bootees knitted painstakingly by Marge during her lunch breaks at the library. A coloured ball, crayons and a packet of chocolate had been cursorily examined and thrust aside in favour of the coveted prize and her mother smiled gently at the child's happiness.

'Baby,' beamed Laura, holding out the doll. 'Yes, we must find a name for her, but first, my precious, we must get you washed and dressed. We can take her to Auntie Vi's if you like,' and she took the doll, followed by a protesting Laura, into the bathroom.

Since that first meeting when the kind-hearted Violet Pomfret had taken pity on Margot Chase's desperate situation, their friendship had grown and the mother and child were accepted almost as part of the family. It would be unthinkable for them to spend Christmas alone and they were to join Vi and her daughter Jean, with husband, Harry, and the twins, for the festivities. Violet worried privately about Marge. On the surface she was coping well, but she had not come to terms with her grief and shut out any attempt to get her to face it. She would not talk about her 'husband', hoping, presumably, that in this way she could erase the hurt from her memory, but there would come a time when the child would want to know about her father and would also wonder why she had no grandparents. From the brief conversations they had had about families, she had learned that Marge's parents had been killed in a road accident and that she had been brought up by an aunt, her only other relative, who had also died. Apparently the young man was estranged from his parents and, though he had known about the baby before he died, had not told them about it, or indeed, about Marge. Violet had urged her to contact them, but, whether from pride or possessiveness, Marge had refused, saying she preferred to manage on her own. Violet's husband, a Major, had been badly wounded on the Somme in 1916 and died a few months later, leaving her, at thirty-five, to bring up their small daughter alone, so she understood the feeling of betrayal and anger with the deceased, but that phase should have passed by now. Granted, she had been well-provided for financially, with a comfortable home and help from both sets of parents, advantages which Marge did not have. She had not taken a conscious decision not to marry again, but practically a whole generation of young men had been wiped out and there were many women in her situation. Marge was intelligent, lively and person-able. She obviously took pride in her appearance; well-groomed, her hair fashionably bleached and styled, her clothes neat and smart. Several men had glanced in her direction, only to be given the cold shoulder. It was as if she had built a wall around herself and pulled up the drawbridge at the first sign of an approach. It was not natural and, while she would not want her to rush into a relationship, she hoped that the girl would at least get to know men of her own age and perhaps allow herself to have some fun, instead of keeping them all at arm's length.

Breakfast over, it was time to clear the snow from the path. Muffled up against the cold, Marge put on her wellington boots, fetched a spade and, followed by an excited Laura, began the task. Most of the neighbours were already out and the scraping of spades filled the air, interspersed with Christmas greetings called over fences and the shrieks of children tumbling blissfully in the snow, making slides in the road and throwing snowballs. The boys next door were building a snowman and Laura, fascinated, pleaded to be lifted over the fence.

'Let her come, Marge,' called their mother. 'She'll be all right.' Turning to the boys as her husband lifted the little girl over the fence, she warned, 'Behave yourselves, you two, or no Christmas pudding!'

The boys looked sheepishly at each other, hoping that none of their friends would see them letting a girl join in their play, but were soon gratified by her cries of admiration for their handiwork and allowed her to put in small pieces of coal for buttons. Marge found an old red scarf, they put an old cap on his head, stuck a twig in his mouth for a pipe and the snowman was finished. Laura clapped her hands and squealed with delight as the boys acknowledged praise from the adults and accepted a bag of sweets from Marge, who had managed to clear the path down to the edge of the road while they had entertained the child. All that remained now was to sprinkle some ashes from the grate to prevent slipping on the path and drag Laura away to get ready to go out. By now the local Council had cleared most of the snow from the roads and Marge, in her wellingtons, carrying her shoes in a bag, steered the pushchair the short distance to Violet's house. The others had already arrived and amid a flurry of greetings and peeling off outdoor clothes, they were quickly absorbed into the warm festive atmosphere. While Marge stowed her presents with the pile already under the tree, Laura and the twins chattered happily and incoherently, showing off their new toys. The artificial tree looked quite splendid decked with tinsel and glass baubles sparkling in the coloured lights and a fairy perched hazardously on the top. Marge relaxed in a corner of a large sofa in front of a cheerful fire and Harry, Jean's husband, handed her a glass of sherry.

'Bliss,' she murmured contentedly, as the first warming sip slid down her throat. Violet, who had refused to let anyone help in the kitchen, from where enticing aromas teased their appetites, joined them and, having exhausted the topics of weather and children, the talk turned to their anxieties about the war.

Harry had failed his Army medical because of flat feet and poor eyesight, much to Jean's relief, though he had some feelings of guilt as, one by one, his friends were called up. He ran a small but profitable brassware factory and realised that its days were numbered as his craftsmen disappeared and that it would probably be taken over for the manufacture of munitions or army supplies. So far, despite a few scares, the only German bomb to fall on British soil had been in the Shetlands in November, when, during a raid on British naval bases, a bomb had gone astray, killing a rabbit. But people were in no doubt that the war was creeping ever nearer and anxious eyes watched the skies whenever the sound of an aircraft was heard. News of the British Expeditionary Force in France was optimistic, though, according to Violet, stories were filtering back from wounded soldiers returning home of dreadful conditions and lack of ammunition. More and more men were being sent over every week and regiments billeted at Barnard Castle were on stand-by to go at any time. She had stayed in contact with some of the lads they had met at the Christmas party and regularly had them to tea, so she was up to date with the news. Incidentally, she added, she had invited some of them to come round in the evening. They were having Christmas Dinner at the Barracks, where their officers would be waiting on them and were free from duties for the rest of the day.

Lunch was perfect. A plump chicken, stuffed with chestnuts and surrounded by crisp roasted potatoes, was served with dishes of steaming vegetables. The rich plum pudding, thickly covered in rum sauce, was pronounced irresistible and, bursting with food and good humour, they called a truce with the mince pies until coffee was ready. Violet, flushed with success and the heat of the kitchen, was banished to an armchair while the girls cleared the table and Harry, insisting that he worked better alone, set about the washing up. The three toddlers had already been fed at a small table and behaved impeccably, so they were free to eat chocolate and open their presents from under the tree while their parents ate. Now they were getting tired and Laura crept on to Marge's knee, her thumb in her mouth. 'Time for a nap!' declared Jean. 'Come on, Marge, let's put them to bed for an hour.' The twins already had a room in their grandmother's house which they used quite frequently and Laura snuggled under the eiderdown on 'Auntie Vi's' bed. Within half an hour, they were fast asleep and the adults returned to their coffee, just in time to hear the King's Christmas message on the wireless. His words, in his poor voice breaking with emotion, praised the courage of the Navy and the Air Force in their defence of the country over the past four months and sent special greetings to the British Expeditionary Force facing unknown hardships abroad. While he hoped for peace in the coming year, no one knew how long the struggle would last. There would be sacrifices, but the British people would remain staunch in the fight against wickedness. They must trust in God. Harry switched off the wireless and they sat for a moment in silence, each with their own thoughts. Violet was the first to speak.

'Whatever happens, we will just have to get on with it as best we can. All the more reason why we should make the most of this Christmas. No glum faces when those poor boys arrive!'

They opened their Christmas presents with exaggerated care.

'Save the paper, you never know what you might need it for!' Harry was delighted with the bottle of whisky from Marge, vowing to keep it for a celebration when Hitler got what was coming to him, while Jean said the silk stockings were the exact shade she wanted and pretended to swoon over the Al Bowlly record. The mysterious bulky package with Marge's name on it proved to be a fireside tidy, beautifully fashioned in brass by Harry's own hands and she gasped with delight at her friends' thoughtfulness and generosity.

'It'll be nose cones for shells or brass buckles next year, I shouldn't wonder,' he said ruefully as she thanked him profusely. Violet had knitted a warm sweater for her son-in-law, but presented both girls with silk underwear, beautifully embroidered with their initials, saying that, if they were reduced to making do with old clothes, at least they could feel glamorous underneath. In return, she had a pretty cardigan in violet wool from Jean and Harry and fluffy slippers from Marge. The war was for the moment forgotten as they turned on the gramophone and settled back happily to the tender tones of Al Bowlly crooning 'Love Is The Sweetest Thing' with the highly popular Ray Noble Band.

At six o' clock, the sound of male voices singing 'Good King Wenceslas' was heard and a loud knocking on the front door heralded the arrival of Violet's soldiers. Greetings were exchanged and they shyly presented Vi with a large box of chocolates. The children, rested and demanding to be entertained, retreated initially to their mother's skirts, but soon lost their shyness when the newcomers produced sweets and let them play with their army caps. Jack produced his sketchbook and made drawings of animals for them to identify, while Mick provided the appropriate voices. Sometimes he would 'baa' when he should have 'miaowed' and the children protested, collapsing in giggles when he pretended he thought he had made the right noise. Bill took out a white handkerchief and wound it round his hand, teasing out the corners to make ears. He drew a face with whiskers on it and working it cleverly with his hidden fingers, presented a talking mouse, which so held their attention they did not notice his mouth moving as the mouse made comments about each child. Each laughed as they heard the mouse make uncomplimentary remarks about the others and protested when their own turn came. 'Where on earth did you learn to do that?' asked Harry, always on the lookout for ways to occupy the twins.

'My brother has two boys,' smiled Bill. 'It sometimes helps to distract them when they get out of hand.' As he started to show Harry how to fold the handkerchief, Vi brought in a tray of tea and cake and there was a short interval in the proceedings while they munched contentedly.

'How about a sing-song?' asked Jack. 'Can we use the piano, Mrs P?' Andy settled himself at the keyboard and began to play, expertly, a Chopin nocturne, the notes rippling from his nimble fingers, until his companions groaned, 'Not that! Something we can sing to!', whereupon he ran through all the old favourites, 'Nellie Dean', 'Any Old Iron', 'Roll Out The Barrel', new ones like 'Alice Blue Gown' and 'Little Old Lady' and a few Christmas carols. They all joined in heartily, until Jean, noticing the time and the children's drooping eyelids, called a halt.

'Sorry to be a wet blanket, but it's way past their bedtime and I'm afraid we must go. We'll give you a lift in the car, Marge. I know it isn't far, but it's dark and probably slippery underfoot by now.' The car was a luxury since petrol rationing was introduced and Harry, because of the business, was one of the few who could continue to run one. Children and belongings were rounded up, thanks and goodbyes said and the men helped them into the car. Marge had thoroughly enjoyed herself and Violet nodded approvingly, as she heard her thank them for the entertainment and agree they should do it again soon.

Back home, a drowsy Laura snuggled into her bed, clutching her doll. 'Nice men,' she sighed happily, 'Laura like!'

Marge laughed softly. 'Yes, darling. It was a lovely party. Go to sleep now.'

Chapter Nineteen

THE WHOLE COUNTRY was in the grip of the severest winter of the century. The River Thames was frozen over for the first time in forty-five years and in some places even the sea froze. Snowdrifts several feet high prevented traffic from moving and on some days people were unable to get to work. Paths had to be cleared daily and it was a struggle to keep the house warm, eking out the coal ration with nutty slack, which spluttered damply and poured out smoke. Muffled up against the biting winds, Marge put woollen socks over her shoes to keep her from slipping as she trudged with the pushchair to Sally's, then on to the library. She had knitted the shapeless socks, thinking wistfully of Eulalia and her campaign for stump socks, nostalgia for Spain and the sense of loss almost a physical pain. The newspapers were full of the war now, so there was little news, apart from a report of General Franco's Christmas message, which, though he preached the need for unity and the end of the hatred and passion caused by the civil war, made it clear that there would be no general amnesty for his former enemies. Life would not be easy in Barcelona.

The reality of war bit deep as more foods went on ration, first bacon, butter and sugar, then meat, then jam, marmalade, syrup and treacle. There were queues outside butchers' shops, hoping for a bit of off the ration brawn or sausage, or, if they were lucky, a rabbit, to make the meat go further. Housewives swapped and borrowed from each other, grumbling mildly, but proud to feel that they were making a contribution to the war effort. Marge, like many others, had stocked up with tins and jars, but fresh food was a problem and it was difficult to balance shopping and queuing with work. She and Violet took it in turns to shop for both, while the other held the fort at the library. Every day now there were reports of British ships being sunk by German U-boats and regular air-raid alarms over the Orkney and Shetland Islands. The number of British troops in France had risen to 100,000 and units from all over the Empire were being drafted in to serve with the BEF. In England, women were called upon to work in munition factories or join the Land Army to replace men called up for military service and help to increase the production of food to feed the population. Harry Walker's factory was turned over to producing buttons and buckles for military uniforms and more conscripts poured into Barnard Castle as new buildings became available.

Occasionally there was a concert organised by the military and Marge accepted Sally's offer to look after Laura while she enjoyed a night out with Andy, who shared her love of music. She felt comfortable with Andy, who wanted nothing from her but the companionship of someone who understood and appreciated classical music. His mother had been a professional violinist and he had trained as a concert pianist, but realised he had not the talent or commitment to reach the top and had settled for a career in the Civil Service and a lucrative sideline as a pub pianist. He had a girlfriend whom he hoped to marry and, unlike Jack, posed no threat to the young widow. Jack, charming, carefree, funny, was dangerously attractive. Once, she had let down her guard and agreed to go to the pictures with him, which he clearly regarded as the green light and attempted to kiss her in the darkness of the auditorium. Momentarily, she felt herself responding, then, horrified, she pulled away, two red spots of anger and embarrassment burning in her cheeks.

Outside, he put his arm round her and she pushed him away with an exclamation of annoyance. He laughed. She wasn't exactly a virgin, was she? They both knew was what, so why not admit it and let him show her what she was missing? Furious, she slapped his face and ran home, tears of rage and shame streaming down her face.

Next day she confided in Violet. 'You see? They're all the same, only interested in one thing and thinking I'm fair game. I'll never trust a man again!'

Violet sympathised, but urged her not to judge all men by one bad experience. At the end of March, things began to stir as regiments were put on the alert for active service. Violet had continued to have the boys to tea every Sunday, though she had admonished Jack for his behaviour towards Marge and he had apologised. Within a few days they had all gone, their destination unknown. The news from Europe was depressing. By mid-April, Denmark had fallen to the Germans, followed by Norway, where a contingent of inexperienced and poorly armed British troops was heavily defeated and had to be evacuated. A month later, the whole of the Western Front exploded into total war, the Allied armies fighting desperately to hold back the Germans from the Channel ports. The Prime Minister, Chamberlain, resigned and Winston Churchill took over to form a coalition Government. The British Expeditionary Force had crossed from France into Belgium at the urgent request of the Belgian king, but the collapse of the Belgian defences and the retreat of the French in the Ardennes gave them no alternative but to withdraw, fighting all the way back to the Channel ports. With the shock surrender of the Belgian king, leaving the road to Dunkirk unguarded, nine divisions of the British Expeditionary Force moved in and held their ground long enough to allow the remaining troops to get clear. Thousands of British soldiers, guided by the dull red beacon of burning oil tanks, converged on Dunkirk, massing on the beaches as the Navy, augmented by trawlers, ferries and private vessels of every size and description, marshalled them into queues for embarkation. Fighting continued around Dunkirk as French forces held off the Germans. Shelling of the beaches and rescue vessels continued throughout the week-long exercise, killing and wounding to the end, but at last the operation was completed and the troops arrived home to a heroes' welcome. Next day, Dunkirk was surrendered. Though it could hardly be called a victory, a great disaster had been averted and there was a huge boost to morale, as the spirit of the nation rallied spontaneously to Churchill's defiant declaration to the world that, though they would have to face 'blood, toil, sweat and tears', the British would defend their island whatever the cost. In homes all over the land, radios relayed his stirring words, 'We shall fight on the beaches, we shall fight on the landing grounds, in the fields, in the streets and in the hills. We shall never surrender.' The people straightened their shoulders, tightened their belts and raised their chins in pride. Violet Pomfret had heard nothing from any of her 'boys' and had no idea where they were. She followed the progress of the BEF in the newspapers, anxiously speculating on their involvement at the various battlefronts and hoping that they remained unscathed. Pictures of the Dunkirk evacuation and interviews with returning veterans were shown on cinema newsreels and she scanned the screen for sight of a familiar face, but there was none. One day towards the end of June, she was leafing through the local paper in the library when a short item about the hospital caught her eye. Two of the wards had been designated for the treatment of military personnel wounded in battle and one of the patients, badly wounded in France, had trained at Barnard Castle. His name was Bill Somers. Immediately, she went over to Marge.

'The poor boy! And he's miles away from home. We must visit him and see if there is anything we can do.' Marge agreed and contacted the hospital to check that a visit would be in order. Armed with magazines and sweets, they duly arrived and were met by the ward sister, who, satisfied that they were friends of the patient, explained the position to them. She was pleased that he would have visitors, because so far, although his parents had been notified, they had not turned up. He had lost a leg and had other injuries, which though now beginning to mend, had threatened his life. He was still poorly, but he would recover and her main concern was for his psychological well-being. He would need a great deal of encouragement to help him cope with months of pain and to focus positively on the future. Any help that they and other friends could give would be invaluable.

They were shown to his bed, where he lay, eyes closed, his face white as death, with a frame over the lower part of his body to keep off the weight of the bedclothes. Violet spoke his name and his eyes opened, unrecognising at first, then, as he looked from one to the other, his face cleared and he smiled sadly, grimacing towards the frame. They nodded sympathetically, telling him that the sister had told them of his injuries and that they would like to visit while he was in hospital. He was lightly sedated and did not say much, but they learned that he and the others had been taken to Southampton and shipped over to France as reserves, from where they were sent in batches to replace losses in various regiments. He had been ill with influenza when they arrived at the base and the others had gone straight to Norway, leaving him behind. When he recovered, he was transferred to a camp on the Belgian border until the order came to cross the frontier and defend the country against invasion. It was some days before they heard the rest of his story, as the sister interrupted, saying that visiting time was up and Bill needed to rest.

At first it had been wonderful, the Belgian people greeting them enthusiastically as the tanks and lorries rumbled through the villages. Girls threw flowers and people rushed out with coffee, mugs of beer, cakes and chocolate as the advance into Louvain continued with only minor encounters with the enemy. Then all hell broke loose. They came under continuous heavy fire from tanks and dive-bombers as the Germans fought unsuccessfully to dislodge them. There was vicious hand to hand fighting when the Germans managed briefly to gain control of the railway station and had to be driven out with bayonets. Bill shuddered with revulsion as he relived the shock of seeing a man die, the eyes looking straight into his with an indescribable expression of puzzlement and pleading before glazing over as he gasped and fell. Automatically, he wrenched back his rifle and stood looking at the blood dripping from the tip of the bayonet until someone yelled at him to move. He had killed a man.

The fighting went on all day with assaults from tanks and dive bombers, but the British held their ground until news came of that the French front had been penetrated and their army was falling back. To avoid the BEF being left isolated, the command to withdraw was given and under cover of night the operation began. As they left, the engineers carried out massive demolition, leaving the Germans high and dry, and the BEF took up new positions on the River Scheldt. Two divisions and an armoured brigade were detached and sent to Arras, among them Bill Somers, to deliver a counter-attack on the German army which was storming its way southwards. He could not remember the details of that horrific encounter, though he learned later that the small British detachment, having inflicted heavy losses on the German army, had only just managed to fight its way out. He had been inching his way along a hedge towards a gun position, when he saw a plane diving towards him. He closed his eyes and heard a loud ripping noise as the bomb exploded, hurling him over the hedge. In a blur of smoke and flames, he felt a searing pain in his leg and blacked out as he landed heavily on his back.

When he woke, he was on a stretcher, *en route* for Boulogne, where he was transferred to a hospital ship for an operation to repair his torn calf muscle and remove pieces of metal from his back. The port was under fire and the town was being evacuated, cargo boats waiting to take women and children out of the danger zone. As they waited on the quayside, enemy planes mowed down the queues with machine-gun fire. Despite the large red crosses displayed on the hospital ship which was embarking wounded soldiers, it came under attack and as he was being lifted from the stretcher a salvo hit the deck. They got Bill below to the operating theatre and he was just being lifted on to the table, when another shell hit the bulkhead, destroying most of the surgeon's equipment and blowing off part of Bill's injured leg just below the knee. The leg had to come off. With only a cut-throat razor and no anaesthetic, the surgeon poured a bottle of rum over the leg and set to work.

Back in England, he spent several weeks in a military hospital where a 'tidying up' operation was performed on his leg and the metal removed from his back. Because of the increasing numbers of wounded arriving for treatment, men were being transferred to hospitals all over the country and Bill found himself back at Barnard Castle. Weak and still suffering from shock, he was haunted by thoughts of comrades who had fallen and dismay at his own participation in the destruction of human life.

He had not yet begun to think about his future. Marge, as the harrowing details emerged, gripped the seat of her chair and felt the sweat pouring down her back, reliving that moment before the blackness swallowed her up. The whine of the shells, the sound of rending timbers as ships broke up, the smell of burning oil and the sight of the sea on fire. In her head that last imploring cry as their hands were pulled apart in the waves and now this new dread. Did she just drown or ...? Oh, please God, I had not thought of anything worse, let her not have suffered even more.

Next day Violet was seething with indignation. She had been to visit Bill at the hospital and his parents had turned up. Instead of being thankful that her son was alive, his mother had seemed more concerned at the prospect of having to look after a disabled man, saying she could not possibly cope and he would have to go into a home. Violet had taken her to task, saying that he would be perfectly capable of looking after himself once his wounds had healed and he was fitted with an artificial leg and that she must not upset him by talking like that in front of him. He needed to have his confidence built up. The little woman, bleak-faced, shuddered as she buttoned up her coat and shook her head.

'I can't do it. I've got his two sisters to look after, so I can't even keep coming up here to see him. And people will stare. He won't be able to work and what woman will have him? I can't have him on my hands for the rest of my life.'

Violet could not believe what she was hearing. She turned to the father, a tall, thin, weary looking man, who shrugged miserably, gesturing towards his wife as he said, 'I've told her. He can't help it, but she won't have it, so that's that.'

Coldly, Violet surveyed them. 'Your son is a very brave young man, who has made a great sacrifice to keep this country safe for people like you. I pity you for your mean, selfish stupidity and I think Bill will be better off without you. Good evening!' She turned on her heel and left, shaking with rage and disbelief.

Next morning, she related the encounter to Marge, who was equally shocked. Had not the doctor or the sister explained Bill's condition to them and the fact that he would recover to lead a normal life? Violet was sure that they had, but there were people who could not cope with disability and, clearly, Bill's mother was one of them.

'How will he react?' asked Marge. Violet did not know. She could only hope they had not conveyed their thoughts to him. At least let him get stronger, she prayed, before he has to face this. The next day they visited him together and there was no sign that he had been upset by his parents' visit, so presumably nothing had been said about the future. He seemed cheerful, having enjoyed a game of chess with a man injured at Dunkirk, who would be staying in the hospital for a few more weeks.

Chapter Twenty

FRANCE HAD CAPITULATED and the Germans occupied the Channel Islands. The threat of invasion came ever closer as air raids intensified, bombs falling nightly, mainly around the coasts and in the industrial Midlands. By now, every town and village had its Home Guard, a civilian force of men too old, too young or graded unfit for military service. Armed with whatever they could get hold of, guns, kitchen knives, staves, they drilled and trained in the evenings and weekends, kept watch on coasts and open spaces and prepared to deal with enemy parachutes or planes coming down in their area. In Barnard Castle, Harry Walker, who had volunteered immediately the call went out, had been made a sergeant. Sally's Tom and Marge's next-door neighbour, Bob Sharpe, were roped in and they all went off enthusiastically on their secret exercises, referred to indulgently by their wives as little boys' games.

There were frequent raids over the North East coast and when the sirens went, Marge wrapped the sleeping Laura in a blanket and carried her down to the Anderson shelter. Usually the all clear went after a short time and they trundled back to the house without the child waking. Raids were mostly carried out at night, but one day in August, during a lunchtime attack over Hartlepool, a German Messerschmitt, pursued by RAF fighters, was shot down and crash landed close to Broomielaw railway station, three miles from Barnard Castle. The sirens had sounded just before one o' clock and people rushed in panic to the nearest shelters or dived for cover in fields and hedges. An hour later, when the all clear sounded, there was great excitement as news spread through the town that a German fighter pilot had been captured. Harry and his mates were furious that it had happened during the daytime, when they were at work, so that the glory fell to a few old men and the ARP.

'We'll never hear the last of it!' grumbled Harry. 'Bloody ARP! Always trying to put one over on us and Jerry's given it to them on a plate!'

At the hospital, Bill had been examined by an army surgeon and told that there was nothing more they could do for him. His back and stump were healing nicely and he was managing well on crutches, having been fitted for an artificial leg which would be ready in a few days' time. In the meantime, he would be discharged and could go home, the Army having no further use for him. He would be entitled to a war pension and could see the Army Welfare Officer if he needed any help with his claim.

'Lucky you!' smiled Sister as she wrote up his chart. 'You'll be able to see your sweetheart again soon. Don't tell me you haven't got one!'

Bill shook his head ruefully. 'No. I got a letter from her soon after I arrived here. She gave me the push.'

Sister paused, glancing sharply at his face, but he did not seem unduly concerned. 'Oh, well. Plenty more fish in the sea!' she said. 'What about work?'

He had already resumed studying and would soon be fully qualified as an accountant, so there shouldn't be a problem. He could do it standing on one leg, he joked. When Violet heard the news she was dismayed. She had known it would happen, of course, but not so soon. She had become very fond of him, almost as if he were her own son, and she did not want to lose him, certainly not to his selfish mother. She confided her fears to Marge, adding that she was thinking of offering to have him as a lodger in her house. Marge said it was a kind thought, but warned her not to be upset if he wanted to go home, reminding her that he had a brother and sisters as well as his parents and his mother might change her attitude once he was home.

Next day, Violet went alone to the hospital and talked at length with Bill about his future plans. It was clear that he was in no hurry to return to Eastbourne and she outlined her proposal that he stay at her house, at least until he was fully mobile. He could continue his studies and in return for his board and lodging, he could help with light tasks around the house. He was quite overcome with gratitude, though concerned that he might be a burden. Not at all, she assured him. There was plenty of room and it would be nice for her to have company. He would have the house to himself for most of the day, so he could study in peace and have friends round whenever he wanted to. If there were any mobility problems, he could always count on Harry to help. It was settled.

The hospital arranged for him to have a Morrison shelter, so that, in the case of an air raid, he could stay in the house with the steel top to protect him. Marge and Jean helped to prepare for his arrival, placing a bookshelf in the larger of the spare bedrooms, removing rugs that might cause him to trip and a stool by the bath so that he could get in and out. Harry fixed a rail over the bath for him to hold on to and another by the downstairs toilet. He also produced a sturdy little table from the factory for him to use as a desk. Violet, critically surveying their handiwork, nodded her approval and on the following Saturday he moved in. He was still on crutches, though his new leg had arrived and he had to wear it for a few hours each day to get used to it. Little Laura, part of the welcoming committee, stared round-eyed as he entered the room, then, having walked all the way round him, looking at the space where his leg should have been, stood solemnly on one leg until she overbalanced. 'Want sticks!' she declared indignantly when they laughed. Marge had been slightly concerned about the child's reaction to seeing for the first time someone with only one leg, but she need not have worried. When Laura realised that Bill could not move around like everyone else she appointed herself as his personal assistant, bringing things to him and fussing round him, arranging the cushion on his chair, shooing off anyone who threatened to usurp her authority. Bill, visibly moved by her solicitousness, readily obeyed when she brought her book and demanded a story, amid hoots of laughter and comments that he was being wrapped round her little finger.

Apart from a few spills, when Harry had to pick him up, Bill was pleased with the new leg and practised assiduously until the time came when he could wear it without irritating his stump. Marge, to the admiration of the others, helped by knitting thick socks to go over the ones provided by the limb fitter, thinking sadly to herself of Eulalia and how she would have been pleased to know that her idea was still proving useful. She and Laura had fallen into the habit of spending most Sundays with Violet and Bill, whose patience in entertaining the child with hand puppets, stories and drawing games seemed limitless. When Marge chided her for pestering, Bill protested that she was like a tonic and he always felt better when she was there. He had confided to Marge that he often felt pain in the missing leg, phantom pains, he said, pointing to an empty space where his calf should have been, such a strange feeling when his head told him that it was not possible. Marge knew that feeling. Her other self was gone, but the pain in her heart remained and that presence, like a phantom, was always near. Soon Bill was able to get around using a walking stick. He had kept in touch with friends he had made in hospital and would meet them for a game of chess or a drink at the pub. Violet had introduced him to some of her friends in the business community and it was not long before he was offered a job with a firm of accountants, with the prospect of advancement when he finally became chartered. He insisted on paying rent to Violet and was still able to put aside some small savings. His studies were going well and he found no problem in settling down with his books in the evenings after work, determined to do well. Sometimes, at the weekend, he and Marge would go to the pictures, while Violet stayed with Laura. Occasionally, if the weather was fine, they would take the little girl on a bus ride into the country. They got on well together, talked about books and films and argued about politics. If he did not come, Laura fretted and would not be appeased by her mother's attempts to distract her with games or visits to see the twins. Violet watched their relationship with pleasure and a slight kindling of hope that it might develop into something more, though she was well aware of Marge's fear of commitment and would not have dreamed of saying anything to her on the subject.

Once, on the way home with Bill after he and Marge had been out for the evening, she had hazarded, 'You like Marge, don't you, Bill?' and he had readily agreed, adding that he enjoyed seeing Laura, too.

'I don't suppose I shall ever have one of my own,' he said wistfully and Violet looked at him sharply.

'Whyever not?' He said it was unlikely that any woman would look at him now and she rebuked him, telling him not to be silly, he was young and there was plenty of time, though her hopes fell as it seemed plain that Marge was not giving him any encouragement.

By the end of the year, prospects of an early end to the war seemed bleak. Towns and cities all over the country were devastated by bombing raids day and night, leaving families distraught in the wake of death and injury having to cope with the added trauma of homelessness. Stoically, people rallied round to help each other and there were those who felt that the spirit of community and friendship engendered by the hardship almost compensated for the suffering they endured. Food was scarce with nearly everything now rationed and few luxuries available even for those who could afford them. All over Europe, Africa and the Far East, British forces fought on land, in the air and on the sea, the newsreels reporting the toll with pictures of wounded men returning in droves. Violet had continued to visit soldiers in hospital long after Bill had left and had recruited several friends to help her, organising them on a rota basis so that men far from home would not feel neglected. Bill sometimes went along to talk to men who had lost a limb to give them encouragement, knowing the desolation they suffered when faced with the realisation that their young lives would never be the same again and the fear that their disability would close the door to the prospects and pleasures they might have expected. He would like to do something to help them, he told

Marge after a particularly arduous session with an eighteen-year-old boy who had lost both legs and wanted to die. If there were some sort of club, where they could talk to men with similar problems and share their knowledge and talents to help each other, it would give them a purpose in life. Marge thought there might be such a thing. There was a man who came into the library sometimes who had lost an arm in the first war and spent a lot of time studying pension law so that he could advise men on their claims. She would talk to him.

Spring arrived and Marge's life had settled into a well-organised routine. She was now fully qualified as a librarian, Laura was a bright, happy three-year-old and she was surrounded by good friends. She was even growing vegetables in her back garden under an agreed plan with Sally and the Sharpes next door to plant different varieties so that they could swap amongst themselves. The women exchanged recipes to make use of whatever food they could get and cannibalised their old clothes to make new ones for the children, often surprising themselves at their ingenuity. She had introduced Bill to the man she knew from the library and he was now involved in the local branch of the British Limbless Ex-Service Men's Association, which took up one evening every two weeks in addition to his visits to disabled men. Things were going well for him at work, he had passed another of his examinations and there was an air of self-assurance about him. He still made time for the Saturday visits to Marge and Laura and they saw him at Violet's at Sunday tea, but his life was now very full and Marge was almost envious of his sense of purpose.

On one such Sunday, Violet had a surprise for them. She had heard from Andy. He had been injured in Norway, not seriously, but being unable to hold a rifle because of a stiff shoulder, had been discharged from the army. Back at his Civil Service job, he also helped out in the ARP and had done some work as a photographer, recording scenes of the London blitz for a magazine. When a landmine fell on Jermyn Street, he had been helping to clear up and the porter, searching the flats, found the body of the crooner, Al Bowlly, who had returned late from a singing engagement and gone to bed rather than go to the shelter. His body was unmarked, but he had been killed outright by the blast. Apparently his death had been reported in the *Daily Mirror*, but the ladies in Barnard Castle had not seen it and Jean and Marge were shocked and sad. Violet was more concerned about Andy facing danger daily as he carried out his duties. He said he was due to get married in June, provided the church didn't get bombed. He had heard nothing of his old mates, though he often thought of them and wondered if Violet had any news. He asked to be remembered to Marge and hoped that all was well in Barnard Castle. Bill was delighted to hear that he was home and said he would write to him. It was no surprise to him to learn that Andy was doing professional work as a photographer, reminding Marge of his great interest in films and his ambition to be involved in some way in that industry.

Chapter Twenty-one

THE LIBRARY HAD NEVER BEEN BUSIER, the demand for books growing rapidly as people found time on their hands in the dark evenings. There was an insatiable demand for books on current affairs, the last war, modern Germany and Hitler's *Mein Kampf,* as they sought to keep up with the complexities of the situation in Europe. Violet and Marge were on their own since Janet, the junior, had been called up as a land girl and it was impossible to find a replacement. After being on her feet for most of the day, snatching time to queue for food and spending an hour or two with Laura before putting her to bed, Marge was too tired to do anything but put her feet up and listen to the wireless. Once a week, Sally came round and they spent the evening together, sewing, chatting, planning for summer outings now that the nights were becoming lighter and soft spring breezes wafted the scent of flowers and freshly mown grass through the air. One April evening, Sally was clearly bursting with excitement. 'Guess what!' she exclaimed without waiting for an answer. 'I'm going to keep chickens!' She laughed as Marge raised her eyebrows in astonishment. 'It's easy,' she assured her. 'I've applied to the Council to register as a poultry keeper and they will give me a special ration card so that I can buy bran and corn to feed them. Of course we have to build a little hut and a chicken run, but Tom says he can get enough wood and chicken wire and some of the neighbours will help. Just think, we'll have fresh eggs and some to spare for friends. So long as we don't sell them, we can do as we please with the eggs and, of course, there will be the odd bird for cooking when they stop laying.' Marge was intrigued, saying she would look in the library for books about poultry keeping. The children would love it. In no time at all the preparations were made. An old door and some bits of wood were transformed into a hut raised on bricks, with a hatch door leading into a wide chicken run roofed with wood covered with felt and fenced with chicken wire to keep out foxes. A door at the back of the hut permitted entry so that eggs could be taken from the nesting boxes while the hens were out and Tom had fixed a piece of string to the hatch door leading to the chicken run, so that once the chicks were in the hut at night he could release it, shutting the door and keeping them safely inside. Now for the chickens. They had decided to buy a dozen day-old chicks instead of hens already laying, taking a risk that there might be more than one cockerel among them. If that happened, there would be constant fighting, so only one cockerel would be kept, any more being fattened up and killed. Marge saved all her vegetable peelings and took them round to Sally to be boiled up with the corn and bran. Tom appeared with cardboard boxes with holes in and Lucy and Laura waited breathlessly while he took the lids off, squealing with delight as the fluffy yellow chicks spilled out, cheeping, into the run. Scooping two up, he put them carefully into the children's hands and they gazed in rapture at the tiny creatures. 'Don't squeeze them!' warned Lucy, as Laura stood transfixed, her little hands clasping the protesting chick. For the next few weeks, the chickens provided a constant source of entertainment as the children watched them grow, gave them all names and tried to remember which was which. They clamoured to feed them, laughing as the silly little creatures tumbled over each other, squawking, to get to the bran mash. When the new-laid eggs began to arrive, Laura savoured hers slowly, claiming proudly that her favourite chicken had laid it specially for her.

On a lovely Saturday morning in June Marge was up early and had done her chores in preparation for a picnic with Laura and Bill. 'Come on, sleepy head,' she called as she went into Laura's room, but the child, normally bouncing with energy on days like this, lay listless in her bed. When Marge reached to lift her from the bed, her body stiffened and began to shake in a convulsion. Marge, trying not to panic, turned her gently on her side. In a few moments the shivering stopped and she whimpered softly, shielding her eyes with her arm when Marge drew back the curtains.

'Darling, what's the matter?' asked Marge anxiously.

'My head hurts and my eyes,' whispered the little girl.

Marge, terrified, told her to lie quietly while she went to get help and ran down the stairs to call Brenda Sharpe next door. As she reached the gate, she saw Bill coming down the street. He was early and started to explain as she rushed towards him, white-faced, gasping, 'Oh, thank God you're here. It's Laura.'

He touched the little forehead and felt her pulse, his face grim. 'It's serious. I'll get the doctor.'

He moved incredibly quickly despite his disability and went to the telephone box at the end of the street. When he returned, he said quietly 'He won't be long. Just try to keep calm so that she doesn't get upset.'

The doctor, having already been apprised of the symptoms by Bill, quietly asked Laura to bend her knees, but she shook her head in pain when she tried.

He turned to Marge. 'I am concerned,' he said. 'This could be meningitis and we must get her to hospital as soon as possible.'

He went to telephone to make the arrangements while Marge and Bill wrapped Laura in a blanket and carried her downstairs. When the doctor returned they put her into his car and whisked her into the hospital, where the diagnosis was confirmed. There was no treatment, the doctor told them, they could only wait and hope. Marge was in a state of shock, gazing helplessly at her child lying limp as a rag doll while the fight for survival raged silently inside the tiny body. After all that had happened, was she to lose the one thing still holding her life together, one more cruel twist that Fate still had in store? The hours ticked by. Bill, his face strained with worry, gently pressed a cool damp cloth on the child's forehead or held the little hand, talking softly to her about the things she loved, repeating nursery rhymes, telling her favourite stories. From time to time the doctor or a nurse came in, checked her temperature and sighed. No change. Day turned to night and they kept their vigil, taking turns to leave the bedside and go to the cloakroom to splash cold water on their faces or walk up and down to keep themselves awake. The nurses brought cups of tea, but they could not eat, their faces grey with worry.

It was just after midnight when her eyelids fluttered. Bill had been talking to her about the chickens, telling her that he had been talking to them and that Hetty, her favourite hen, had promised to lay a big brown egg for her when she came home.

'Chick, chick, chick, chick, chicken,' he sang quietly in her ear, 'lay a little egg for me.'

A tiny croaking voice wavered in response, 'Chick, chick …' and he turned to Marge, tears streaming down his face. 'Quick, get the doctor, she's wet through with sweat!' As he straightened up from his examination, the doctor nodded.

'That's it. The crisis is past. She's going to be all right.' Marge collapsed against Bill, burying her face in his chest as she sobbed in relief. The nurse quickly sponged the child's body and made her comfortable.

'Let her sleep now,' she said. 'You both look as if you need a rest. Go home and come back after breakfast. It will be a while before she is fully recovered, but she is out of danger and there is nothing more you can do tonight.'

They walked through the dark streets, feeling their way cautiously, the tap of Bill's stick making an eerie sound in the stillness. An ARP warden looked at them curiously as he wished them goodnight, but there was no-one else about as they reached the house. 'I'll come for you about half past eight,' said Bill, turning to go as she fumbled for her key.

'Oh! Couldn't you stay?' she asked, pleadingly. 'I am afraid to stay by myself tonight.' It was nearly two o'clock and Bill had earlier telephoned Violet from the hospital to let her know where he was. Going in at this time would only disturb her.

'All right,' he said, 'but you must go and get some sleep. I'll rest in a chair and we'll talk in the morning.' Gratefully, she dragged herself off to bed and was surprised on waking to find that it was six o'clock. She washed and dressed quickly and went downstairs. Bill was already in the kitchen making tea and went to freshen up while she cooked eggs and made toast. They had not eaten for nearly twenty-four hours and had not realised how hungry they were.

Back at the hospital, Laura lay listlessly against the plumped up pillows, managing a faint smile as they approached the bedside. Her skin was cool and her hair had been brushed. The nurse, taking Marge aside, told her that Laura had spoken, was able to stand and there was no sign of any permanent damage as sometimes happened with meningitis, but she was very tired and needed a lot of rest. They would keep her in hospital for three or four days, at the end of which they would be able to say with certainty whether her recovery would be complete. No, she did not know how she had caught the disease. It was something that could attack any time, particularly young children. Laura, well-nourished and strong enough to fight the infection, had been lucky. Mummy and Daddy could spend half an hour with her each morning and evening, but not let her try to talk much. Marge blushed, looking covertly at Laura, who was holding Bill's hand, then decided against correcting the nurse's assumption. She hoped Bill had not heard.

The next few days passed in a blur, but somehow Marge managed to cope with her duties at the library, Bill and Violet taking turns to accompany her on visits to the hospital. When Laura came home she was still very weak and could not walk far, so Sally came round to look after her. Marge was overcome with gratitude for the kindness they all showed. It was like being part of a family, she told Bill. He grinned ruefully.

'Depends on the family,' he said.

'Oh, Bill, haven't you heard from your parents?' she asked, ashamed that she had not thought of his problems.

'Not since Christmas and then it was just a card hoping I was keeping well. I have written several times, but they have not replied. I did get a letter from my brother a few weeks ago, so I know they are all right, but I don't think I figure in their lives any more. Violet is more like a mother to me than my own.' Marge smiled.

'I know. She is wonderful, isn't she? But for her I don't know how ...' Her voice tailed off and he squeezed her hand as Laura called her from the couch. She went to the kitchen to fetch orange juice and Bill went over to the child, lifting her into a sitting position so that she could drink. Laura held on to his sleeve.

'Nurse thought you were my daddy,' she said, her eyes fixed on his face. 'Will you be my daddy?'

Shaken, he could only stammer, 'Well, that would be very nice, but you can't choose a daddy. Only a mummy can do that.'

Laura, looking over his shoulder, opened her mouth to speak and he turned to see Marge holding the glass of juice in her hand, pink with embarrassment.

'Now, Laura, drink up and I'll get you ready for bed. You are very tired.'

The child protested feebly, but her eyelids were drooping and she allowed herself to be carried off to bed, having claimed a goodnight kiss from Bill.

When Marge returned, she was still visibly flustered. 'I'm sorry about that,' she said, meeting Bill's quizzical gaze. 'But she is still only a baby and doesn't understand what she is saying.'

'Doesn't she?' he retorted. 'She's a bright child and when she sees other children with their fathers or talking about their fathers, she wants to know why she hasn't got one. You never talk to her about him and it's not as if there were grandparents or family to keep his memory alive, so she thinks the job is still open!'

Marge sat down wearily, pushing back a strand of hair from her forehead.

'I just wanted to bury the past and make a fresh start for both of us. We have no living relatives, so she is missing out on aunts and uncles and cousins as well, but there is nothing I can do about it.'

Bill, exasperated, slapped the arm of his chair. 'You are an attractive, intelligent, healthy young woman. What is to stop you marrying again and possibly raising a family? I'm not suggesting that you do it just to please Laura, but surely some day you are going to want a normal relationship with a man! I can understand that you might not consider me, with my one leg, as a prospective husband, though you could do worse. I love both of you and I could look after you. One day, I will have my own business and make enough money to keep you in comfort.'

Marge, silent, buried her face in her hands.

'I'm sorry,' he said. 'I should not have gone on like that. Please forget what I said. Don't let it spoil our friendship.'

She put out a hand, her face wet with tears. 'You don't understand,' she whispered. 'You don't really know me. I can't marry anyone.'

He looked puzzled, then realisation dawned. Her husband must still be alive and she had run away. No, she told him, wrestling with the admission she could no longer avoid. She had never been married. She had made a mistake and had to pay for it. Unable to face the degradation, she had left before the neighbours found out that she was pregnant. It was easy to make a clean break because she had no real friends in the area, having been at boarding school until her aunt died, and none of her friends lived locally. There was no question of marrying the child's father. He was dead. Apart from himself, only Violet Pomfret knew the truth and she begged him not to reveal it to anyone. Guilty though she might be, she still had some pride. Marriage would mean producing her birth certificate revealing that she was single, so a prospective bridegroom would have to be told in advance that she was an unmarried mother. He would lose respect for her and the wedding would be off. There was pain and shame in her past, but it must remain a closed book and she would never talk about it to anyone, even a husband. How many men would accept that?

Bill tried to collect his thoughts. She sat, eyes downcast, twisting a handkerchief in her hands, like a child awaiting a reprimand, scared, guilt-ridden, but defiant. He wanted to take her in his arms and kiss away the tears, but was afraid of being accused of taking advantage. He could almost have laughed with relief, but understood the devastation she must have felt as a well brought up girl, barely out of school, with no family to help her face a judgmental society. If he sympathised, she would probably think he was condescending.

'We all have things in our past that we are ashamed of,' he said. 'I am twenty-five years old and I was not exactly an innocent youth when I went into the army, so who am I to judge you? You were just unlucky. Anyway, there are worse things than that. I killed a man, probably several men if the truth were known. I have to live with that.'

'You had to. He was trying to kill you,' she interjected.

He shook his head. 'I don't think he wanted to kill me any more than I wanted to kill him. That's not the point. What I am trying to say is that we cannot alter what we have done in the past. What matters is what we make of ourselves in the future. I don't want to know about your past. I know what you are now and that is good enough for me. You have worked hard, earned respect in the community and you are a good mother with a child anyone would be proud of. Violet thinks the world of you and she is no fool. Maybe it's time to put the past behind you and really make a fresh start. You say I don't know who you are, but sometimes, Marge, I wonder if you know yourself.'

She looked up sharply as he rose to his feet, leaning on his stick. The corner of her mouth twitched nervously.

'I'm off now,' he said. 'Think about it. I shall not mention it again unless you raise the subject. I will respect your confidence and there is no reason why we should not go on just being friends if that is what you want.'

Before she could summon her voice to reply, he was gone.

Chapter Twenty-two

VIOLET HAD SET OUT THE MORNING PAPERS in the reading room when Marge arrived for work. Glancing up as they exchanged greetings, she noted the haggard face and guessed that the girl had not slept. Bill had come in early last night and gone straight to his room, which was unusual, so it did not take much to deduce that they had quarrelled. Affecting not to notice anything amiss, she carried on with her tasks until Marge came in to discuss the list of new publications. Having established that Laura was well, she remarked that it was now weeks since the bombing raids had stopped and, according to the papers, instead of being relieved, people had lost the camaraderie it had brought and were beginning to grumble again about the shortages and rationing.

'At least Andy will have had his wedding in peace,' she concluded.

'When was it?' asked Marge.

'A week last Saturday. I sent a card, but I have not heard from him. I expect they are still on honeymoon.' A tear fell on the publication list and she looked with concern at Marge's woebegone face.

'My dear, what is it?'

'Oh, Vi,' she wailed, 'I don't know what to do. I seem to make such a mess of everything.' She glanced at her watch, noting that there was still half an hour before the library was due to open, and sat down to hear the account of the previous night's conversation.

'The little minx,' she exclaimed, stifling a giggle, as Marge recounted how Laura had asked Bill to be her daddy, then became serious as the rest of the story unfolded.

'You were right to tell Bill the truth about your situation,' she said slowly, 'and I can assure you that he would mean it when he said it made no difference to him. I agree with him that, for your own sake and for Laura's, it is time to stop dwelling on the past and think about the future. I know that he cares deeply for you and you could not ask for a better father for Laura. What are you going to do?'

Marge did not know. She liked Bill very much, enjoyed his company and felt at ease with him, but she did not love him. Violet understood that she had been hurt, but she was still very young and surely she was not going to spend the rest of her life mourning the romantic image of a dead man?

'No,' she said, 'it certainly wasn't that.'

Then what did she mean by love, asked Violet, because if, as she suspected, she meant wild passion, that sort of love was not in itself a sound basis for marriage, unless it was rooted in friendship. In any case, it rarely happened outside story books and she could waste a lifetime waiting to be swept off her feet. On the other hand, though Bill was a fine young man with a good head on his shoulders and would undoubtedly make a success of his life, she would not want her to marry him for the wrong reasons and perhaps break his heart. He deserved better than that.

Stung, Marge replied that she had no intention of taking advantage of him. That was the reason for her hesitation. He had never until now given her cause to think that he was interested in anything more than friendship with her. She did not know whether he loved her or just felt sorry for her and Laura. Did she know, asked Violet, that his girlfriend back home had dropped him when he lost his leg? Not that it bothered him, she added, he was no longer interested in her, but maybe he thought Marge might be put off by it too. Marge replied that his disability was of no consequence and that she felt that she could do as much for him as he could for her. Certainly at the present time, her financial position was better than his, as she owned her own house. Laura adored him, but what if they had other children? Would he still feel the same way about her?

So she was at least considering it, thought Violet, as she dismissed her concern that he would put other children before Laura. She should take her time and be quite sure that she knew what she wanted before making a decision, but not take too long about it.

'He is attractive to women, you know,' she said, hesitantly. 'He will not be left on the shelf for long.'

Marge nodded. Sally had mentioned seeing him going into the cinema with a nice looking girl a couple of weeks ago. She had replied that he was not her boyfriend and could do as he pleased. She had said nothing to him about it. Pressed, she admitted to Violet that she had felt a twinge of jealousy.

'There you are, you see! Your feelings for him are probably stronger than you realise, but time will tell'. She looked at her watch. 'Heavens! It's half past nine. Time to open the door.'

156

It was two days before she saw Bill again. He came into the library to exchange some books and smiled as he asked after Laura, showing no sign of embarrassment. After chatting for a few moments in between customers he turned to go, pausing to ask, 'Saturday OK then? There's a good film on if you fancy it.'

She nodded happily as she waved goodbye.

Violet, watching discreetly from behind a filing cabinet, smiled to herself. It was going to be all right. Marge left for home with a lighter heart. Laura had not repeated her startling request. She was getting stronger every day, taking an interest in her toys and asking Sally when she could see the chickens again. Bill was coming on Saturday, as usual, and it remained to be seen whether the child would return to her objective. This time they would both be prepared and, if she did, Marge was determined to let him know that the door was not closed.

Laura was still weak and unable to walk far. She refused to go in a pushchair, so there was no question of an excursion on Saturday and they had to think of other ways to entertain her. It was a beautiful summer day and Marge spread a blanket on the lawn for her to sit on, while Bill cut out shapes from old newspapers which, unfolded, turned into a line of dolls or animals. As he turned and snipped, she would try to guess what would emerge and clapped her hands when she recognised a shape. Soon the garden was littered with newsprint and Marge laughingly called a halt, saying they would be in trouble for wasting paper. They played 'I-Spy', then Bill read stories to her while Marge made a picnic lunch, which they ate from a trestle table which Bill had placed in the shade of a tree at the bottom of the garden. The little girl, hot and tired, was visibly wilting and Marge carried her indoors, where she fell asleep on the couch. They cleared up the garden and Bill washed the pots while Marge made coffee which they drank in the kitchen, listening to the wireless. Violet arrived for tea, bringing a pot of homemade blackberry jam, the last she had saved from the previous year, and some sweets for Laura, who, refreshed from her nap, transferred her attention to her favourite 'auntie'. Tea over, the good lady shooed out the young couple.

'It's such a lovely day. You should have a walk before you go into the cinema. I'll put her to bed.'

It was cool by the river, though the midges were a nuisance and they soon retreated to the main street, Bill struggling slightly up the steep slope. It was still too early for the cinema.

'Drink?' he suggested as they came to a public house, and they sat outside with glasses of beer and lemonade, passing the time of day with acquaintances who stopped to chat, until it was time to join the cinema queue. The film was 'The Divorce of Lady X', starring Laurence Olivier and Marge had been eager to see it since its release in London the previous year, when it received excellent reviews. Made in colour, with splendid sets, it was a light, frothy extravaganza and she sighed blissfully over the glamorous clothes worn by Merle Oberon as the calculating heroine. When Bill tentatively took hold of her hand, she did not withdraw it and turned slightly towards him with a shy smile before returning her attention to the screen. They walked home hand in hand, talking animatedly about the film, the music, the acting and the gossip about the stars. It had been a lovely evening and when, later, they went upstairs to look at the sleeping Laura before Bill left with Violet, he kissed her swiftly and gently on the lips. It had been so long, she mused, since a man had been so close to her, she had almost forgotten the sensation. It was rather nice. Over the next few weeks their relationship blossomed slowly. Bill was anxious not to rush her and the subject of marriage was not raised, though friends had begun to notice and made sly comments in their presence. Marge had changed, they noted. There was a sparkle in her eye and she laughed more frequently. Laura was completely recovered with, thankfully, no after effects from her illness and the three of them spent happy hours together at the weekends. One day, when she was inconsolable, having broken the arm off her beloved doll, Bill had mended it and she had flung her arms around his neck.

'I do wish you could be my daddy,' she breathed, 'then you would be here all the time and not go home when I go to bed.'

He glanced nervously at Marge, but she was smiling.

'Well, little one,' he said, 'we'll have to think about it.'

Later, when they were alone, he took her hand. 'I can't go down on one knee, Marge, but I am asking you, with all my heart, if you will do me the honour of becoming my wife.'

She hesitated, looking into his eyes. 'First,' she said, 'there is something else you should know which I have not told you.'

He waited, his face tense with anxiety.

'My name is not Marge, it's Margot. Vi thought it was too posh and christened me Marge, but either way, if it's all the same to you, I accept.'

They collapsed, giggling, as he covered her face with kisses.

There was no point in waiting, they agreed. Bill would have liked a church wedding, but they were both relative newcomers to the area and though he had occasionally attended Sunday morning service, Marge was reluctant to have the Banns read out, revealing her status as 'spinster', so Bill went next day to make the necessary arrangements with the registrar. The wedding was fixed for three weeks hence. Violet was delighted and threw herself into the preparations. It would be a very small affair, with only Sally and Tom and Jean and Harry in attendance, with their children and Laura, of course. They would have to let Bill's parents know, but there was no chance that they would want to come. Marge, thankful that she had kept all the London clothes, trawled through her wardrobe for something suitable to wear and found a pretty crepe dress in palest pink with silver piping at the neck and waist and tiny silver buttons on the elbow-length sleeves. It was much more sophisticated and expensive than anything she could buy locally. She had lost some weight and found to her delight that it fitted her perfectly. She breathed a sigh of relief. Sally, highly impressed, pronounced it divine, but there was a problem with shoes. The dress demanded high-heeled court shoes, preferably in the same shade of pink, but the only ones she had were black, apart from an old pair of white high-heeled sandals. She could dye the sandals, suggested Sally, either pink or silver. She would take them to the cobbler to see what could be done. What about a hat? Sally thought it should be a wide-brimmed picture hat, but where to get such a thing in Barnard Castle? Jean came to the rescue. She had a halo hat in natural straw which could be dyed to match the dress. Laura had to have a new frock, too, and Sally, clever with her needle, made one for her from a remnant of white organdie trimmed with rosebuds which Marge had bought a year ago and never got round to making up.

The wedding, on the day before the Bank Holiday weekend, took place in brilliant sunshine. The bride looked lovely in pink and silver, the groom proud and nervous as he placed the platinum ring on her finger. Sally, as Matron of Honour, was sophisticated in her dress of oyster silk and a small tilted hat in deep pink setting off her dark curls, while Harry, conscientious in his duties as best man, fussed around arranging the little group for Jean to take photographs with her Brownie camera. Violet had excelled herself, producing a magnificent repast from saved rations and raiding her store cupboard for pre-war tinned salmon, ham and fruit. There was even a wedding cake, thanks to the eggs from Sally's chickens, though without icing, as that was forbidden as a waste of sugar. To toast the happy couple, Harry produced a bottle of champagne he had been keeping for years for a suitable occasion. Laura, pirouetting in her frilly new frock, suddenly stopped in front of Bill.

'Daddy!' she exclaimed excitedly. 'My Daddy!' She held up her arms to be picked up. He hugged her tightly, his eyes shining with tears as he looked over her shoulder at Marge.

'My two girls,' he said quietly, as she moved to his side and linked her arm in his.

Violet had insisted that they should have a honeymoon and Harry drove them to a charming little hotel only five miles away. Laura was happy at the prospect of spending spend three days with the twins and waved them off without a murmur. At the hotel, as they changed their clothes to go for a stroll before dinner, Bill felt suddenly shy about his leg, worrying that the sight of it might upset Marge, but she teased him, saying that it was the bride who was supposed to be nervous and she was not in the least bit squeamish. Their walk was delayed as she proved her point to the satisfaction of both of them and, relaxed, they dined in candlelight over a bottle of good wine to the accompaniment of a violin playing a romantic serenade. As they raised their glasses to each other and he made a toast to 'Mrs Somers', Marge reflected that this was indeed a new beginning. She would face the future with a different name and no longer alone. Together they would build a successful life and the past, with its ghosts and torments, would be buried.

Chapter Twenty-three

LEUTNANT KARL-HEINZ ENGEL surveyed the scene in disbelief. His battery, marching with an infantry division, had forged its way from village to village towards Stalingrad, driving the occupying Russians before them. In broad daylight on a freezing morning, a group of Russian infantry, armed only with rifles, was advancing across open ground. The German barrage of mortars and machine guns drove them back, but time after time they returned to the fray until over five hundred men were hurling themselves suicidally into the attack. Karl-Heinz brought up his artillery and opened fire, but they kept on coming until they were annihilated, the snow stained red from the blood of hundreds dead and dying. He felt no satisfaction as they rounded up the remnants as prisoners and went about the sorry business of collecting gloves and padded jackets from the corpses to help keep their own men warm. It had to be done quickly as the corpses froze instantly in the sub-zero temperature and clinked like pot dolls when disturbed. Worse was to come. Before he realised what was happening, the prisoners, twelve in all, had been herded into the woods and shot. His protest against this flouting of the Geneva Convention was met with derision. There were insufficient men available to look after prisoners. If he was to survive, he must learn that such ideals had no place in this brutal war. When he graduated from the Kriegschule it was the proudest moment of his life, the realisation of his boyhood dream to serve the Fatherland. Not twenty years old and with no actual experience of battle, he soon found himself, along with other young officers, on a supply train bound for Rostov to join an artillery unit in the Sixth Army. He knew that there was heavy fighting in Stalingrad and that he would be going into a dangerous situation, but he had no idea how bad it was, because the real situation was not reported to the German public. It had been necessary to draft in inexperienced young officers like him, because so many first class veterans had been killed or had fallen victim to the deadly climate.

It was October when he arrived in Stalingrad to be briefed by the Oberleutnant, Helmut Behr, and almost immediately found himself in circumstances for which no amount of training could have prepared him. He knew that he was asking too many questions of men who already had more than enough to do and he learned quickly to keep his eyes and ears open and work things out for himself. First the interminable rain, then the mud, turning the earth into a quagmire through which nothing on wheels could move until the roads had been corduroyed with small tree trunks laid side by side to provide a solid surface. Then the lice. They were everywhere, picked up from the peasant huts they requisitioned and a constant torment, with no chance of delousing facilities for months as the soldiers scratched arms, legs, stomach, armpits, writhing restlessly in their blankets at night. By November, there was a hard freeze, but the men still had no winter clothing and, in a temperature of 12 degrees below zero, Fahrenheit the danger of frostbite became a serious concern. The snow blew almost horizontally in blizzards, preventing any movement, as the men piled on all the clothing they could find, icicles forming on ears and noses, the cold a more deadly killer than the Russians.

Everywhere there was death. Russian soldiers, clad in their quilted uniforms, felt boots and gloves made from animal skins, would appear from nowhere to ambush a patrol or blow up a hut where men were huddled for shelter against the biting cold. Bloated animals lay dead, limbs sticking up grotesquely out of the frozen snow, with human bodies, German and Russian, mutilated and left carelessly strewn around, gruesome, obscene. Any semblance of human dignity was rapidly diminishing as soldiers squabbled over scraps of food looted from starving peasants or tried to wrench felt boots from Russian corpses stiffened like marble. Frostbite was decimating the regiment as casualties were sent back to field hospitals with toes, fingers and feet frozen, until only a couple of batteries remained.

They were preparing to move in order to join up with another group two villages away, when they heard mortar fire coming from the wood. Two men set out on horseback to investigate, but were blown into the air as a salvo of rockets, fired from a truck, blasted into the camp, followed by another as men dropped to the ground. Clods of earth struck the young officer in the face as he tried to estimate the damage and he was flung against the wall of a barn which was already burning. Suddenly the noise stopped and when the smoke cleared he staggered to his feet and set out to regroup the men. He found himself alone. Blown beyond recognition, limbs torn from charred bodies, bits of torso clinging to pieces of equipment, identity discs missing, they were all gone. Sickened, he tried to heap them together, though burial was impossible, then paused, anger suffusing his brain as the bitter realisation overwhelmed him. Leaders like the Führer were willing to see millions of poor, decent, trusting men slaughtered for the sake of power. He had had enough.

Just walk away, he told himself, get the hell out of here before another unit comes through. Let them assume that everyone died. There was not much left of the stores, but scrabbling around in the debris he found a handful of lentils, some sugar and, miraculously, half a bottle of rum, stuffing them into a saddlebag with a pan for heating water, a few packets of cigarettes which might come in useful to barter for food, and matches. He hesitated over a Russian fur cap and a pair of felt boots one of the men had looted from a corpse, then put them on, grabbing a couple of blankets, which he threw across his shoulders. Field glasses, a pistol and a compass completed his kit and he made his way carefully towards a thick hedge which ran along a frozen stream away from the woods in the direction of a village they had occupied previously. Checking that he was not leaving footprints in the hard-packed snow, he ducked under the hedge and took stock of the situation.

He felt reasonably confident of his tracking and orienteering ability, giving silent thanks for having been allowed to roam freely in the mountains of Majorca with childhood friends who taught him the basics of survival and how to navigate using the stars and geographic features to guide him. Here there were the added factors of freezing temperatures, snow masking the physical details of the terrain and the danger of attack by soldiers from both sides. Still, with a bit of luck, he reasoned, there would be people willing to help a fellow human being in trouble to find an escape route. Had not he himself been actively involved in such operations in Majorca? A flash of pain seared his brain as he remembered that last time, when Republican planes had blitzed Palma harbour, not only sinking the battleship *Deutschland,* object of his youthful adoration, but killing the two young English women he had just escorted to a German ship which was to take them to safety. In those days he had believed naively that Germany was the avenging angel, saving a nation from tyranny, but in the past months he had witnessed unthinkable cruelty and acts of brutality by German soldiers, not just against enemy soldiers, but against women and children, too. He had not encountered any real hostility from the Russian peasants they had met on the march, just ordinary people wanting to be left alone. As a deserter, he might be looked on with sympathy. If he ran into a German unit, he would be shot.

Squeezing through a gap in the thick hedge, he found that he could creep along the bank of the stream shielded from the road. There was an open field on the other side of the stream, but he should be able to spot any movement in time to lie low and there was less chance of soldiers on that side of the hedge. Dusk was falling and with it the temperature. He must find shelter for the night and, remembering a cluster of derelict huts and a barn they had passed a few days ago, he made his way to the spot. All was quiet as he lay in an old foxhole scanning the area. The ground was freezing as he slithered quickly to the barn and the icy wind blew through the rotting doorway, but he found an old piece of tarpaulin to cover himself, took a long swig of rum and huddled in a corner to wait for morning. He slept fitfully, jolted awake from time to time by the wind rattling the loose timbers or the cry of a fox in the distance. Suddenly, still half asleep, he sensed that someone or something was watching him and terror prickled his skin, shocking him into awareness as his eyes, gummed up with sleep and grime, tried to focus on the apparition. It was a child, heavily padded from head to foot in fur and quilting, black eyes unblinking in the little round face staring at him. Hardly daring to move, he ventured a smile and whispered a greeting in Russian. The child vanished and he dragged himself to his feet in trepidation, gathering his belongings and praying that he could get away before the alert was given. As he reached the door of the barn the child reappeared, holding out a chunk of bread. There was a pain in his stomach from hunger and he took it gratefully, past caring whether it might be poisoned, the child watching gravely as he devoured it. The child, he could not tell whether it was a boy or a girl in the bulky clothes, turned and motioned to him to follow. Hesitating, he realised that there was no point in trying to get away, now that his presence was known. He followed painfully, his limbs stiff from the cold and the long night on the floor of the barn.

There was no sign of life as they walked past the dilapidated huts, a burned out truck and a few old farming implements rusting in the snow. The child stopped in front of a dugout, from which a thin trail of smoke came from a crude pipe on the roof. Inside, an old woman, stirring a pan over a stove, turned and looked searchingly at Karl-Heinz, then pointing with her ladle to a chair by the fireplace, returned to her task. For a few moments he sat in uncomfortable silence until the woman wiped her hands on her skirt and spoke rapidly to the child, who ran to the cupboard and fetched a bowl, into which she ladled steaming broth made from potatoes and turnips. He ate gratefully, his bones warmed by the soup and the fire and when he handed back the empty bowl, stammering his thanks as best he could in Russian, she nodded, her eyes softening, as she replied in German, 'You are welcome, but it is not safe here. When my son comes back tonight we will help you. Katya is my grand-daughter,' she added, putting her hand on the child's shoulder.

'I came here from Germany many years ago, after the war.' Startled, he glanced round the humble living quarters and her rough peasant clothing and she smiled ruefully.

'It was not always like this. My husband was Russian and we were both teachers in Kiev until he became ill with tuberculosis. We moved out here so that he would have clean fresh air and he worked in the fields while I taught the village children, but it was too late. He died soon after and I could not go back to Kiev because my baby son was not strong and it would have been difficult in the city to find someone to look after him while I worked. Here he was always close by.'

She explained that most of the villagers worked on farms, tasks being allocated on a daily basis by the local commissar. Pay was poor and mostly by receiving food such as potatoes, chickens or meat in return for services. Her son could not keep up with other workers, so he cut wood in the forest and sold it round the villages, earning a little extra by running a service for people who wanted to trade goods they had made for things from other villages. He had married, but his wife had died in childbirth seven years ago, leaving his mother, Gerda, to bring up Katya. A few weeks ago, Russian soldiers had swept through the village, taken all the able bodied men for the army and burned the houses because they thought the inhabitants had given food and shelter to Germans who had gone through earlier. Her son had been spared because of his disability, but their house was burned and they had to move into the dugout. Others were hiding in similar places, fearing the return of soldiers, Russian or German.

'You think I would have been better off in Germany,' she said, 'but my husband would have been denounced as a Communist and we would both have been killed. Besides, how comfortable do you suppose life is in Germany now that nearly all the cities are being destroyed by bombs?' The jingling of harness and the soft snorting of a horse outside brought Katya to her feet and she ran to the door to greet her father, almost pulling him into the room as she chattered excitedly, pointing to Karl-Heinz. A small, slight man with twinkling eyes, laughing as he removed his fur hat and used it to brush the snow from his jacket, he nodded to

Karl-Heinz and limped to a chair at the other side of the fire while his mother explained the situation. Trying not to stare, Karl-Heinz noted the club foot and the curve of his spine above the shoulder when he removed his jacket. Mother and son talked rapidly and at length in Russian, before she returned to the stove to bring him a dish of broth. As he began to eat, she turned to Karl-Heinz.

'Serge can take you on the sledge as far as Kharkov, which will take two or three days, then you will have to make your way towards Kiev and from there to the Polish border.' He could not travel in his German uniform or carry any incriminating papers, so he must be able to pass himself off as a Russian. Clearly, Serge's clothes would not fit him, but, somewhat apologetically, he produced the Russian quilted jacket and felt boots from his saddle bag and Gerda dragged an old chest from under a bed, pulling out a long peasant blouse and some old baggy trousers which must have belonged to her husband. These were larger than Serge's, but not quite long enough and she set to work to insert a piece of material from another pair at the waist. Hidden by the blouse, it was a passable job, but there remained the problem of language. Karl-Heinz was a natural linguist and had already acquired a smattering of Russian, but not enough to pass for a native and they decided that he must remain silent, acting the part of a mute, almost a simpleton.

The next morning, dressed in his disguise and carrying a knapsack containing some dry food, his precious field glasses and pistol strapped to his waist under the bulky clothes, they were ready to go. He lay in the sledge, covered with a blanket while Serge piled wood on top of him, so that he would not be seen as they passed through the villages. Slowly they set off across the snow, the two horses straining to get into their stride. Serge called out the occasional greetings or exchanged a few words with people he knew until they were clear of his territory, then he stopped and Karl-Heinz joined him behind the reins. Serge spoke German well enough to carry on a reasonable conversation and the time passed pleasantly enough, with no sign of soldiers. They rested overnight in an empty barn which Serge had used before and another full day's travel brought them to the outskirts of Kharkov. Unbelievably they had crossed the front line with no challenge from either side, though there had been a heart-stopping moment when they met a group of Russian soldiers who insisted on sharing a bottle of vodka with them. Serge set him down with directions for the route to the border.

'That should see you through,' he said, handing him a package containing rough rye bread, cheese and a small flask of vodka. Karl-Heinz thanked him, expressing concern for his journey back home, but was assured that he had relatives in Kharkov who would be pleased to see him and give him a bed for the night. The two men embraced briefly and he watched as Serge turned the sledge towards the town. The adventure had begun.

Chapter Twenty-four

His MIND WAS MADE UP. The war had been over for almost a year and it was time he went home to Germany. Propping himself up on his elbow, Karl-Heinz gazed sorrowfully at the sleeping Janecka. When he arrived in Poland over two years earlier, exhausted, starving and filthy after deserting from the Eastern Front, she had hidden him and nursed him back to health before introducing him as a relative of her late husband. He had been trying to steal eggs from a barn, when he heard the door close quietly behind him. Turning, he saw a young woman with tousled blonde hair, arms crossed over an ample bosom, sturdy legs planted slightly apart on bare feet, her bold blue eyes regarding him steadily. Blushing, he began to stammer an apology, but she stepped towards him and placed a hand over his mouth and a finger to her lips warning him to be quiet. After looking around outside, she beckoned him to follow her and led him into the house, where she gave him soup and bread. While he ate, she boiled up pans of water on the stove, filled a tin bath which she had lugged across the floor and told him, in German, to take off his clothes. As he hesitated, she disappeared from the room, but was soon back with clean garments and clicked her tongue impatiently for him to get into the bath before it got cold. She brought soap and scrubbed his back, then held up a thin towel and helped to dry him, her eyes running appreciatively over the muscular young body, until, red with embarrassment, he pulled on the fresh clothes.

For the next few months he remained hidden in a loft reached by a ladder from the top of the stairs, allowed down to pad around the house, but scurrying back to his lair if anyone called. Janecka brought food and drink in between work on the smallholding and at night she would creep into his bed. Karl-Heinz had been shy at first. It had been a long time since he had been close to a woman and then it had been only the clumsy fumbling of adolescence. Janecka, some fifteen years older than the young refugee, lost no time in completing his education. She was beautiful, blonde hair tumbling over her face, firm, creamy flesh cool against the heat of his body, arms and legs downy soft like the skin of a ripe peach and the wide, sensual mouth exploring, caressing. There had been other men, since her husband died, she told him. Bees round a honey pot, but old, grizzled widowers and lecherous married men after a romp in the hay. Not like him. Soon she would let it be known that a relative was coming to stay and they could live openly, running the place together.

That seemed a long time ago. He had worked on the land, helped to build up the business and fed her insatiable sexual appetite. She was possessive, jealous if she saw him talking to other women and had begun to talk of marriage. Karl-Heinz, indebted, was not ready for such commitment and had begun to think that it was time he went back to Germany to try to find his parents. Today he would be on his way. She stirred in her sleep and rolled over, throwing her arm across his chest. Gently he pulled away, placing a pillow under her arm and, gathering up his clothes, crept out of the room. Dressing hurriedly, he picked up the bag he had packed and hidden, made a final check to see that she still slept and left the house.

It was very early and he saw no-one as he crossed the field to the road and set out on the long walk to the railway station. Breathing hard, he increased his pace and had been going for almost twenty minutes when he was almost knocked down by a wagon coming out of a farm gate. The driver offered him a lift and in a short time he was boarding a train for Poznan. Settling into his seat, he looked around at the other passengers, but they were all strangers. He was free! Watching the scenery roll by he felt a twinge of remorse for not having had the courage to tell Janecka, but he knew that there would have been a scene and that his attempts to thank her would have been received almost as an insult. Nothing she could have said would have deterred him and actual words of rejection would have been more hurtful than her own thoughts of him as an ungrateful bastard. It was the second time he had deserted, he recalled uneasily, then dismissed the thought from his mind. These events had been an interruption in his life and he must resume that life to fulfil his destiny as a German citizen in his native country.

In Poznan he wandered around until he found a cheap lodging house and set about enquiring how to reach the German border. There seemed to be an appreciable number of foreigners in the town centre, many of them Jews, their dead eyes past grieving as they trudged the streets looking for work or searched the passing faces in the hope of finding a lost loved one. He needed to move on. It must be less than a hundred miles to the border, he reckoned, as he went into a café and ordered vodka.

The refugee camp was just outside the border and he had wandered in unchallenged, joining the queue of applicants outside a guarded tent. He had no papers and the guard brusquely ordered him to stand to one side for questioning. Watching as others were taken one at a time into another tent, he realised that the guards were French, controlling the sector following the German surrender. They would be suspicious of a German without papers and on the look-out for Nazi spies. It would be unwise to confess to being a deserter from the Eastern Front. Even if they believed him, they were soldiers and unlikely to sympathise. He spoke French fluently from childhood years spent in that country during his father's diplomatic career and decided to pose as a French citizen, living in Germany since the war ended, who had been robbed and stranded in Poland after visiting relatives there.

The interrogating officer leaned back indolently in his chair, flicking ash from his cigar as he signalled to Karl-Heinz to sit down. He smelled of cognac and belched silently as he picked up his pen and raised a weary eyebrow, waiting for yet another tale to begin. Karl-Heinz, drawing on his memory, gave his name as that of a French friend of his father, whose house he had visited many times. By the time he had finished his story of having gone to Germany to try to track down a missing relative and become involved with a German girl, the Frenchman was nodding and winking. Waving expansively to a junior officer to bring him an entry permit, he called to a passing colleague to come and meet a fellow countryman. Greetings were exchanged and the new arrival, a tall, anxious-looking young man with a nervous cough, sat down and began to talk about the lack of civilised society in Germany and his longing to go home. He asked where Karl-Heinz came from. Thinking quickly, the first town which sprang to mind was Limoges and his heart fell as the officer's face lit up. Why on earth had he not got in first and asked the man about his home? It took only a few minutes before it became clear that Karl-Heinz knew nothing of Limoges or its inhabitants. Despite his attempts to explain his ignorance by saying that he left Limoges in childhood and lived in Paris for most of his life, the atmosphere turned distinctly chilly and the interrogator tore up the permit with a flourish. Guards were summoned and Karl-Heinz was escorted off the premises and out of the camp.

He leaned against the high fence and lit a cigarette. Two men, loading sacks of rubbish on to a wagon, shook their heads sympathetically and he grinned, holding up his hands on mock despair. After a brief conversation with his colleague, the driver strolled over to Karl-Heinz and offered him a lift into the town. On the journey he regaled them with a humorous account of his interview. He was a good mimic and, having themselves experienced the high-handed attitude of the French guards, they roared with appreciation at the discomfiture of the interrogator he had so nearly taken in. A bottle of vodka was produced and by the time they arrived in the town the wagon was weaving precariously to the accompaniment of raucous songs from its occupants.

His new friends accompanied him to a small boarding house, sparsely furnished, but scrupulously clean, where they were greeted by a neat pink-cheeked little woman who looked as if she herself had been freshly scrubbed.

'My sister, Rosa,' explained the driver, Stanislav, ducking as she aimed a good-natured blow at his head, admonishing him for being drunk. They went inside, where it was quickly settled that Karl-Heinz could have board and lodging at a very reasonable rate. He had some money and paid in advance for his first week. Arranging to collect him early next morning, when they would introduce him to their boss, they left.

He unpacked his few belongings and lay on the hard bed, considering his situation. He had blown his chance of getting across the border from here, but if he found work he could do worse than stay for a while among these agreeable people until he learned enough about alternative routes to enable him to formulate another plan. He must have fallen asleep, because the next thing he heard was a furious knocking on his bedroom door and Rosa's voice calling anxiously, 'Mr Engel. Please come down! Staczyk will be here soon and if you want work you must be ready.' He rolled stiffly out of bed, banging his knee on the iron frame, and groaned, his mouth dry, his tongue thick from the vodka. A jug of water, stone cold, stood in a bowl on the wooden table and he splashed his face and neck, then hurriedly pulled on his clothes and went downstairs. Two men, his fellow lodgers, sat at the table, eating in silence. They looked up as he entered the room and acknowledged him briefly, exchanging names, then returned to their plates. Rosa, pouring tea from a large pot into thick white mugs, handed him a plate with a chunk of dark, grainy bread spread with lard. He had just finished the bread and was gulping down the hot, sweet tea, when his benefactors arrived. At the dump, he waited with Pavel while Stanislav spoke quickly to a wiry little man with white hair, who looked briefly in his direction then nodded and signalled to him to approach. The work was menial, just sorting and burning rubbish and sweeping up, with a chance of a driving job later. Karl-Heinz, grateful for anything, accepted and, waving goodbye to the others, followed his new boss into a shed, where he was provided with overalls, brush and shovel, a few brief instructions and left to get on with it. He took off his own clothes and folded them carefully, replacing them with the overalls. At first the foul smell made him retch, but he soon became inured to it and, characteristically, applied himself with enthusiasm to finding the most efficient way of sorting the piles of assorted waste, extricating anything worth saving, burning or breaking down the rest. Absorbed in his task, it was over two hours before he looked up to see the boss watching him approvingly. He drank the proffered bottle of warm beer and returned to his task, having accepted the man's invitation to take a bowl of soup with him at lunchtime.

By the time the wagons returned at the end of the day, the site had begun to look structured and he had made another friend in Waldo, his employer. The pay was not much, but life at the dump was interesting enough, with people coming and going all day, looking for bargains and spare parts. Some of the regulars were foreigners, Jews and other stateless persons like himself, trying to scratch a living, always hoping that, if they could survive, they might one day return home. They liked to talk, in the hope that someone, somewhere, might have news of a lost relative and Karl-Heinz, himself anxious about his parents in Germany, listened to their stories, sharing their despair that so many doors seemed closed against them. Back at Rosa's, he wolfed his meal of pork and potatoes and went out drinking and playing cards with his new mates and Rosa's husband, Stefan, a large, cheerful man who worked on the railway. So the pattern continued. The other men were all married and had their domestic duties to attend to, but generally one or other at least was available for a night out. Karl-Heinz was subjected to good-natured chafing about finding a girlfriend and was beginning to feel restless when, one bright spring morning, Wanda walked into his life. The sun was high in the sky and he had taken off his shirt as he sweated over the pile of metal he was hammering in the yard. Straightening his back to shift the hammer to his other hand, he heard a low, pleasant laugh and turned to see a young woman regarding him with interest.

'So you are the Wonder Boy!' she said, as he attempted, blushing, to cover his bare chest with his arms. 'I was looking for my uncle, but he does not appear to be around. Perhaps I can talk to you while I wait?' She was about twenty years old, he guessed, small, dark and pretty, with a captivating smile and a curvaceous figure. Her voice, soft and slightly husky, sent a thrill of excitement through his celibate body and, wiping his hands on his overall trousers, he introduced himself. By the time Waldo returned, about half an hour later, apologising to his niece for having kept her waiting, they were deep in conversation and had made arrangements to see each other that evening. It was the beginning of a passionate and stormy relationship.

Chapter Twenty-five

FOR THE FIRST TIME in his young life Karl-Heinz was in love. The world was a wonderful place and Wanda the angel of his dreams. He continued to work hard at the dump, but his mates hardly saw him in the warm summer evenings which he spent mostly with her, wandering among meadows carpeted with flowers, making a secret love nest under a hedge and, sometimes, if it rained, going back to her uncle's shed at the dump, for which she had acquired a key. She was beautiful, soft and feminine, teasing him gently with alluring glances from limpid blue eyes under the dark, silky lashes which fluttered like moths on her warm cheeks, her smile demure as he stammered endearments in the still unfamiliar language. He ached with desire for her and she played on his emotions, sometimes passionate and yielding, sometimes teasing, keeping him at arm's length, refusing even a kiss. He would plead and rage as she leaned back indolently, her supple body tantalising in the tight dress, her laugh mocking as she gloried in her power over him. On Saturday afternoons they would go to the shops, where he spent all his spare money on trinkets and flowers for her, or tea at an expensive café. She would set her heart on some frivolous object, pouting prettily if he demurred at the price, rewarding him with a swift kiss when he relented. She seemed to have no concept of the value of money and wrinkled her nose in distaste if he expressed concern that he must keep enough to pay for his board and lodging, saying he was boring.

From Waldo, her mother's brother, he gleaned that she lived with her parents and two younger sisters who were still at school and that she worked at a leather factory packing goods for despatch, but she evaded his questions beyond saying that she hated her job and she would not be drawn into inviting him to the house to meet her parents. She would never see him on Saturday evenings or on Sundays and there were times when, having arranged to meet him, she failed to turn up, his demands for an explanation producing sulks or indignation at his presumption. Jealous and hurt, he would hide his feelings and pacify her with some little gift, rewarded by the warmth of her forgiveness. As the months went by without his becoming any the wiser about her activities or her feelings, he became irritable. With no money to spend on himself, he could not afford to drink with his friends and when he could not see Wanda he walked around the streets or sat alone in his room, reading. He lost his appetite and began to look pale and thin. Rosa, worried, asked Stanislas to talk to him.

'What would be the use?' was his reaction. It was unlikely that he would listen. They all knew what the problem was, but he was sure it would be over soon. From what he had heard of the girl, she was a flirt and maybe worse. She would find someone else and dump Karl-Heinz. He would get over it and things would revert to normal. Let nature take its course!

Karl-Heinz's nature, however, had in it a tendency to curiosity as well as an analytical streak. Besotted though he was, he could not avoid an urge to find out what she did when she was not with him. It was not that he distrusted her, but surely it was reasonable to expect her to confide in him after all this time. He had tried casually to engage Waldo in conversation about family weekends, but either he knew nothing or was not prepared to be disloyal to his niece. After a particularly trying Saturday afternoon with Wanda, he made up his mind to settle the question, whatever the consequences. Next morning he rose very early and walked over to the lane where she lived. Opposite the house was a field with a large hedge, behind which he positioned himself at a point from which he could observe the house and anyone approaching it from either direction. Though barely light, it promised to be a dry, bright, autumn day. There was dew on the grass, but he had brought a waterproof cover to sit on and settled down to wait. Nothing stirred, the only sounds the song of birds and the distant whirring of a tractor as the farmer began his daily chores. It was some two hours before the door opened and he craned forward in excitement as a man and woman, both middle-aged, and two young girls emerged, all dressed in their best clothes and presumably on their way to the church. The bells were ringing and other families were soon walking up the lane, laughing and chattering as they greeted each other. There was no sign of Wanda. He waited until the lane was quiet again and debated whether to risk knocking at the door, but decided against it. Taking an apple from his pocket, he bit into it and prepared for a further vigil. The family returned from church, people came and went in the lane, but she did not appear. By the middle of the afternoon, he was stiff and cold and still had no idea whether she was in the house or not. He gave up and went home.

Over the next two weeks he watched carefully. On days when he knew that Waldo would not be at the dump until later, he waited, hidden from view, near the factory where she worked to observe her comings and goings. She was always among the last to arrive, alone, sauntering as if she had all the time in the world. Once or twice he managed to get away early enough to see her leave, usually alone, though on one occasion tossing a laughing remark over her shoulder at a group of girls who pulled faces and giggled behind her retreating back. She turned in the direction of her home. Then, on a day when she had refused to meet him in the evening, he watched her leave the factory and walk in a different direction towards the town. Following at a discreet distance, he saw her enter a building, a smart hotel in the main shopping area. He waited, affecting to study a display of art and curios in a shop window, but half an hour went by and she did not emerge. At the risk of discovery, he approached the hotel and looked through the glass door into the lobby. Apart from a receptionist at the desk, it was empty. He saw her twice that week, when she was her usual charming, maddening self and he felt an almost impersonal satisfaction at having observed her without her knowledge. He arranged to meet her on Saturday afternoon, when he bought her some satin ribbons and laughed and joked with her over tea in the café, then, when she kissed him goodbye, instead of going home, he followed her. She did not look back and went straight to the hotel.

While he pondered on his next move, a boy in uniform dashed out and almost knocked him over.

'Hey, where's the fire?' he asked affably, as the boy gasped his apologies.

'Lucky it was me and not that young lady who just went in!' The boy agreed. The boss would have had him for that, he said, grimacing. A few zlotys established that the 'boss' was not the owner of the hotel, but a wealthy businessman whose connections were widespread and impressive, in short, concluded Karl-Heinz, a black market racketeer. He learned that the man stayed most weekends at the hotel and on the odd night during the week. And the young lady? The boy nodded, sniffing. She was usually with him, he confirmed, stuck-up piece who never gave a tip! Karl-Heinz laughed and gave him a friendly cuff. 'Best be on your way, then, before someone misses you,' and the lad fled. The bitch! He should have been desolate at such betrayal by the woman he had idolised, but he was almost exultant at having exposed her little game and smiled ruefully to himself at her audacity. She had not been joking when she told him she would never marry a poor man like him. Well, she had

had her fun, but so had he and though he might never meet another who could stir his soul as she had, he was young and alive and that was really all that mattered in this godforsaken world. Quietly he returned to the evenings of camaraderie with his friends. Staczyk nodded and winked and reminded Rosa that he had told her it would work out. Wanda fumed and fretted when, despite all her wiles, Karl-Heinz, without giving any indication that he had found out her secret, politely declined to go out with her, saying that he was busy. Suspicious, she turned up at the dump several times. Evoking no response, she resorted to making derisive remarks about his performance and insinuations about his sexuality to anyone within hearing distance, until Waldo, now cognisant of the situation, warned her to stay away. Life returned to normal and Karl-Heinz continued to work at the dump over the winter months until the first signs of spring stirred his blood and he became restless. He needed more mental stimulation and another attempt at the border. It was time to move on.

He had enjoyed the brief exercise in detection and began to move around, offering his services to people who wanted information for various reasons. His enquiring mind and experience of life beyond his years, gave him the tools for the job and his background, education and the fact that he spoke several languages fluently, added to his credentials. He charged only a small fee, was soon impressively successful and word spread until he found that the potential clientele was sufficient to occupy him almost full-time. The odd dalliance sustained him while he sought to regain his identity, but he was wary now and avoided intense relationships. It was some years before he eventually managed to return to Germany, by which time his parents were dead, but he had moved around the borders, increasing his expertise, until the time came when he could afford to open an agency in his native land.

Chapter Twenty-six

LAURA WAS DOWN EARLY and joined Hans and Dieter on the hotel terrace for breakfast. She always loved this part of the day and the leisurely buffet meal, temptingly displayed, in the cool morning air. She accepted a glass of freshly squeezed orange juice from the waiter and ordered coffee, looking doubtfully at the heaped plates of the two men, before selecting an *ensaimada* and some fruit.

'You will never reach the top of the mountain on that!' crowed Dieter. 'Hans, fetch her some of those lovely warm rolls at least. And how about champagne with that orange juice?' She held up her hands in mock horror as the young German, small, lithe and tanned, jumped to his feet.

'All right, just one roll, but no champagne. I had more than enough last night!' Dieter smiled, nodding.

'Wasn't it a great evening?' he said. 'We all enjoyed sharing in your Silver Jubilee. It is hard to remember that not so long ago our countries were fighting. War is so,' he waved his fork round in the air as he sought the word, 'vulgar! They should have mass parties on the battlefields instead of killing each other, the winner being the side with the most left standing when the drink runs out!'

'I think my father might have agreed with you on that,' she said. He was dark, muscular, a little older and taller than his friend, invariably charming and ready with a jest or a friendly remark. Such a loss to the female population, she sighed to herself. Others were arriving as Hans returned with rolls and jam, which he presented with a flourish.

'Eat up,' he insisted, wagging his finger. 'No lunch until we get to the top and we have to help to carry it!'

It had begun to cloud over and a few spots of rain fell as the little group, chattering and laughing, crowded on to the hotel bus which was to take them to Soller, where the walk would begin. Pepe, the guide, distributed packets of food and bottles of wine for the men to carry in their rucksacks scornfully dismissing the notion that it would be a wet day. Laura settled happily next to Frances, a young woman with whom she had become friendly the previous year. Frances, a doctor, had been travelling with two friends, both lecturers, and the four single women had spent some time together round the pool. Lisa had since married, but Frances had returned with Jennifer, who had sprained her ankle and was unable to manage the walk. Karl-Heinz sat with Max, a retired English doctor, well over seventy years old, who had been coming to the hotel for over twenty years and left his wife sitting in the gardens each day while he went walking alone. Amid greetings and banter, with a wave of encouragement from a few onlookers, the door was closed and the bus rolled slowly down the slope to the Soller road.

Tumbling from the bus, they set out in small groups behind Pepe and before long they were toiling up the steep mule path from Biniaraitx. As usual on the walks everyone mingled, dropping back or catching up to chat as they walked. The rain held off, but the clouds remained, mercifully shielding them from the heat of the sun. The path wound round the side of the mountain, giving glorious views of the orange groves and an excuse for frequent stops to admire the scenery or take photographs. Laura loved the mountains, so quiet and peaceful, yet alive with birds and insects, the contrast of towering rocks against shaded woods of oak and pine, the beauty of the views from the peaks and plateaux. However many times she wandered up the trails, she was always struck by some new aspect, a shaft of sunlight casting a different angle on a rock, or a waft of scent from an unseen flower nestling among the undergrowth. There was a place where she liked to sit alone on the stones of an ancient ruined wall, watching crag martins flitting in and out of the thousands of holes in the sheer rock face across a dell. Today they were to make the ascent to L'Ofre, which she had not previously done and she looked around to see how the rest of the group was coping. Once or twice she had begun to talk with Karl-Heinz, but each time someone had interrupted and she decided to forget it for the time being and just enjoy the walk. The sun had broken through the clouds and the heat was rising as the trail grew steeper. Passing the Ofre farm, where a spring bubbled softly, they left the trail to climb the last two hundred metres, helping each other to negotiate the rough footholds up the steep incline. The views from the top were breathtaking, Soller, sparkling in the lovely valley, bounded by high mountains, as well as Pla de Cuber and some of the highest peaks in the mountain range. Beside her, she heard Jennifer's gasp of delight.

'It's magical! I was not sure I could manage that last bit, but I am so glad I did.' Laura agreed and they gazed in silence for a few moments, before someone declared it was time for lunch and they scrambled down to where Pepe had earmarked a picnic site. As they unwrapped the food and poured the wine, Karl-Heinz sat down beside Laura.

'It seems unlikely that we shall get the chance to talk privately,' he said. 'Shall we dine together this evening?' She agreed and he said mysteriously that there was someone he would like her to meet if she was free next day. He would not be drawn beyond saying that it was a friend of Bill's.

Lunch over, they began the descent by another path towards Orient, where the bus would meet them on the road down. With the sun still glinting through thickening cloud, they made their way steadily downhill, admiring the different views and congratulating each other on having all completed the ascent. As they drew off the road into the hotel drive it began to rain and they cheered exuberantly as Pepe raise his thumb triumphantly. Exhausted now, Laura went straight to her room and ran a hot bath into which she sank gratefully for a long soak before dinner. Karl-Heinz had the package and she looked forward to finding out what was in the document written in Spanish, but she could think of no link with her own family and wondered if it might be something her father had been keeping for someone else. Presumably that was why Karl-Heinz wanted her to meet this friend.

He was waiting by the door of the dining room when she went down. It was too wet for dining on the terrace and the head waiter showed them to a table in the corner of the room. She had not known much about his early life, other than that he was head of a detective agency, and asked what had attracted him to that sort of work. He told her briefly of his war experiences and the unsuccessful attempts to return to Germany. It had taken ten years before he was able to establish his identity and claim his birthright and during those years he was a stateless person, with no home and no qualifications. He had to live on his wits or starve. There had been one or two women who helped him, he confessed wryly, but at that time there were many people in Eastern Europe wandering around looking for lost relatives after the war par-ticularly because of the holocaust. As a deserter escaping from Russia past two hostile armies, he had developed acute powers of observation, quick reflexes and a good knowledge of human nature, so he put his talents to use and provided a service for tracing missing people.

The fact that he spoke English, French and Spanish fluently was an added bonus. Word of his successful cases spread and he was able to make a modest living. When he finally convinced the German authorities of his identity, not admitting his desertion, of course, but claiming that he had been left injured among dead comrades during the retreat, he had set up in a rented office, advertising his services as a private detective, specialising in tracing missing persons and divorce work. It was an immediate success, particularly on the divorce side! He had met his wife, Ute, a few years later, when she asked him to provide evidence on which to divorce her first husband. That had lasted fourteen years and he had not needed to employ anyone to know that she was unfaithful, so the marriage had been brought swiftly to a conclusion.

Coffee came and he withdrew the package from his pocket, extracting the Spanish document. It was typewritten on thick, plain paper and appeared to have been a confession by a young woman concerned that she might die. Laura listened, puzzled, as he translated. 'To whom it may concern. I, Margarita Rosario Federica Martinez, have committed a terrible crime and must leave Spain to avoid bringing shame and danger to my family. I was wilful and foolish and deceived my parents who loved me. They warned me against Vicente Alvarez, but I would not listen. He betrayed me with another woman. I saw them and waited until she left, then confronted him. He laughed at me and when I told him I was pregnant, he was cruel and cast me aside, telling me to have an abortion. He cared only for his ambition for power in the Communist Party. I was overcome with shock and rage and hardly knew what I was doing, but I saw his gun lying on a chair and I picked it up and shot him. He was dead. I do not think anyone saw me there, but it would not have been long before he was found and I could not have faced questions without giving myself away. A refugee organisation helped me to escape to Majorca and my dear friend is with me.

'She is in the same situation. She is innocent and good, but I was a bad influence. We are going to England, where we can help each other and make a fresh start. I can never go back. My family will think that I am dead and it is better that way. I have been to the Cathedral this morning to pray and make my confession. I do not want my child to know who its father was, but if I should die and the child lives, it has a right to know the truth. I cannot undo what I have done, but I would like my parents, Ramon and Teresa Martinez, to know that they are in my heart and in my mind. May they and God forgive me.' Laura, stunned, sat in silence.

'There is no date, no signature,' he said. She recovered her composure.

'How awful! That poor girl! But do you think it is genuine? And why should it be in my father's possession? I cannot believe that he knew her or he would have said something. Was he keeping it for someone else?' Karl-Heinz nodded.

'I think so,' he said. 'Now for the rest of the package.' He drew out the rosary. 'She would have used this at the Cathedral'. The photograph was of a small family group, a dark handsome man, blonde wife and a pretty girl aged about ten, presumably their daughter. Laura had never seen it before she found the package and had no idea who they might be. Karl-Heinz waved the last piece of paper, clearly excited.

'This is an exit permit, allowing someone to leave Spain on the authority of the German Consul. It is signed by my father!' Laura looked blank and he hastened to explain the coincidence. His father had been the German Consul in Majorca during the Spanish Civil War, when it became difficult for foreign nationals to leave because of suspicion that they might be Spaniards from the opposing side trying to escape. Majorca was in the control of the fascists, with German and Italian troops operating from the island against the Republican mainland. People who had offended against the communist dominated Republican regime often tried to use the island as an escape route and his father would help by issuing exit permits, usually on German ships, if he was satisfied that they had a genuine case. Though only a boy of fourteen at the time, Karl-Heinz had sometimes been involved and, in fact, he remembered very clearly the day that Palma harbour was bombed and the battleship, the *Deutschland,* sunk. He had escorted two young women to the quayside and seen them on to a German ship, which was also blown up in the attack. It was thought that there were no survivors, but it now seemed that one, at least, of the girls, had escaped. In the circumstances, they would not have contacted anyone to say that they were safe. The name on the permit was Miss Margaret Martin, described as a student, of London, England.

'I still don't understand,' said Laura, bewildered. 'What connection could there be between her and either of my parents?'

Karl-Heinz poured more coffee and caught the eye of a passing waiter, asking him to bring two cognacs. 'The coincidence stretches almost beyond the imagination,' he said quietly. 'The man I want you to see tomorrow is Father Rafael, the priest at Deya. He is the son of Ramon and Teresa Martinez and he believes that the young woman calling herself Margaret Martin was his sister, Margarita Martinez, and that she was a friend of your mother. It is also probable that your mother was with her when she left Majorca. Did your mother ever mention her or the fact that she lived for a while in Barcelona with the Martinez family?'

Laura was shaken. 'She never mentioned having been to Spain. I remember her telling me that she had a friend at school who was Spanish and that she had died in an accident at sea, but I cannot recall her mentioning her name. How do you know that my mother was with her in Spain?' He held up her mother's birth certificate and the Higher School Certificate showing the name of the school.

'The friend named in the document was Margot and she had been staying with the Martinez family in Barcelona for almost a year. Rafael never met her, but I contacted the school Margarita had attended in England and their records confirmed that there was a Margot Chase in the same form. The photograph is of Rafael's parents and his younger sister, Eulalia. These documents prove the connection.' He had made further enquiries, he told her. Having obtained Margot's old address from the school's records, he had contacted the present owners. Fortunately the property had changed hands only twice in the last forty years and he had been able to establish the date when it was sold by Margot Chase. It was in September 1937, just over three months after the bombing in Palma harbour and three months before Laura was born in Barnard Castle. The dates tied up. Somehow, Margot had survived. It was strange, mused Laura, that none of this had come to light during conversation when the priest, Karl-Heinz and her father met so often over the years. He agreed. In the ten years he had known Father Rafael, not once had he mentioned his sister and he himself had said nothing of the incident involving the two girls, though each knew that the other had been on the island at the time. Bill knew that the priest was from Barcelona, but had never referred to his late wife having been there, possibly because he was not aware of it. When he spoke of her he called her 'Marge', which one might think was short for 'Marjorie', but, even if he had used her proper name, there was no reason to suppose that it would have triggered a question in the minds of any of them. When they spoke of the Spanish Civil War, as they spoke of World War Two, it was usually about the political aspects or their personal experiences on the battlefield.

It was very late. The restaurant had closed and the waiters were preparing the tables for breakfast. Laura's head was reeling. Karl-Heinz stood up.

'We have probably come to a dead end and may never find out how Margot survived and was rescued, but Father Rafael is grateful to you for bringing the package to light and he is looking forward to meeting you.'

She smiled. 'He must keep the package, of course. I wish I could be more helpful. I have brought an old photograph of my mother with a school friend who might possibly be his sister, but I cannot be sure.

'Until tomorrow, then.' They said goodnight and she went to bed, her imagination aflame with the fate of the luckless Margarita.

Chapter Twenty-seven

S HE HAD HARDLY SLEPT, tossing and turning as the implications of Margarita's confession slowly dawned on her confused brain. Clearly, what was meant by 'We are both in the same situation' was that Margot had also been pregnant and that she, Laura, was the result She could hardly wait to put the question to Karl-Heinz as they walked up the steep cobbled streets to the village, and he, having calculated the date on which he had last seen the two girls, said he had already reached that conclusion. Did she know who her natural father was? She did not. She had only ever seen a shortened form of birth certificate, which showed William Somers as her adoptive father. Surely she must have wondered? No, Bill was the only father she had ever known and she loved him. It had never occurred to her to try to trace her real father or even to question her mother about him. She had a vague notion that he had been a soldier, but, as far as she was concerned, he did not exist. It was hot and they paused, sitting on a garden wall where bees and hummingbird hawk moths hovered busily among the lantana bushes and the splash of a duck alighting on a tiny pond was the only sound disturbing the stillness of the morning. Laura, plainly shattered by this new image of her mother, seemed close to tears and Karl-Heinz, taking both her hands in his, said softly that she must not make harsh judgements. People behaved differently in wartime, he told her, the awareness that life might end at any moment caused them to cast caution to the winds.

'Tell me about your mother,' he said, gently. 'She must have been a very resourceful lady to have coped alone with the problems she faced. I know that Bill loved her and never got over her death.'

She sighed, a slight frown puckering her brow.

'Yes,' she said slowly, after a moment's contemplation. 'Her parents were killed in a road accident when she was a child and she was brought up by an aunt, her only living relative, who never married. She went to boarding school and expected to go on to university, but her aunt died just as she was about to leave school, so her plans were shelved and she had to sell up and fend for herself. She was always busy, restless, unfulfilled, I suppose. She gave up her job at the library when my brother was born, by which time Dad had started on his own as a chartered accountant and was doing well, so they had no financial worries. After the war, she began to take an interest in social problems in the area and became a local councillor and a magistrate. She ran a Wolf Cub pack to keep the local kids off the streets and make them take pride in being responsible citizens. Dad was Chairman of the local Branch of the British Limbless Ex-Service Men's Association and she ran jumble sales and coffee mornings to raise funds for them. She loved us, but she did not always have time to listen, not like Dad. As a teenager I could never talk to her about my emotional problems, because she seemed to put up a barrier and when my marriage failed and I needed comfort and support, she was cold, distant. Dad made excuses for her, saying she had had a hard life before I was born. Now I am beginning to understand just how hard it must have been when she lost everything and everyone close to her in such tragic circumstances. Why did she not confide in anyone?' Her voice faltered and Karl-Heinz said quietly that it was not uncommon for someone who had been traumatised to block out the experience from their conscious memory. They may want to keep away from anyone or anything which reminds them of the incident. In suppressing their feelings and maintaining control, they may find it impossible to accept emotional weakness in others. Survivors often felt guilty that they had been spared when others had died and these two girls had been so close that it would have felt almost like losing a part of herself.

If Margot was rescued, not actually having seen her friend die, she might have cherished a hope that one day she would turn up and that could be why she had kept the package. There was no point in conjecture. The important thing for Laura to remember was that, against the odds, her mother had lived and had worked hard to make a decent life for her family. She should be proud of her. The priest's housekeeper admitted them and led them into a cool room, lined with bookshelves, a large oak desk taking up most of the floor space, with a small, wooden cabinet, a rather shabby brown leather sofa and two deep armchairs the only other furniture. Father Rafael would be with them in a few moments, she explained in Spanish to Karl-Heinz as she invited them to sit. Laura felt nervous. It must have been a shock to him to receive this sudden reminder of a family tragedy after so many years. Would he be able to tell her anything about her own mother and, if so, how would she feel? She swallowed hard and cast a despairing glance at Karl-Heinz, but he just smiled and gave her an encouraging nod. Footsteps and the sound of voices outside heralded the arrival of the priest, closely followed by the housekeeper, bearing a tray with glasses and a decanter of sherry, which she poured and handed round as Karl-Heinz made the introductions. Lunch would be served in half an hour, she said firmly as she left the room. Rafael Martinez was a man of some sixty-odd years, slim, straight-backed, his wavy hair quite grey, his smile warmly sincere as he offered his condolences on the death of her father, with whom, he told her, he had spent many a happy hour.

'This is such a coincidence,' he said. 'I did not know your mother, but she lived with my family for almost a year and they were very fond of her. My father died five years ago. My mother is frail and I did not want to excite her too much until I had more information about Margot, but I have spoken on the telephone with my sister Eulalia, who was thrilled to hear that Margot survived. She wanted to come over to meet you, but she is still working as an eye specialist at the hospital in Barcelona and could not get away.' Laura, still unable to grasp why her mother had made no attempt to contact the family who had been so good to her, began to apologise, but he stopped her, saying gently that it was not possible to imagine the effect on the mind of someone who had survived such a horrendous experience. They must rejoice that one, at least, of the friends had survived and he would tell her as much as he could of her mother's life in Spain, but first, they must repair to the dining room or lunch would be cold and his housekeeper would scold him! Maria beamed approvingly as they entered the dining room, a small plump, woman of indeterminate age, dressed in black, her grey hair drawn back severely into a tight bun, her starched white pinafore spotless. Bustling around, she soon had them seated at the long refectory table and vanished into the kitchen, while Rafael poured wine into crystal glasses. She had looked after the house since his predecessor's time, nearly twenty years ago, he explained. As long as he did not interfere or upset her routine, the household ran on oiled wheels and he was content to abide by her rules. After the war, he had been ordained in Palma Cathedral, then spent some years in Valencia and Madrid. He had always loved Majorca and when he heard that the priest at Deya had died, he had begged to be given the appointment, having no ambition to be anything but a good parish priest. Karl-Heinz complimented him on the wine, a good Rioja, and he laughed, holding up the glass in a toast to his guests. 'It is one of the perks of the cloth! One of my parishioners is a wealthy wine merchant and very generously keeps me supplied. In return, I pray for his soul!'

Maria placed before them plates of *pa amb oli*, local farmhouse bread, fragrant with olive oil, with chunks of *sobrasada*, the red spicy Majorcan sausage, and cheese. It was delicious and Laura ate appreciatively as she listened to the two men discussing the merits of various wines. Rafael waited until the next course appeared, a steaming dish of roast Majorcan lamb, delicately flavoured with garlic and herbs, before beginning his story. He had been in Valladolid when the rising began and, though the fascists, who supported the Church, quickly gained control, news of atrocities committed against priests by Republicans alarmed the elders and they dispersed the novitiate to places of greater safety. He was sent to Majorca, but on his way to Valencia, having got a message through to his parents, he managed to have a rendezvous with his mother at a old charcoal burner's hut in the mountains behind their house just outside Barcelona. She had brought him food and money and news of the rest of the family. Margarita, who had been at school in England for two years, had brought home a friend, an English girl, whose aunt, her only relative, had died, leaving her to plan her future alone. It had been too late to prevent them from coming when the trouble began in Barcelona, but they seemed quite unaffected by it and Margot was a lovely girl who quickly became part of the family and helped with refugees in the city and at the hospital. He reached Majorca in safety, where he stayed with the local priest in Deya, hearing nothing more from his family until after the bombing of the harbour. On that fateful day, the whole island was shocked by the sudden attack and the scale of the devastation. He had gone to the Cathedral in Palma to pray for the dead, but had no idea that his sister was among them. It was two weeks before the priest broke the news, having received a message from people in Palma who had been involved in arranging their escape. The family had been informed through the escape route and, knowing that he was on the island, had asked for him to be contacted.

He was introduced to a lady in Palma, Dona Mercedes, who explained briefly why the girls had fled, though she did not know the circumstances in which the man had been killed. He had gone to the place where the remains of those recovered were held and personal possessions from suitcases and lockers dragged from the wreckage were displayed, but few bodies were identifiable and most had gone down with their vessels. Eye-witnesses had seen the girls boarding the *Amadeus* and he was shown women's clothing and shoes, among which was a blouse, with Margarita's name tape sewn into the collar, presumably a requirement of her English school. There was no report of any survivors from the *Amadeus*, which had been blown savagely apart before she sank. Perhaps the worst part of it was that his parents were unable to mourn openly, because they could not reveal that the girls had been leaving from Palma harbour without arousing suspicion and endangering the people who had helped them to escape. Laura gave a little sob and Rafael paused, his face lined with sorrow, as he reached over to touch her hand.

'I am sorry, my dear, do you wish me to go on?'

She nodded. 'It is worse for you, your sister – it is just such a revelation to me that all those years she kept those dreadful memories to herself.' She asked if he had known the whole story before he saw Margarita's confession. He replied that he had known through Maria Calhoun, the assistant matron at the hospital to whom the girls had gone for help, that she had shot Vicente in a jealous rage, but they had not known that she was pregnant. Nor had they known about Margot's condition, another reason, perhaps, why she had felt unable to make contact with the family. Maria came in to clear the table, smilingly acknowledging their thanks as she placed coffee and a large bowl of fruit on the table and a decanter of cognac in front of Father Rafael, who, despite Laura's protest, poured out a generous measure for each of them. As Maria departed, silently closing the door behind her, Karl-Heinz asked how long it had been before Vicente's body was found and whether suspicion had fallen on Margarita after she left so suddenly. Rafael shook his head sadly.

Vicente was found early the next morning, but he was not dead. He had hit his head on the table as he fell and was knocked unconscious. Weak from loss of blood from the wound in his chest, it was some weeks before he recovered. In the first place the woman he had been with was questioned, people having seen them together. Vicente had too much pride to admit that he had been shot by a woman and made light of it, saying that he had had a quarrel with a jealous husband over a little matter in Madrid. It was a question of honour, no harm had been done and he did not wish to pursue it. When Franco took Barcelona, ending the civil war, Vicente was among the communists and anarchists shot in recrimination. Laura shivered.

'Poor Margarita. What could she have seen in such a man?' Rafael said that Vicente came from a good, highly respected family. His father and Dr Martinez were close friends and the children had grown up together, gone to the same schools, shared holidays, but that in his teens Vicente had changed, becoming lazy and arrogant. Perhaps he felt that he could not attain the academic standards his parents expected of him, but had ambition and saw an opportunity to achieve power in the emerging

Communist Party. He was handsome and could charm the birds out of the trees if he were so disposed. Margarita was headstrong and was probably attracted by the glamour of a dangerous situation. Laura, her hands cupped round the bowl of her brandy glass, as if looking into a crystal ball, sighed gently as she swirled the amber liquid.

'I don't suppose,' her voice faltered, then she said firmly, addressing the priest, 'I never wanted to know while Dad was alive, but was my – I mean, if my mother ...' Rafael interrupted her.

'Your father? Maria Calhoun is fairly certain that he was a young Swedish man who was in Barcelona to compete in the Popular Olympiad when the rising began and stayed to join an International Brigade. Eulalia remembers that she was seeing a Swedish lad called Sven and Maria had seen Margot with him and was sure that they were more than friends. Apparently he was a very nice young man. The day after the girls had left, he appeared at the hospital asking for her and was very upset when he heard that she had gone.' Laura wondered how Margot could have left without at least leaving a message for him. Rafael shrugged. There would not have been much of a future for them at that time, he conjectured. So many of the Brigaders died in the fighting, but, if Sven escaped, he would have returned eventually to Sweden and would soon have forgotten about his short romance. Better for him to think she had lost interest than to be worried about becoming a father in such troubled times. Karl-Heinz reached out and took Laura's glass from her, reminding her that she had a photograph to show Rafael. She delved into her handbag and pulled out the picture of two smiling girls wearing school uniform and passed it to the priest, who gazed at it silently, a shadow of pain crossing his face as he passed it to Karl-Heinz, saying softly,

'That is my sister. It must have been taken shortly before they left school. How happy they looked!' Karl-Heinz said ruefully that he could not really remember the two girls he had escorted on to the ship so long ago. 'Which one was your mother?' he asked. Laura, still rummaging in her bag, produced another photograph, this time of her mother's wedding to Bill.

'I thought you might like to see this one with Dad,' she said, handing it to Rafael as she turned to Karl-Heinz to point out Margot. A strangled cry from the priest made them both turn to see him clutching the photograph, his face white as a sheet, as he gasped,

'Margarita. This is Margarita, my sister.' Karl-Heinz took the photograph from him, held it against that of the two girls and pointing to the one she had just identified, looked questioningly at Laura.

'My mother,' she confirmed. 'Margot.'

Karl-Heinz drew her gently to her feet, his arm supporting her.

'Your mother,' he corrected her, 'Margarita!'

Stunned, the three of them stood in silence, their eyes fixed on the photograph.

Chapter Twenty-eight

THE PRIEST WAS THE FIRST TO RECOVER. He crossed himself, his lips moving in a silent prayer, then, placing a hand on the shoulder of each of his guests, he suggested that they go into the other room. 'I have something to show you,' he said, as he settled them into the armchairs, then went over to the desk, where he opened a drawer and took out a photograph in a silver frame. Slipping it quickly from the frame, he handed it to Laura. 'It was taken in England, a few weeks before she left school. There is a message on the back.' Laura gazed spellbound at the attractive young face smiling confidently into the camera. The hair framing the face was dark and there was a mischievous sparkle in the eyes which she could not recollect having seen before, but she was looking at a picture of her mother. Slowly, she turned it over. 'To my dear brother, so you will not forget me in your prayers. All my love. Margarita.' It was written in her mother's hand.

'I knew that she bleached her hair,' was all she could think of to say. 'Even when she was very ill, she insisted on having the hairdresser come to the house to do it.' Karl-Heinz remembered that both girls had been blonde when they boarded the *Amadeus* and Rafael confirmed that Dona Mercedes had told him of Margarita's disguise. Why had she continued with it for the rest of her life? It was as if she had tried to transform herself as nearly as possible into her dead friend when she assumed her identity. Laura shivered, her eyes wide with apprehension as she looked at the two men. 'But she was not who she claimed to be. Nor am I! Or Michael, though he, at least, knows who his father was. Oh, what have I done? Michael said that no good would come of my meddling.' Hollow-eyed, deathly pale, she sat hunched in her chair, her fingers fluttering nervously at her lips. Karl-Heinz rose from his chair and moved silently to the window, his thoughts conjuring with the legal implications. Rafael leaned forward and gripped her hands. 'You are still the same person. Your mother was your real mother, whatever she called herself. I believe that she meant you to know the truth one day or she would not have kept the documents all those years. Please try not to think too unkindly of her. It has been a great shock for you to find out this way, but I thank God that he led you to me.' She smiled shakily, her brain still reeling. There were so many questions, so much still to talk about. She took a deep breath, then the words tumbled out as she attempted to understand. Her mother, high-minded and highly respected, was an impostor who had assumed someone else's identity and deceived even her husband and children beyond the grave. How could she have allowed them to live in ignorance all those years? Or had Bill known and been a party to it? Why had she never tried to contact her family after the Civil War ended? If she had done so, she would have found out about Vicente and they would have been reunited.

Karl-Heinz stopped her. 'I am sure that Bill knew nothing. It is difficult for you to comprehend, but I know only too well what it is like to lose one's identity. She was nineteen years old. When the ship was blown up, she was already in a state of shock. The explosion, the loss of the friend who was her only support at a time of great stress, the fact that she had no passport and could not return to Spain, would have been enough to challenge the sanity of most people, but she was a survivor and there was an obvious solution. She took it. She knew that Margot had no relatives and that there was no-one with a claim on the estate, so no actual harm was done to anyone. It may have been illegal, but I do not think it was immoral. Once the step had been taken it would have been difficult for her to extricate herself. I would not be surprised if she submerged her own personality to the extent that she came to believe that she really was Margot Chase.' Laura looked up sharply.

'You think her mind was affected, that she was schizophrenic or something?'

'No.' He shook his head, a wry smile on his face. 'When you have been on a battlefront, faced death, killed, witnessed some of the atrocities that human beings do to each other, you see things in a different perspective. The main objective is survival at all costs. Alone, on the run, you have to rely on your wits. Deceit becomes second nature. I drew on it freely for several years, I can tell you. So did many others, like Willy van Hoek and even Rafael.' He glanced at the priest, who nodded. 'If we had not, we would have died. Bill would have done the same if he had had to. We often talked, the four of us, about what war does to people's integrity. Your mother did what she believed she had to do to ensure her survival and yours. She, Margarita, earned love and respect by the way she conducted her life in Margot's name. Think about that, Laura!'

Laura, contemplating the dilemma of the young girl, alone in a dangerous and hostile world, unable to trust or confide in anyone, was mortified to think how ready she had been to condemn. Shyly, she turned to Rafael.

'I am sorry. It is just beginning to dawn on me what a remarkable person she really was. It is so sad that she was never able to trust anyone enough to share her pain. She worked hard to provide a secure, happy life for us and succeeded. There were no grandparents or other blood relatives, apart from Dad's brother and his sons, who we hardly ever saw but we were surrounded by surrogate aunts and uncles who loved her and looked on us as family. How she must have longed for her own people in Spain!' Rafael sighed heavily. It saddened him to think that his sister had not felt able to trust him, a priest, enough at least to let him know that she was alive. She could have contacted him easily enough through the Church at any time after the end of the war. Many Spanish people had lost loved ones in those dreadful days, he told her, some never found out what had happened to them and, certainly, few were fortunate enough to discover, years later, a direct descendant. His mother had longed for grandchildren, but with Margarita gone, Eulalia remaining unmarried and himself a priest, it had seemed that it was not to be. She would be thrilled beyond words when she learned the truth.

Laura smiled. The prospect of a family with blood ties to herself was wonderful. Then the thought occurred to her that the blood was Spanish. Her father had been Vicente Alvarez, a monster who had rejected her and ruined her mother's life. 'That man, my –', she swallowed, looking worriedly at Rafael, 'my father. He was presumably executed for having taken part in atrocities like those you spoke of. I know that you said his family were respectable, but ...' she broke off, embarrassed at the thought of meeting them. Rafael shook his head sadly. She must understand that Vicente and his comrades had not been the only perpetrators of cruel, inhuman deeds. Both sides had committed equally appalling acts of violence against their fellow countrymen. Even in Majorca, where the islanders were normally warm-hearted and kind, there had been fascist witch hunts for suspected socialists, who were rounded up and shot, or taken on *passeillos*, short walks, to a promontary near Valldemosa, from where they were pushed to their deaths on the rocks two hundred metres below. He had himself seen bodies, dead and dying, sprawled on the rocks below and, to his shame, had not dared to try to help for fear of execution, though some of the monks from the nearby monastery would climb down the cliffs to administer the last rites, under the pretence of collecting samphire from the shore. They had even managed to save one or two lives at great danger to their own.

As for Vicente's family, they were delightful, decent people and he broke their hearts. When he was executed, they could not bear the shame and moved away from Barcelona, telling no-one where they were going, not even Rafael's father, who had been perhaps their greatest friend. They did not know that he had been seeing Margarita, let alone that she was pregnant and had no idea that it was she who had injured him, so it would seem best not to seek them out, even if that were feasible. Relieved, she agreed.

'It feels so strange to think that I am not even English. Michael is Bill's son, so he is half English, but my blood is entirely Spanish, though I know nothing of the country or the language!' Rafael laughed.

'Well, almost. Your blood is certainly more Spanish than mine! My mother is English, so I am only half Spanish, while you have just a quarter of English blood in your veins. Now! We must think what to do next.' Karl-Heinz stood up, suggesting that they had talked quite enough for that day. Rafael had work to do, he said, and there was a lot to think about. They both needed time to sort out their own feelings before dropping the bombshell on their families. And it would be a bombshell! They should consider whether it would hurt rather than heal, whether they should continue to keep the secret which Margarita had so carefully protected all those years. Laura looked anxiously at Rafael, but he shook his head. 'We do not have the right to keep it from them. I am in no doubt that this was meant to be and I am sure that my family will want to know the truth. You, Laura, must decide what to do with regard to your brother.' She assured him quickly that she would prefer to share the news with Michael and they agreed to meet in two days' time, Rafael having established that Laura would be staying in Majorca long enough to meet his sister, Eulalia, if it could be arranged. Shyly, she embraced Rafael and they stepped out into the early evening sunshine to walk down the village, back in the real world, she thought as they mingled with smiling tourists who sauntered around as if nothing had changed, while her own world had just turned upside down. Karl-Heinz said he had some business matters to attend to in Palma next day, but that he had arranged to play snooker with Willy van Hoek at his house later, followed by dinner. He was sure that they would be delighted to see Laura and, if she liked, he would telephone Tilly to confirm that she would accompany him. What a splendid idea, she agreed enthusiastically. There was no-one in whom she would rather confide than Tilly. She would love to talk to her.

She was down early for breakfast, having skipped dinner the previous night, unable to face food after the excitement of the day and Maria's substantial lunch. The smell of fresh warm bread aroused her appetite and she had just piled her plate with rolls and an *ensaimada*, when Frances and Jennifer appeared, eyes rolling in mock horror at this blatant disregard for her figure.

'We missed you at dinner last night,' said Frances, looking anxiously at her pale face. 'Are you all right?'

'Yes,' she assured her. She had spent the day seeing some of Dad's friends and had enjoyed generous hospitality at lunch, so she had not been hungry. It was a bit upsetting to have to go over it all again, but they had been so kind to him and she felt that it would have been wrong to come to Deya and not visit them. She would be out again tonight, she added, dining with her friend, Tilly. Jennifer's ankle was much better, she said in reply to Laura's enquiry, but she did not yet feel up to walking far. The three of them spent the day lounging on sunbeds, reading, chatting, splashing about in the pool. They shared a bottle of wine and some fruit at lunchtime and Laura slept for an hour in the shade of an umbrella, waking refreshed and relaxed. She bathed and dressed, then sat on the balcony, glancing at her watch from time to time, eager for Tilly's reaction to her story. Karl-Heinz was waiting in Reception when she emerged. As they walked towards the car park, he asked how she felt. She squeezed his arm, excitedly.

'Bewildered,' she admitted. 'My imagination keeps running away with me, but it is already beginning to sink in that this is really happening and there is no going back now. To begin with, how do I break the news to my brother?' Not on the telephone, he advised. She should wait until she got home, when she could do it face to face and would have news about further developments with Martinez family. The van Hoeks greeted them with hugs and kisses and ushered them into the lounge, where Willy brandished a bottle of fine champagne, saying they must celebrate Laura's return after such a long absence. The pleasantries exchanged, Tilly said they would eat later, after they had talked. She shooed the men out to the snooker room, then sat down by Laura, her kind face full of concern.

'My dear, Karl-Heinz has told me briefly of your amazing discovery. It must have been a great shock to you.' Laura nodded.

'I still don't know I feel about it. Karl-Heinz has been wonderful, but there are things – feelings – that I can't just dismiss as coincidence. I need to talk to you, Tilly. You are the only person I know who will understand.' Tilly listened, her blue eyes wide as the story unfolded, an involuntary gasp escaping her lips as she took in the details of the sinking of the *Amadeus*. 'Oh, the poor child!' she whispered.

'But it's so weird, Tilly. Not a hint over all those years, not even a deathbed revelation, yet all the people who could piece it together just happened to end up in the same place and as friends, never having had any idea how each of their lives had touched hers at times and places so far apart.' Tilly smiled enigmatically. 'There are many things in this world which cannot be explained by logic. People call me fey, but I believe that there are forces beyond our comprehension pushing us in the direction of the truth when it needs to be told. We should not ignore them.'

'But I wonder if it was right to disturb the mud after all this time. I admit it is exciting for me to contemplate having blood relatives, but has it opened up old wounds for Rafael and his family? They now have to face the uncomfortable fact that she chose not to tell them that she was alive. His mother is eighty years old and I understand that she is not in good health. The shock could kill her!'

Tilly touched her cheek. 'No, no. It is right, I am sure. I know Teresa Martinez. She comes over to stay with Rafael for a few weeks every year in the Spring and for Epiphany. She is a remarkable person and an accomplished musician. Five years ago she performed in one of my charity concerts here in Deya. I remember there was a classical guitarist and a visiting quartet from Argentina. She gave a piano recital, then at the finale, as an encore and a tribute to the quartet, she launched into a medley of Latin American music, equally competent in the rumba, samba and tango as in her own classical field. When she came off the stage there were tears in her eyes and I asked what was the matter. She replied that, for some reason, she had included a paso doble and it had brought back memories of an occasion, many years ago when, in the middle of the Civil War, she had taken her elder daughter and a friend to a performance of that dance. It had been a wonderful, happy evening, but it was almost the last time she had seen them – they died in a tragic air raid a few days later.' Laura had been sitting silently, leaning forward, elbows supported on her knees, her chin cupped in her hands, as she listened, fascinated. Frowning slightly, she sat upright.

'When was this?'

Tilly thought for a moment. 'I can tell you exactly when it was,' she declared, 'because it was my birthday, the first of May, 1972.'

With a catch in her throat, Laura whispered, 'That was the day my mother died!' She was pale, shaking. 'There is something else. I couldn't say anything to Karl-Heinz, because it sounds silly, but last night I dreamed I saw my mother, young, laughing, twisting and turning in a sort of dance. I called out to her and she turned, but it was not her face. Then there were two of them. They beckoned and I followed, first one, then the other, trying to catch up with them, but whenever I got near enough to touch them, they spun together, round and round until they seemed to merge into one and I woke up, crying to my mother to come back. The window was open and the curtain was blowing slightly. I went to close it and in the distance I could hear girls' voices, tinkling laughter carried faintly on the breeze. I stood there for a while, straining to listen, but there was no more. I tried to tell myself it must have been a sheep's bell, but I know it was not.' Tilly, her hands clasped, her eyes shining, breathed, 'But don't you see? This is what she wanted. At last the record has been put straight and she is free. She is at peace.'

They sat in contemplative silence, as Willy and Karl-Heinz entered the room. 'Let's eat!' cried Willy, rubbing his hands. Tilly jumped up, leading the way into the dining room, where she busied herself with her duties as hostess. 'When did you manage to do all this?' asked Laura, as they took their seats at the beautiful oak table gleaming with glass and silver and laden with a variety of tempting cold dishes.

'I didn't!' chuckled Tilly. 'Willy had it brought down from the res-taurant and Caterina, one of the waitresses, who often helps me, set it all out while we were talking. Now, help yourselves to hors d'oeuvres while I get the casserole out of the oven. Pour the wine, please, Willy.' It was always a joy to be in the company of the van Hoeks, who had a instinctive flair for putting people at their ease, and Laura, thankful to have been able to share her anxieties with Tilly, felt light-hearted and almost giddy with happiness as the four of them raised their glasses in a toast to friendship. They talked warmly of Bill and she felt a sudden conviction that he would have been pleased to know that she had found her family. The others agreed and the talk turned to the Martinez family.

'You told me about Rafael's mother – my grandmother,' she added, shyly. 'Have you met his sister, Eulalia?' Karl-Heinz said that he had met her once. She was about his age, he thought, about fifty-two or fifty-three, a strikingly handsome woman, clever and with a nice sense of humour.

'Yes,' agreed Tilly, 'Lallie, they call her. Both she and Rafael have their father's looks. Even at eighty he was a very good-looking man.'

'I wonder why she never married', mused Laura. 'Rafael said that his mother had longed for grandchildren.' Willy said that she and Rafael had also inherited their father's dedication to their professions and, of course, Lallie had stayed at home to care for both parents. 'As you did, Laura,' he added.

She nodded. 'Yes, it is surprising how the years pass. I shall be forty in a few months' time. I thought my life was settled until two days ago and here I am with the exciting prospect of a new identity.'

'Ha!' cried Tilly 'There is truth in the saying that life begins at forty. I should know. That is how old I was when I met Willy.' Her husband beamed affectionately at her.

'I was a little older than that, so I had waited longer,' he said, 'but it was worth it. Is there a man in your life?' he asked innocently. It did not seem an impertinent question and Laura laughed.

'Not at the moment. I haven't had much time for socialising and, well, my short experience of marriage left me wary about trusting a man again.' Karl-Heinz looked indignant. 'It is not only men who can't be trusted', he said. 'As one who has been let down several times by unfaithful women, I would need a lot of persuading to risk it again!' There was a short exchange of light-hearted banter about which sex took fidelity more seriously, until Tilly exclaimed, 'Your mother learned to trust again. She and Bill were happy, weren't they? It just needs the right person!' Laura, just slightly tipsy by this time, giggled.

'I,' she announced, covering her glass as Willy moved to refill it.

'I,' she began again, as the others looked expectantly at her, 'am a Spanish person!'

'*Olé!*' they cried in happy unison.

On the way back to the hotel, Karl-Heinz asked if her talk with Tilly had helped.

'Oh, yes,' she said fervently. 'You always know that she will give an honest opinion and she makes everything seem so straightforward. I feel much better now.'

He wondered aloud whether Rafael had contacted his sister and Laura turned towards him anxiously.

'You will come with me tomorrow, won't you?' she asked. 'I still feel a bit awkward on my own and your knowing Rafael so well is reassuring.'

'Wouldn't miss it for the world!' he replied. 'It would be like reading a book and finding that the last chapter is missing.' He parked the car and they walked towards Reception, the gravel scrunching beneath their feet. 'None of this would be happening without your help,' she said. 'You are the only person who could have made the link and I can still hardly believe the chain of coincidence that led to it. Not that Tilly regards it as coincidence,' she added. He stopped. 'Who knows? I am an old cynic, but I have to admit that Tilly hides a lot of sense under that rather zany exterior.' She nodded.

'Seriously, though, I realise that I am taking up a large slice of your holiday and I must not be selfish. You will tell me if I am making too many demands on your time, won't you?'

He laughed, took both her hands in his and stood looking at her worried face. 'Dear Laura. I am enjoying every minute and I will be there for you as long as you want me to. I hope you are not trying to get rid of me, because, if you are, better stay clear of Tilly! Did you not see the gleam in her eye when we were talking about the right person? I am sure she is making plans!'

She felt herself blushing in the darkness, then giggled. 'We must watch out then!' They stood quietly, facing each other. 'Look, Laura. This is not the time, but when all this is sorted out, I would like to spend some time with you, if you agree. I can always find a reason for coming to England or we could meet here. I am sure you will be coming over to see your new family.' She smiled shyly, her hands tightening in his. 'I would like that very much,' she said softly.

He saw her to her room, kissed her gently on the cheek and turned to go.

'Goodnight. I will see you tomorrow.' He paused. 'Spanish person!'